EXTINGUISHED WORLDS:

WHAT GOES AROUND

PATRICIA GILLIAM

Copyright © 2022 PATRICIA GILLIAM

This book is a work of fiction. Names, characters, places, and incidents are the products of the author's imagination or are used fictitiously. Any resemblance to actual persons, living or dead, is entirely coincidental.

All rights reserved. No part of this book may be reproduced in any form or by any electronic or mechanical means including information storage and retrieval systems without permission of the author, except by a reviewer, who may quote brief passages in a review.

ISBN: 9798377081456

ACKNOWLEDGMENTS

Special thanks to Jerry Cornell, C. Andrew Nelson, and the entire team involved with Adventurous Ideas. I've loved being a part of this project.

Thanks to Matthew Rose for proofreading/editing.

ADVENTUROUS IDEAS™

EXTINGUISHED WORLDS: WHAT GOES AROUND

EXTINGUISHED WORLDS: WHAT GOES AROUND

CYCAD COVE ARCHIVES: ACCESS GRANTED_LEVEL 1

With most stories, it's best to start from the beginning.

I can't—not without breaking out a convoluted flow chart with color-coded push pins and a whole lot of string. I'll try my best to keep my part in order from my perspective, though.

Even with that, time travel and dimensional hopping can be confusing at times. When we first met, I knew a lot less than I do now.

Keep whatever else I manage to send you through this island—sometimes called Orchid and other times Perilous. It's all relevant but may take time to piece together.

I've also discovered a few worlds where it doesn't exist and never did. None of us seem to be there, either.

It all boils down to this: Earth—our Earth and a lot of ones similar to it—are still in danger, and I'll do everything in my ability to protect them and our family.

No matter how many tries it takes.

CCA File 00001_AGG2031617_NWOI

Message from Caleb [last name illegible]
Dated June 30th, 1908
Recovered on Orchid Island, Northeast Quadrant
Logged June 17th, 2031 by Dr. Adira Greene-Gregory

Digital media card enclosed, manufactured circa 2003.

CHAPTER ONE

MY EARLIEST CLEAR MEMORY was having the wind knocked out of me when I was eight years old. I didn't know who or what collided with me just before that, but it sent me tumbling across a hot sidewalk.

It was the middle of summer in Cycad Cove. My eyes had to adjust, like maybe I'd been coming up to ground level from the subway. Scrapes on my arms and knees healed just as I noticed them. This startled me, but I was relieved, too.

Traffic on the intersection near me had stopped. As I rolled onto my back and gasped for air, a dozen brightly-suited heroes surrounded a bulky man hovering several stories above me.

The villain wore dark tactical clothing and didn't notice me sprawled out on the sidewalk below him.

None of them did.

"I'm telling you it was an accident!" the villain shouted. A warning blast from a hero's laser vision struck a bank headquarters behind him, shattering a glass pane. I cringed and covered my face, but a faded green canvas awning diverted the shards before they reached me. The villain's tone turned furious. "Oh, forget it..."

He retaliated with reddish balls of energy from his palms, keeping the heroes at a distance. One melted clean through an abandoned car's hood, including its engine block. Another made a hole through the laser vision hero's cape and caught it on fire.

The air smelled like burnt plastic and metal.

Terrified, I scrambled into a nearby alley, trying not to draw attention from either side. After a few minutes, the villain seemed to have worn himself out. I edged back to the corner of the bank building and tried to get a better look.

A female hero in a blue sparkled uniform raised her hands and attempted to negotiate. "We just want to talk, Roman! If what you're saying is true, you need to calm down and come with us willingly. Please."

Roman didn't buy it and scowled at her. "I've heard that before, Rodoxian, and it took my lawyers this long to get me cleared! I'll pay for the damages today, but I'm not going back to some facility filled to the brim with murderers and psychopaths! Not for this. All of you just stay the hell away from me!"

Everyone froze in place, and the air around all of us rippled—like multiple iridescent bubbles compressed together and about to burst.

This was bad—really, really bad.

I could sense what was coming, but I couldn't run away.

"Roman! No!" Another hero in a red uniform yelled. He managed to pull Rodoxian clear from the rippling area. The other heroes followed and shot upward above the city's skyline.

Then Roman flew away—as if he had to struggle to escape, too.

I wasn't so lucky. A split-second after everyone else was gone, a cascade of energy waves imploded the skyscraper above me. I saw it falling toward me just before I lost consciousness.

***

I woke up in complete darkness and couldn't move my arms or legs. My mouth felt dry, and my stomach ached. Metal creaked all around me. Ice-cold droplets of rainwater pelted the top of my head and trailed down my neck and back.

"Help! Somebody, please help! Please!" I shouted for as long as I could, but debris muffled my voice. I strained until I could barely hear myself.

Then I started crying.

Nobody was coming for me. I was panicked and alone and confused by how I'd even gotten downtown in the first place. I couldn't remember where I was before. I couldn't picture my mom and dad's faces or remember their voices anymore.

There was still something important—enough for me to have repeated it dozens of times out loud to myself.

319D Gregory Street...355-667-

The creaking grew worse, and something huge toppled over. This created a small pocket of space where I could reach up with my right hand.

Footsteps crunched the rubble above me.

"Oh no...kid? Are you alive?" a guy asked in an uneasy tone. "Can you hear me?" The footsteps got quieter, like he was backing away.

I took in a breath and shouted one more time. "Yeah, I'm alive, but I can't move! I need help."

He came back. "Okay. Okay, give me a minute. Even with an amplifier, this will take me a while. Let me know if you feel any heat, and I'll stop." He made an initial blast then continued in a calmer tone. "My name's Dominic Averelli. What's yours?"

"I'm Caleb," I replied, frustrated that my last name refused to pop up from my brain. "I know I'm Caleb..."

It turned out my rescuer didn't have a suit and cape—or even a police officer or EMT uniform. Dominic was fifteen at the time, barely seven years older than me. He'd witnessed the fight and wanted a jump on salvaging any tech lost in the aftermath.

I was an unexpected complication to his day, but he used his laser vision to cut through the major debris and then dug me out the rest of the way.

Once I was free, I held my hand out to him. "Thank you."

"No problem, kid." He shook my hand but suddenly seemed distracted. His overstuffed backpack looked as if he was about to go mountain climbing in the middle of the city. "The ground is a lot more stable about three blocks that way.

Can you fly or walk far enough to get clear on your own? I can't carry you plus all this gear, and I can't afford to leave it behind. Somebody would take it before I could make it back. Do you understand?"

I nodded, still in pain and a little disoriented. "It's okay. You can go on—do whatever you're here to do."

He readjusted the straps on his backpack and started to walk away. "Good luck, kid. Be careful."

"You, too," I replied then asked before he got too far. "I think I was supposed to wait here, but have you ever heard of Gregory Street?"

He turned around and pointed to his right. "That's uptown—lot of apartment complexes and part of the college. The bus system can get you there for free once you get to a clear street. Is that where you live?"

I shrugged. "Maybe..." It didn't feel quite right—like home—but I didn't know how else to explain it. "I think it's important, but I can't remember why."

"Well, don't wait around here for too long." He looked up, causing me to look up, too. The bank building was completely demolished, and several others nearby were heavily damaged. Those all looked vacant or had possibly been evacuated while I was trapped. "The city heroes and Roman were playing Skyscraper Jenga up there, and both sides lost." His tone turned reluctant. "Was your family here with you? Parents?"

"I...I don't know what happened." I'd seen people with amnesia in TV shows and movies, but this felt different. "We might have lived at 319D on Gregory Street. I think I remember some phone numbers, too."

I gave him both numbers, but they went to generic voicemails.

"If you know a kid named Caleb, he's safe. Call me back on this number, and I'll let you know where to meet him." Several minutes passed, and police sirens blared in the distance. Dominic cringed. "Look, maybe they made it out alive but lost their phones. I—" One of the damaged buildings began to buckle, and he scrambled to grab me. "Hang on!"

He unlatched and dropped his backpack and tried to fly us clear. A stinging cloud of debris overtook us within seconds, forcing him to land in a narrow alley.

As everything settled, he sat me down against a brick wall and collapsed beside me. We were both hurt then—covered in a mix of concrete dust and blood—but we were alive.

"You okay?" He wasn't angry or upset—just seemed genuinely worried about me.

"I think so." I coughed and nodded. "All of your stuff, though...I'm sorry."

He started laughing, trying to cover being nervous or panicked. "It's not your fault. The problem is it wasn't just *my* stuff." His cell phone rang a few minutes later. He groaned but then answered it in an exaggerated cheerful tone. "Grandma? Hi—I was just about to call you. About those fancy mineral sensors I borrowed this morning...I'll make it up to you as soon as...Look—I almost just died and found a little kid! Can you cut me a break for once? There might even be a reward when his uptown *hero* parents crop up. We're near the corner of 17th and Central. A ride would be appreciated unless you want us to limp there. Thanks."

Based on the old woman's agitated replies, I wanted to run again—but I had no idea where to go. "Your grandma sounded angry. Maybe I shouldn't—"

"Oh, we're not actually related," Dominic explained. "It's more of a nickname to irritate my boss. We'll still be safer at her shop tonight than out here, though. Just don't expect milk and cookies when and if she shows up. Keep quiet and let me do the talking."

Considering Dominic had just saved my life, I was reluctant to ask any questions. It took me a while to calm down and work up the nerve.

"Is your boss a villain?" I asked. He half-smiled but didn't answer me. "Are you?"

He shrugged. "Depends on your definition. We don't hurt or kill innocent people, and scavenging is mostly permitted by the city. I find Grandma the tech she needs. She repurposes it and sells it to people who couldn't afford it otherwise. Then I get my cut from the overall deal. That's all. I started out when I was five—and it's been a lot better than living on the streets or taking my chances with a foster home."

"What happened to your parents?" I asked.

"Oh, they're villains—as in the really horrible kind." He sighed at my wide-eyed reaction and looked down at his phone. "They were locked away almost ten years ago, and I don't talk to them anymore. I'm a lot better off now, but I was pretty messed up for a few years without knowing any better—kept running away from anywhere I was placed before Grandma found—"

Tires screeched, and a horn beeped multiple times—causing a few dazed pedestrians to scatter. An armor-plated delivery truck barreled down the alley and screeched to a halt.

When its side-door opened, a little old lady with wide-rimmed glasses was in the driver's seat. She'd used a stack of engineering textbooks to boost her height, and the gas and brake pedals had extensions so she could reach them.

"Wow, Dominic. For once, you weren't lying. Well, are you two getting in or just going to stand there all day?" Once we were inside, she shut the side door. "You're both splitting the bill when I have this thing detailed—and for my equipment you lost, Dominic, with interest."

Dominic gestured for me to sit in one of the rear seats. "Don't let Grandma fool you. Once you get to know her, she sort-of grows on you—like a parasite or mold." He didn't care that she'd heard him, and she tapped the brakes and caused us both to fall off-balance. "Better buckle up—and closing your eyes helps with the motion sickness and general feelings of terror."

I nodded and tried to sound calm, but my voice came out shaking. "All right..." If I'd made a mistake by going with them, I was too late to do anything about it.

Realizing joking wasn't reassuring me, Dominic changed his tone and helped me find one side of my seatbelt. "It will be okay, kid—seriously. We'll watch the news and keep trying your mom and dad's cell numbers. Maybe get a ride to your place tomorrow in case they think you'd go there. Reward or not, we'll get you back to them or somebody who can help you—I promise."

"Don't push your luck," Grandma snapped from the front, but then her tone changed, too. "You know, it might actually be worth my trouble. The last thing Dominic needs is his own pint-sized henchman. He's been enough hassle on his own, and I'm so close to finally getting him booted out for good."

Dominic grinned as he took a seat across from me, and he hung on to a welded metal bar during the sharper turns. "You'll miss me and you know it—especially whenever you need anything off a shelf higher than five feet."

I started to catch on to their banter and relaxed a little. "Thank you. Both of you."

I didn't have my full abilities yet and had no idea how things would play out. I'd lost my family—and gained a much stranger one. How it all connected didn't come crashing down on us until ten years later.

The worst part is I saw it all before it even happened.

EXTINGUISHED WORLDS: WHAT GOES AROUND

EXTINGUISHED WORLDS: WHAT GOES AROUND

CYCAD COVE ARCHIVES: ACCESS GRANTED_LEVEL 1

When I was a teenager, scientists believe a meteor exploded in mid-atmosphere over Tunguska.

It looked as if the entire sky had split open. Your grandfather and I even saw multiple suns. Then the shockwave hit us. Other than a few scratches and a temporary loss of hearing, I was fine. It flattened the surrounding forest for kilometers. Our reindeer herd was stunned but returned to their feet, mostly uninjured.

Papa was a farmer, a quiet man who worked hard and just wanted a peaceful life. Even though we'd been standing right beside each other, the blast had slammed him into a tree braced by an embankment. There was nothing I could have done to save him, but I still tried...

Superstitious murmurings following his funeral caused me to leave our village—people claiming we'd offended some spirit or god. I held my tongue for the sake of my mother and sisters, but a vengeful rage began to build inside me.

I vowed whoever did this—whatever had murdered him—would be revealed to the world and then pay, if it could be killed. Three nights later, I packed some supplies and started hiking toward the blast's epicenter.

I never saw your grandmother or aunts again.

That was a hundred and thirteen years ago.

CCA File 4200005_AG20211217_RG_PA

Recorded interview of Dr. Roman Greene
Conducted by Adira Greene, age 16
December 17th, 2021
Access Restricted to Level 2 or Higher

CHAPTER TWO

IN SPITE OF TECHNICALLY kidnapping me, Grandma did everything she could to locate my parents. When she took Dominic and me to Gregory Street, 319D was rented by a retired couple who'd never seen me before.

"There was a hero and his family who lived here prior to us, but they abandoned it in a hurry—left some furniture and personal belongings behind when we first moved in, but we turned everything over to the property manager years ago." The gray-haired woman who'd answered the door gave me a sympathetic smile but shook her head. "You don't resemble any of them, Caleb—not from the photos I remember. I'm sorry I can't be of more help, but my husband and I have lived here longer than you've been alive."

I nodded and didn't try to argue with her, more confused and disheartened than anything. "Thanks, anyway..."

The Cycad Cove local news had published nothing about a missing child, and there were no reports of any heroes or villains dying in the fight. Other than the phone numbers that still weren't being answered, I had no more leads to follow.

"Do you want to try the police next?" Grandma asked me on our way back to her shop. I thought it was bizarre she was even offering me the choice and shrugged. "Think it over. If you were running from someone or something, maybe the answer will come back to you. Until we're sure, making things worse for you could make things worse for Dominic and me, too—from a safety standpoint."

"You said something about you were supposed to wait there—as in near the bank?" Dominic asked once we returned to the delivery truck. I had remembered saying it but couldn't recall why. "Maybe if we keep going back there, you'll figure something out."

I eventually chose to stay with Grandma and Dominic over taking my chances with total strangers. Dominic started taking me with him on salvage jobs, hoping someone who knew me might spot us working.

One day we returned to the shop, and Grandma handed me a very authentic-looking birth certificate. It had everything I'd told her and Dominic, with the exception of my last name.

"You need to go to school soon, Caleb—so you don't draw any attention to yourself, or more importantly, me," she explained. "Pick a last name. I'll take care of the rest—take the costs out of what you find me later."

Turns out, that was basically the same deal she'd made Dominic. Anything else he needed later to survive, he basically earned, even as a kid.

I couldn't think of a last name on the spot. "What's yours?"

"Not relevant," Grandma replied, her tone turning irritated. The whole time I'd been there, I'd never seen any mail addressed personally to her—just 'Current Resident' or the shop's name, which was Cycad Cove Recovery & Repair. "Just pick something. We don't have all day on this."

I looked at Dominic. "Averelli?"

He frowned and shook his head. "Don't do that—just trust me." He thought a moment. "How about Caleb Gregory—like the street? Will that work?"

I didn't hate it, but it would take time to learn to respond to it. "Sure." I handed the certificate back to Grandma. "If I ever do remember, can we change it?"

She nodded but laughed. "Yeah, as long as you pay for it."

***

Days and weeks turned into months and years. By the time I was eighteen, I'd basically given up on ever finding

EXTINGUISHED WORLDS: WHAT GOES AROUND

any answers.

"Hey, kid—check this out." Dominic walked over a mound of demolished debris and passed me a visor.

The thing looked expensive, and I tried to be careful handling it. "Nice anodization job on the casing. The mirrors look intact, too. Could it work with your laser vision? Like an amplifier?" I handed it back to him.

"Let's find out. Stand back and look away for a sec."

This made me nervous, considering we'd seen accidents happen with recovered equipment. "Be careful. It may not be safety rated for—"

Dominic laughed. "You sound like you work for superpowered OSHA. Worst thing this could do to me is make my eyes itch if I use it for too long. It's everybody else I have to watch out for—don't want to blind or burn anyone by accident." He cut cleanly through a thick piece of sheet metal as if it was nothing and then stopped so I could see the result. "Oh, this is awesome! This had to belong to Cyndero. I bet he's really missing it right now, too. Best he can do with his natural powers is play dual laser pointer with a cat or catch paper on fire—same as me."

I nodded. There weren't many people—hero or villain—in Cycad Cove with that ability. "Are you related? Maybe he'll pay you more for returning it than you'd get in a resell."

Dominic frowned and didn't seem to like the idea. "He's probably my distant cousin or something—not that he'd care. I'm not returning or reselling it. I'm going to change out its casing and serial number once we get back and start using it to make our jobs easier. If it looks like crap on the outside, he won't believe it was ever his." He put on the visor and turned away from me again.

Something went wrong.

A broken mount caused one of the mirrors inside the casing to change angles, and Dominic didn't notice in time. Instead of his laser vision being directed out the exterior port like before, the beams bounced and redirected back into his face after being amplified about twenty-fold.

He didn't yell or scream in pain. He just collapsed...and I stood there paralyzed in shock.

Then I shuddered involuntarily. The air rippled, and I saw Dominic inspecting the visor again.

He was still alive and began to repeat what he'd just said. "I'm going to change out its casing and serial number once we get back and—"

"No! Don't!" I tackled him before he could finish. The visor fell out of his hands and clattered across the ground.

Dominic got to his feet before I did, more annoyed than angry. "What is wrong with you? If any of those mirrors are broken now, the whole thing will be useless." He crouched down to pick it up again.

I panicked and scrambled to explain. "It's already broken! I saw it kill you—I mean, it could kill you if you don't repair the mounting array first."

He raised an eyebrow but at least didn't put the visor on again. "Calm down. I'm fine." He sounded more concerned about me than he did about almost dying. "You had one of those early-warning visions again?"

"Yeah..." I'd tried to describe them before, but this was the first major one that had happened around him. "I didn't know how to warn you the first time around, and I don't have a lot of time once reality catches up and starts to repeat again."

"You see things twice? First time, I died. Second time, you just stopped me."

I nodded. "It's a lot worse when it's somebody else getting hurt—instead of me just tripping or falling on something. I can't always change what happens, either. You still could have..." I trailed off, the original outcome still lingering in my head. "I'm glad you're okay."

"Thanks—I think." Dominic groaned and stretched as he stood. "I'll look this thing over at the shop before I try it out again—promise. Just use your words next time. I'll believe you. Just wish you'd envision us finding an open safe full of untraceable cash or something good once in a while."

"Yeah...me, too." Any visions I could somewhat control were usually boring—like déjà vu for several minutes at a time. "This just hit out of nowhere. I still haven't quite got a handle on them."

He looked down at the visor again then back at me. "No wonder you're so jumpy lately—and I'm beginning to feel like the Sean Bean of minor villains. Am I really that stupid—where you're having to divert me from getting myself killed every other day?"

I shook my head. "It's not that often—and this isn't exactly the safest career to begin with. People get hurt all the time, even when they're careful. It happens."

"Well, I want better soon—for both of us. All jokes aside about saving your life and you owing me, you don't have to stay in this after you graduate. Your grades should get you into a two-year college, and you can get scholarships from there if you can focus. Hell, by then you may be able to look ahead at your test answers before you even take them. Just be smart about it and foul up an answer or two just to keep the instructors off-guard."

I laughed. "I'm more worried about my identification getting flagged."

"That shouldn't be a problem. Grandma's fake ID guy is good. I mean, she's been ninety years old in public record for at least the past two decades, and nobody's ever bothered her about it."

"That we know about..." I sighed. "Hey, we have company incoming."

Dominic tensed. Even though Cyndero's visor was broken, anything of potential value tended to attract other scavengers—not to mention people who didn't approve of what we did in the first place. "Who is it?"

"I'm not sure. I've never seen her around here before."

The girl looked around my age but didn't go to my high school. She could fly but was dressed in normal clothes—jeans, t-shirt, and a jacket. No hero or villain uniform. She also kept her distance from us—eyeing Dominic and then me with a wary expression. "My name is Adira Greene. Which one of you is Dominic? Your grandmother sent me—said you're independent contractors and not her employees. I have a job I want to run by you."

Dominic quickly slipped the visor into his pack before he

responded. "We're not exactly set up for repair work out here. If you drop something off at the shop with your contact info, I'll have it back to you within a week—just depends on the problem. Grandma's usually happy about getting her cut from the referral. Is it something hazardous she doesn't want to store?"

Adira shook her head. "I don't need a repair. This is a salvage op. It's just the location and details will require some discretion. It's in an area normally restricted to the general public, but we're in the process of obtaining a permit. We've gotten them before without issue."

"Where?" Dominic asked.

She hesitated. "Can your friend be trusted?"

"Caleb's my little brother—and we're losing daylight. You can either tell me the details or wait until we're finished up here. I don't have time for games."

She crossed her arms, and her tone turned frustrated. "It involves Orchid Island..."

This confirmed that she wasn't a local. It's not that our tourism bureau was a bunch of liars. The restricted island just off of Cycad Cove's eastern coast *technically* had orchids...and high levels of radioactivity...and magma-filled sinkholes that could swallow up the average citizen who couldn't fly.

Even with having powers, 'Perilous Island' was its unofficial but more accurate nickname—and nearly everyone within a fifty-mile radius knew to stay clear of it.

Dominic relaxed but shook his head at her. "Ah, now it all makes sense. Grandma told you to shove off, and now you're trying to bypass her through us. Whatever you're after there, it's not worth it—not that we'd sue her, but you could if someone on your exploration team gets hurt or killed. It's the same with us. We're not tour guides, especially with Perilous. Thanks—but no thanks. Have a nice day."

She flew closer to us, and I noticed she had a faded scar

on her chin—either from a fight or possibly a childhood accident. "We already know the general layout of the island, but we need to recover something specific. You and your brother appear to have the right track record and expertise, and you're fast about it. We're up against a deadline the moment this permit is approved."

"And how many other salvage teams before us did you feed that line to?" Dominic asked. Adira didn't answer. "That's what I thought. Can't spend the money if you're dead."

Giving up on trying to convince Dominic, she looked at me. "What about you?"

I wasn't used to being asked things like this and usually just followed Dominic's lead. "I like being alive, too? It's kind of nice. Sorry, though. I, uh, hope things go well for you and that you make it back okay."

She gave me a skeptical look and focused on Dominic again. "Best we can offer is two hundred each—upfront but held in an independent escrow. You help us find what we're looking for, and the bonus will be worth your while. If either of you change your mind, your grandmother has our contact info. My family has bought suits and other equipment from Maggie for years. I'm not trying to jerk you around on this, but I don't have time for games, either." She started to leave.

"Then you should know that four hundred dollars wouldn't even touch the cost of our basic gear!" Dominic called after her. "That's not including all the extra equipment we'd need! I'm not planning on kids, but I'm already enough of a genetic freak that I don't want to wake up with extra arms or pass on whatever that kind of radiation would do to me."

She turned back around to face us, and she sounded more relieved than condescending. "I think there's been a major misunderstanding. The offer is for two hundred thousand each, and we'll do everything possible to ensure your safety."

Dominic's tone hardened, and he glared at her. "Do you have any idea how long it would take us to legitimately earn that kind of money? And then you just drop in like Archeology Barbie and expect us to risk our lives for something you won't even fully discuss? No way. If you don't get us killed, you'll probably get us imprisoned while you and your team walk away clear with whatever the hell it is you're after."

She shook her head. "I'm going with you—and my father, too. It's that important, or I wouldn't be putting up with this—trust me."

"Who are you?" I asked. "I mean, who's backing you to throw that kind of funding at this?"

"My father's full name is Roman Greene—media dropped his last name even before I was born. He knows both of you—of you, at least. He wouldn't have sent me here otherwise."

I froze. Her father was Roman—as in the villain the heroes had attempted to capture the day Dominic rescued me. I hadn't heard anything on the news about him in years—had no idea what had happened to him, other than he'd left Cycad Cove. I'd never gotten the opportunity to talk to him about what happened before that fight or if he knew anything else about me.

Dominic's shoulders slumped. "I've really just stepped in it, haven't I? You're not trying to scam us, are you?"

Adira's tone softened, and she forced a smile. "My parents started their business not much differently than what you're doing. I get it—and I'm not some spoiled little rich girl trying to buy what we can't earn ourselves. We still need help—smart help—and I would have been more concerned if you'd immediately said yes. We lost my mother on that island, and Dad and I have had our share of close calls."

"Then why keep going back there—at all?" I asked.

This made her uneasy again. "We can't tell you until you accept the job and sign all the legal disclosure paperwork. You can still back out after we tell you, but it would require returning the escrowed funds back to us—minus a small fee we'd give you to keep your mouths shut. It's a safety issue, too. We don't want a mad rush of random people getting hurt trying to find something they won't even understand."

"When would you need an answer?" Dominic asked.

"Depends on when Cycad Cove decides to clear the permit this time. They're more than happy to send out heroes to enforce them the second they run out. For now, it's just a money racket to force Dad to reapply and pay more fees the closer we get to making some progress. He's concerned if we don't succeed this round, we'll get shut out for good—and some competing team will be sent in to follow up on all our previous work. Without going into details, it would be very bad for the world if that happened."

"That doesn't sound ominous at all..." Dominic said to me under his breath and then replied louder. "All right, we'll think it over and get back to you. Out of curiosity, what would be the 'keep our mouths shut' fee—each?"

"Two grand—but I hope you'll at least hear my dad out," Adira replied. "He's not who most people think he is—just runs with the reputation rather than wasting time trying to fight it."

"I know a thing or two about that with my family—our family, I mean." Dominic gestured to me as if pretending we were biological brothers was somehow important—that he didn't want Adira or her father knowing otherwise.

I went along with it and nodded in agreement. Once she left, Dominic started gathering his gear to leave.

"What was that all about?" I asked.

"She's genuine, but her father may be an issue. I remember him now. He used to come into the shop a lot when I was a kid. He and his wife were just like any other customers—and then that so-called accident hit the news. Big court case. Bigger media circus because Roman's wife was apparently loaded. Portions of his story just didn't add up, but there wasn't a body or any other evidence to charge him for murder, either. It didn't matter. Bunch of paparazzi idiots harassed the poor kid, too, but she seems like she's dealt with it."

"I saw part of the fight the day you found me, but I don't remember any of that. I guess I was too focused on trying to find my parents."

Dominic gestured to the area where nearly everything had been rebuilt over time, just not as tall. "All those buildings collapsed because heroes tried bringing Roman in a second time—like something else had set him off, even after he was officially released. You just got caught in the middle of it, but I'm still not sure how I feel about working with him now. Let's go home, and I'll think it over."

CYCAD COVE ARCHIVES: ACCESS GRANTED_LEVEL 1

A man burst up from the water and landed on our main deck, his hands raised in a gesture of surrender. Based on this and his scaled metallic suit, my immediate thoughts went to Neptune or Poseidon—that all of those Roman and Greek myths had some basis in reality.

Naturally, we still drew our guns. As the youngest of the crew, my hands trembled too much for a steady shot. Captain McNabb began asking him questions, though none of us expected an understandable response—much less in English.

'I am from another planet much like yours,' the man explained calmly. He looked human, enough—sounded human, enough—that curiosity began to override our fears. 'My name is Fortis, and I'm not here to harm any of you. Can we talk in your quarters, Captain McNabb? It's very important.'

'I never mentioned my name,' McNabb replied. He looked to all of us, who agreed he hadn't identified himself yet. The rest of us tended to use his title, even in emergency situations.

Fortis lowered his hands to his side and smiled. 'I know.'

CCA File 2700003_BWTS19080706_TS_PA

Private Benjamin Wallace
U.S. Lifesaving Service
July 6th, 1908

CHAPTER THREE

WE FINISHED PACKING UP just before nightfall—when all the city's major trouble tended to start—and took the visor and a few minor finds with us.

When we reached the shop, Grandma had a pot of chili cooking. Dominic tested it then hit it with a short burst of his laser vision—causing a portion to boil over onto the stovetop.

Grandma didn't seem amused and whacked him with a dish towel. "Stop showing off. You'll burn it."

He handed over what we'd found for the day, minus the visor. She paid us both cash upfront—something that almost never happened.

"Are you feeling okay?" I asked.

"I'm fine," she replied, but her tone seemed off. "It's just such a small amount today it's not even worth all the paperwork. I take it you were both distracted by your new lady friend?"

Dominic nudged me. "She's a little young for me, but Psychic Boy here could barely string two sentences together. I made sure to be accidentally insulting enough for him to have a chance."

Grandma half-smiled. "Well, I'm not giving him 'the talk.' You found him. You tell him."

I put my hands up. "That's okay—I'm good. Every health class since fifth grade had that covered. We do *not* need to have that conversation."

"That's probably for the best," Dominic replied. "Samantha was my only long-term girlfriend, and she literally teleported away before we got to that stage—all because I decided to take relationship advice from somebody who hasn't had any action since *The Titanic*."

Grandma held up one finger. The middle segment was slightly crooked as if she'd broken it at some point. "One, all I said was honesty is a good thing if you care about someone—not to dump everything on that poor girl as if it was a joke."

"She asked how long my parents had been married, and I told her the truth!" Dominic replied then mimicked Samantha's voice. *"Oh, that's so sweet. When can I meet them?"* His voice dropped back to normal. "Well, the Cycad Cove Women's SuperMax where Mom's held has a shorter visitor waiting list than where Dad's in solitary at Brunel Heights…poof…gone…blocked my number…never saw or spoke to her again. I really liked her, too, and I blew it."

"It could have been worse…" Grandma said.

"Yeah, and there was room enough on that door for two people."

"Two, I was never on *The Titanic*. Three, that movie wasn't a documentary. Caleb, where are you going?"

It was easier to lie than try to explain what I was seeing outside of our conversation. "I just need some air for a minute. Just yell when the food's almost done. I'll help set the table."

Grandma gave a reluctant nod. After I shut the door behind me, I leaned up against it and could still hear her and Dominic talking. I also saw a brief vision of the future playing out, but it didn't directly involve any of us.

"Is he all right?" Grandma asked. The conversation was more important to me, and I tried to focus on it.

"He's fine—other than the fact he thought he saw me die earlier today…managed to stop it before it happened, too." Dominic sounded more worried than he had in front of me. "These visions or premonitions—whatever the hell you want to call them—they're not just panic attacks like I was thinking before. It's a power, and he's getting overwhelmed by it. Do you have any business contacts who could help him without making things worse?"

"Not anyone I can easily reach right now," Grandma replied.

"Well, you may want to start trying, anyway. I'm out of my depth on this one—not to mention this whole deal with Roman and his daughter. I want to take the job. I really do. Caleb and I could both use the money to get out of this grind—no offense."

"None taken. I also have five-million-dollar life insurance policies on both of you if you don't make it back alive. I win either way."

"Of course, you do." Dominic sighed. "I'll be right back."

I moved away from the door and went upstairs, opening a second door to the rooftop. There's a set of wicker lawn furniture up there, kind of like an outdoor break room. Grandma's shop was originally a tire store and still smelled like one. It's close enough to downtown that I was accustomed to all the sirens at night, but it's far enough away to not have a random hero or villain crash through our walls while we're trying to sleep.

A lot of surrounding businesses had moved out over the years, along with a significant number of civilians. I couldn't blame them. Both sides escalated conflicts to where collateral damage was the last thing on their minds. Even ten years earlier—when Grandma put the word out that a child had been injured during Roman's attempted capture—not a single Cycad Cove hero ever bothered to follow up or help find my family.

Once word eventually reached him, Roman sent Grandma money to buy me some clothes and toys. I was the same age as his kid—as Adira—and he'd actually felt terrible about what had happened. That made the whole world turn upside-down to me. The so-called bad guys cared, and the good guys always seemed too overwhelmed or stressed out to feel anything.

My parents could have been heroes like Dominic believed, but I didn't want that kind of life—not if it was like that.

The rooftop door creaked open.

"Hey. Chili's almost done, and I think we're through with

embarrassing you about Adira for at least the next thirty minutes," Dominic said and then added. "No promises, though."

I sighed and rubbed my face. The visions sometimes gave me migraines, especially if something else was happening right in front of me at the same time. "It wasn't that. Right in the middle of you talking about Samantha, I got a brief flash ahead of me coming up here—thought I'd better actually do it in case it was important."

He frowned, and his tone made me think he was worried I was going crazy. "You're following what these visions tell you to do? It's just images, right? No voices or anything?"

"Other than people having conversations," I said, and he picked up that I'd overheard him and Grandma, too. "When I don't follow them exactly, it's not always bad or anything. I could have stayed downstairs with you, and the vision probably would have changed with the decision. I'm just trying to figure it all out. It's like I'm tapping into something outside of me...bigger than me...a lot bigger..." I pointed at a hero and villain fighting in the distance. One of them had electrical powers, and the other had a glowing orange bubble around her that was absorbing and occasionally redirecting the blasts. "Those two are about to knock each other out and fall, and there's nothing we can do about it from this far away."

About three seconds later, they both dropped below the skyline. I hoped they both survived, but I couldn't make my brain see their outcomes either way.

Dominic's expression was shaken—maybe a little terrified. His words came out slower and more careful than normal. "I want to take this job with Roman. I won't force you to go with us, but—"

"If I stay behind, I'll be too far away to warn any of you." I gestured east toward Perilous Island, which looked faint in the distance. "Even without having full control over this, I don't know if I could live with that."

Dominic started pacing. "It's not as if any accident there would be your fault. You zoning-out to look ahead when you need to be focused in the moment could get you hurt, too.

You don't have to do this just because I am. You have other options—more than I could possibly dream about when I was your age."

"You're not that much older than me. If you still want to go to college or just do something else—"

"I tried for a long time—and I got tired of having doors slammed in my face." His expression turned frustrated. "I don't have a criminal record—not even a juvenile one. One look at my last name...people make the assumption I'll end up wrecking their campus or have some ulterior motive for working for them. They don't trust me from the start, and I don't have the time or energy to waste trying to prove them wrong. It's affected you, too—whether you ever noticed it in school or not. You should have a much better life right now—friends—instead of spending your evenings and weekends digging through scrap with me."

It wasn't as horrible as he made it sound. There were entire days I'd daydream about what my life could have been like if my parents had been located—as if it would magically solve every minor problem in my life—but I thought about the possibility less and less as I got older. Whatever had happened, they were likely dead. I could have been, too—or possibly worse—if the wrong people had found me.

Grandma was practical—not a tyrant keeping Dominic and me around against our will. Even if she eventually kicked us out, she wanted to make sure we both left at the same time.

I forced a smile. "You're my brother. I mean that in every way it matters."

Dominic looked away from me at the island. "Well, I haven't always been that great of one...and you don't owe me anything, Caleb. Seriously. Stay here on this one. Don't feel any damn guilt if I screw up there. That's too much weight on anybody—much less an eighteen-year-old. I wouldn't want it to mess you up for the rest of your life."

I shook my head. "You've always tried to look out for me. I just want to do the same—on something good for once. You get this money, and then you'll have some options, right?"

"I'll have even more if you invest your part, too. May I

interest you in my business pitch, good sir?" He laughed at my reaction. "Crap, I don't even have a Kickstarter page set up yet...give me a few days."

"I'll think about it—if we make it back."

"*After* we make it back," he corrected. "I don't know how any of it works, but a little optimism probably can't hurt you. Just don't go overboard and switch sides on us. Becoming Cycad Cove's pre-disaster detector wouldn't be much of a life."

I laughed. "You mean for the heroes? Yeah, that's never going to happen."

Before he could reply, Grandma yelled from downstairs. "I just finished what little chili wasn't scorched to a crisp! If you two want to order a pizza, you can take it out of the money I just gave you. Dominic, you're cleaning this mess up on the stove—not me."

Dominic looked at me. "I didn't burn that much, which means she ate three-fourths of a pot of chili just to prove herself right. You order the pizza from Al's. I'll go pick it up to save us the delivery fee. We'll eat it up here. I might sleep out here tonight, too." He raised his voice. "If she's as gassy as the last time—"

"Quit being so overdramatic," Grandma snapped from downstairs.

"Plants wilted! Moths and bats dropped from the sky! We had to sleep in our hazmat suits for two nights! Oh, the humanity..." Dominic shouted back. "Back in a minute, kid. I'll risk getting the number from downstairs and call Roman, too—find out when and where he wants us to meet. Wish me luck." He took a deep breath and then went downstairs. "Gah—how can you digest anything that fast! You're not even human, are you? You're some miniature demon warthog who likes watching *Wheel of Fortune*."

Grandma's tone went creepy, almost sinister. "You get any closer on your guessing, Dominic, and I will have to kick you and Caleb both out of here—for your own safety." She returned to sounding closer to normal. "Here's another six bucks. I want some breadsticks. Might settle my tummy. Adira left a business card on the counter. It's still there."

"Thanks..." Dominic replied then hesitated. "So, do I have to call you Rumpelstiltskin two or three times to make you vanish?"

"That's Beetlejuice—and nice try. Go on. It's getting late."

I called the pizza place and waited until Dominic left before I came downstairs. The air was...tolerable compared to what I was expecting.

Grandma forced a smile at me. If there had ever been a mess on the stove, she'd already taken care of it. "There are some things I can never tell either of you, but at least it's fun—most of the time, anyway."

"Did you ever have a family—before taking us in, I mean?" I asked, not expecting to get much of an actual answer from her. Over the past ten years, I'd barely learned anything about her past and just guessed on most of it.

"I know what it's like to be alone and on your own, but I never intended for you and Dominic to get attached to me—at all," she replied. "Once you graduate, both of you need to leave here and go do something for yourselves. In fact, I'd prefer it if you both got as far away from this city as possible. I'd leave if I could, too, but I can't—not for a while longer."

This bothered me. "You haven't really hated us being around this entire time, have you? I've tried not to be any hassle, and Dominic torments you all the time because—"

"I know. I—" She sighed and started to look uncomfortable. "I have to get some work done before we open tomorrow. Enjoy your pizza. Tell Dominic to knock and leave the breadsticks at my office door when he gets back."

"I will." I replied. She shut the door before I could say or ask anything else. "Goodnight."

CYCAD COVE ARCHIVES: ACCESS GRANTED_LEVEL 1

From a historical standpoint, it can be argued that Fortis changed the course of our planet the moment he entered it. If we take him at his word—and I do—he's limited his intervention to averting two global wars and then settled in Cycad Cove to live a relatively normal life.

Relatively normal—considering the recent phenomenon of humans developing supernatural abilities. Flight. Healing. Extraordinary strength, speed, or agility. Overall longer lifespans. There appears to be no common connection in these cases, at least not geographical or socioeconomic.

One prevailing theory is that Fortis's spacecraft affected Earth's water supply when it crashed into the Pacific Ocean—something he didn't intend but has so far not produced any negative side-effects. Documentation is still ongoing, as are sanctioned expeditions to recover the ship for study. Fortis believes there's nothing left to recover after four decades but has offered to assist in the efforts.

The more immediate concern is this: If enough people—some with possible evil intent—gain abilities near or surpassing Fortis's levels, we could enter a new global age of violence and war that he can no longer stop alone. We need to act now and begin recruiting and training individuals who present these abilities. In the United States, this initiative will be a collaboration at the city, state, and national levels. I've spoken with Fortis personally, and he's offered his overall advisement for the program and the opportunity of personal mentorship for anyone who relocates to Cycad Cove.

I will be presenting a formal proposal for Congressional approval later this week.

CCA File 3900009_HMN19480120_PR

President Horace McNabb
Broadcast Radio Address, Recorded January 20th, 1948

CHAPTER FOUR

THE FOLLOWING DAY was the Saturday before Spring Break, which for my high school had been extended to two weeks because of some major repair delays.

All the damage occurred when a sophomore in my physics class, a hero-in-training named Katie O'Connor, decided to confront our school's A.P. Chemistry teacher for being a supervillain.

For the most part, Katie did all the attacking. The lizard monster formerly known as Ms. Watkins screeched a lot but tried to avoid her. They wrecked multiple walls from the chemistry lab to the cafeteria, where I was trying to eat lunch at the time.

Everyone else scattered, but I was so used to watching similar fights and waiting for any gear to drop that I kept eating...until a giant purple lizard arm landed on my chicken tenders and fries. I gave it—tray and all—to an EMT on my way outside. The last I'd heard, Ms. Watkins had survived but had been fired.

So, it startled me that she ended up being our Uber driver to Roman's house. She seemed more embarrassed than angry about the whole situation. "Not that I don't appreciate this far of a trip, guys—especially the money for it—but can't both of you fly? It will take me a couple of hours to drive there, and I may need to make a stop or two to avoid a repeat of what happened at the school. Is that all right?"

If I couldn't string together more than two sentences

around Adira, Ms. Watkins had somehow rendered Dominic speechless. She didn't look that old for a teacher—maybe mid-twenties—but there wasn't an opportunity to outright explain to Dominic that she was also a seven-foot-tall reptile lady.

"We'll still be early, even if you have to stop a few times," I explained. "Our, uh, client warned us there's a security perimeter surrounding his house. We just don't want to get shot down if it targets us by accident or be exhausted from flying and then hiking there with all our gear. How's your arm? Looks like it went back to normal once it got reattached."

Dominic's eyes widened. "Your entire arm got detached? Are you all right?"

Ms. Watkins smiled and nodded. "Oh, I'm fine now. This one's brand new—still tingles a little when I wiggle my fingers, but it won't affect my driving. It just grew back last week, but I kept the one Caleb recovered for research purposes." She looked at me using the rearview mirror, still talking fast. "Sorry about ruining your lunch. It was all one big misunderstanding. Just wish it hadn't gotten me fired. I enjoyed teaching there. I know I never had you in my class, Caleb, but I do remember you, Dominic. You're probably on your Masters or Doctorate by now. Engineering, right?"

In the passenger seat, Dominic's face flushed red, and he rubbed the back of his neck. "I decided to pursue other opportunities—getting ready to start my own business. Space-related tech. Very early stages. That's nice of you, though—probably saw my name on the app to jog your memory, right?"

She laughed. "Oh, I remembered you. Very sharp. Liked to one-up the heroes in the room, especially the smug ones. It's probably a little late now, but I would have been happy to write you a recommendation letter if it would have helped anything. You never asked."

Dominic nodded, but his tone turned sad. "You were nice to me—compared to all my other teachers, anyway. I guess I was afraid if you gave me a recommendation or reference, it would somehow come back to hurt you professionally—given who my parents are."

"Nonsense!" she shouted, causing Dominic and me to jump in our seats. Patches of her skin turned purple and scaled but returned to looking human again as she continued. "I knew who you were from the start. I heard all about it in the teacher's lounge—was warned about you as if they were all doing me a favor. Don't let that one near anything dangerous, or you'll regret it...bunch of awful, condescending...anyway, I didn't care. You can't control what your parents did. I didn't ask for my situation, either. People don't always understand that. Doesn't necessarily make them evil, either, just ignorant. Sometimes success can be the right form of revenge, though. I'm not giving up, either—just doing what I need to do so I can try again."

"What are you researching?" I asked.

"It's classified—somewhat—but I hope it will help a lot of people like me." She went quiet for a minute, apparently trying to gauge how much she could trust us. "That scary monster you saw me turn into? Most people get it all backwards. I turn *human* so I can interact with everybody else. I've developed injections to make it last longer, but they're not permanent. I got a little over-excited conveying some material—lost track of time—and then suddenly a whole classroom of high schoolers freaked out when I turned back. By that point, I couldn't explain I was still in control, and Katie just thought she was protecting everyone. It was my fault for not disclosing everything upfront, but fifteen years is a good run in one place. I'll try again in a few years—different city, different subject, different name. It's getting a little harder now with social media and facial recognition but not impossible..."

The rest of the trip was surprisingly uneventful. She and Dominic ended up talking about advanced chemistry for most of it—not my thing—and the two stops she had to make allowed us to get road trip snacks.

"Well, I hope things go well for both of you, and my number's in that app if you want to stay in touch, Dominic. Good luck with your new company. Looks like we're here. Nice house..."

The walk from the security gate to the actual house looked as if it was at least a mile. Dominic and I got out of the car and grabbed our stuff out of the trunk.

"Thanks! Great to see you again!" Dominic waved to her and then asked me once the car was out of sight. "So...she didn't kill anybody last month, right?"

"No..." I replied. "I think the police released her after she turned human-looking again and explained. Principal Parks fired her, anyway—I guess to keep the school from getting sued or something."

He nodded, his focus still on the road even though the car was gone. "You didn't see her seriously maim anybody, though—not even the hero who tried to fight her?"

I hadn't seen the entire fight but had heard some things later. "A freshman ran through a block wall when he saw her and Katie fighting, but that wasn't *technically* their fault. The guy had powers and healed up later. Why? Are you thinking about calling her once we get back?"

He put up his hands. "Hey, she already knew about my parents and didn't bail on driving us here. I'm honestly more weirded out that she was my teacher when I was around your age than the whole giant lizard thing. As a human, she looks exactly the same as she did back then—like she hasn't aged in eight years." He sighed. "Let's just focus on getting through this first. Follow my lead."

He placed his backpack and duffel bags on the ground and approached the guard shack with his hands raised again. I did the same with mine.

The lead guard was older than Dominic and had buzzed-cut hair, making me think he was former military. "You're a little early. Dr. Greene told us you were coming today. I'm Andy. That's Scott. We just have to search you and your bags for weapons, which I hope you were both smart enough not to bring."

Dominic relaxed and nodded. "Everything except the invisible ones—" Both Andy and Scott drew their guns from their holsters. "Whoa! Hey! Hey! It was just a joke! I—"

I freaked out, and a cold shudder rippled through me—just like when the visor had malfunctioned.

Dominic and I approached the guard shack again, repeating the moment.

"Dr. Greene told us you were coming today—" Andy started.

I interrupted him before it was too late. "You're Andy. He's Scott. My brother is a smartass who does *not* own any invisible firearms. We didn't even know that was a real thing that existed—I swear! Please, don't shoot us."

Both guards tensed but didn't draw their guns this time.

Dominic just stared at me as if I'd gone insane.

A landline phone in the guard shack rang. Andy answered it. "Yes, sir. Yes, sir. You're sure? Okay. I'll take them up in the cart. We'll be there in about five minutes." He hung up the phone. "That was Dr. Greene. He's cleared you both. I'll give you a lift up to the house. No flying within the gated area unless it's an emergency—got it? There are sonic guns and a force field active right now. You definitely don't want to get knocked out and end up as a snack for Ziggy."

"Huh, Adira didn't mention having a dog. Is it friendly once it gets to know you?" I asked.

Something massive roared from one of the locked garages near the guard shack. I shuddered again, but time didn't go backwards like it had before. Fear seemed to have some connection to making the ability work, but it was still inconsistent and not something I could just consciously make happen.

Dominic looked at Andy. "Can I at least make a 'My Little Kaiju' joke without being shot?"

Andy relaxed but seemed slightly annoyed. "It's not that we don't have senses of humor, but this isn't the time and place for it. Do you both understand? There are people out there willing to kill us to get through that gate. It's happened before...same reason the Greenes don't get out in public often. They don't want innocent people caught in the middle of this mess."

"Who's targeting them?" I asked. "Is it heroes or someone wanting the same thing they're after?"

He shrugged. "You two figure that out, and Dr. Greene will probably pay you a lot more to watch his back than dig in the dirt."

From the outside, Roman's house looked more like a museum than a traditional mansion. It had massive columns and two wolf statues near the main door. I counted seven security cameras—including one drone—covering the front entrance alone. Andy told us to remain in the golf cart until he rang the doorbell.

Roman answered personally, not a butler or another guard like I was expecting. I thought my childhood imagination had made him much bigger than he actually was, but he took up most of the entryway. "Come on in, boys. Leave everything in the cart you don't immediately need. Andy will get it squared away for you. I just want to talk with you both."

Even though he seemed friendly, almost casual, it was difficult not to feel intimidated. He towered over a foot above Dominic, who wasn't short, and I realized I'd have to keep my neck angled up just to maintain a normal conversation. When he shook our hands, I was pretty certain he could palm a basketball with the same grip I could hold a baseball.

"It's nice to finally meet you, Dr.—" I started.

"Oh, just call me Roman. Everybody else does—except for Andy...great at his job—little too formal sometimes. Anyway, the doctorate was earned, so Cycad Cove University just denounced me about a decade ago instead of stripping it from me. I think they got offended once I stopped sending them money, but it was either pay all my lawyers' fees or lose everything. I could live almost anywhere, but this has been Adira's home her entire life. My wife, Nadia, loved it here, too, so I fought to keep it. I'll give you the short tour on the way up to my office. Some of it's relevant to what I need you two to help me find."

It took me about five minutes to realize it wasn't so much a tour as a bizarrely polite interrogation. Roman had already done extensive research on both of us compared to what we knew about him.

"You're a little over eighteen now, correct, Caleb?"

"Yes, sir."

"When was your birthday?"

"February 17th."

"Of what year?"

I humored him—giving him the current year minus eighteen years.

"Ever wonder why you hesitate on that? Have to work it out?"

I laughed nervously. "Pretty sure it has something to do with getting hit on the head when I was eight—not that I blame you for any of that. I saw the videos later. You were dodging everything the heroes were throwing at you, and you were way outnumbered."

Roman nodded. "I never wanted anyone to get hurt that day, but it was the principle of the situation. I still appeared for questioning later—voluntarily—as opposed to being dragged in by those rent-a-heroes Cycad Cove keeps on their payroll. I was angry, too—already upset about losing my wife on that island. Nearly getting framed for what happened just made it worse...and Adira having to go through all of it, too. I meant to follow up years ago on your situation, but I'm assuming none of your biological family ever came for you?"

I cringed. Dominic and I rarely talked about this kind of stuff anymore—same as the topic of his parents. "No, sir. No one ever came."

Roman's attention went to Dominic. "And you found Caleb in the process of—how can I put this—recovering my tech for me so I could buy it back later?"

Dominic nodded but shuddered. "I borrowed some proprietary sensors from Grandma without asking her first. I knew how to operate them—that they could locate your tech—but I wasn't familiar with exactly how or why they worked. She's always been secretive about that—I'm assuming for good reason. Your suits and gear a decade ago were years ahead of what most heroes and villains are using now. I admit—I was curious to get a look at it, even if you paid Grandma a premium later to keep it out of everyone else's hands."

Dominic and I hadn't found any of Roman's tech in years, but Grandma never mentioned why she had a unique deal with him. She'd never seemed afraid whenever his name came up. If they weren't friends, they at least respected each other.

Roman brought a device the size of a cell phone from his jacket pocket and approached a large meteorite fragment inside a glass case. The device began beeping and then beeped faster as he got closer to it. "Nadia and I found this together over twenty years ago. The radiation it's emitting is harmless to us but detectable with the right equipment—comes from an extremely rare mineral we were later able to extract and integrate into our tech. I have a little hypothesis that might get all of us some answers."

He walked away from the meteorite and then approached us. Within a few steps, the beeping increased again.

Dominic's tone went nervous. "Wow, no wonder those sensors gave me so much trouble that day—kind of like using a metal detector wearing steel-toed boots, right? I guess my laser vision set it off—"

Roman shook his head. "Step away from Caleb—please. I won't hurt either of you. I just want to confirm something."

I concentrated and managed to get a brief vision ahead of Adira and I talking at the security gate. Roman wasn't lying. "It's okay, Dominic. We'll be fine."

Dominic still seemed skeptical as the beeping continued. "Okay...so, I found Caleb while looking for your tech—but he's obviously not a meteorite full of some space mineral. How's his body emitting the same radiation?"

"Ever take him to a doctor on a regular basis?" Roman asked. "Powered or otherwise?"

Dominic frowned and shook his head. "His powers healed him up before it seemed necessary, but Grandma had one of her contacts check over him because of the concussion—legitimate medical doctor, but those visits were all off-the-books. There didn't seem to be anything wrong with him physically by that point, and if this radiation is as harmless as you claim—"

"Where did you and your wife find that meteorite?" I interrupted.

I got another brief flash ahead of his answer but didn't

attempt to take back the question.

It was the entire reason Roman had sent Adira to find us. "Adira hates the name, but I grew up knowing it as Perilous Island."

EXTINGUISHED WORLDS: WHAT GOES AROUND

CYCAD COVE ARCHIVES: ACCESS GRANTED_LEVEL 1

Out of our original crew, McNabb and I are the last remaining survivors. He's a two-term president now and doing well in the position. People who still claim Fortis's influence got him elected probably aren't wrong, but he's no political puppet—and Fortis isn't some B-movie Martian dictator. They're not perfect, but I'm not either. Overall, I'd still trust them both with my life.

The year after I returned home from my final tour, I sensed an earthquake several minutes before it hit. I was alone at the time—dismissed it as coincidence—and told no one else about it. This continued happening for months. Trying to get my mind off of it, I went on a fishing and hunting trip in Montana with my cousin and his friends.

I had a nightmare on the second night, and the ground below our tents rose into a mound over twenty feet tall. Nobody was hurt, but my cousin and his buddies—and later the local authorities—were suddenly terrified of me.

The way I saw it, I had two options: Voluntarily get help to figure all this out and learn how to control it—or end up getting locked away against my will if I kept ignoring it.

McNabb came up with the name Terrashield—not me—but I get that branding was important at the time. It's to the point the people closest to me now don't ever call me by actual name. I suppose it's the same with most heroes—for our personal safety, mostly.

Cycad Cove feels like home now. I'm just not sure where everything is heading at the global level—if a normal life is still possible for people like us. I hope so.

CCA File 4900014_BWTS19520917_TS_PR

Benjamin Wallace/Terrashield
September 17th, 1952
Cycad Cove News-Sentinel Exclusive Interview (Scanned Microfiche)

CHAPTER FIVE

BEFORE ROMAN COULD SAY anything else, Dominic moved between us. "If you're just putting everything on the table so we understand your situation, we're good—but if this is about using Caleb for some sort of science experiment—"

"My wife was the scientist—not me," Roman replied, and he seemed offended by the accusation. "I'm not out to get either of you harmed or killed—which is why I waited until Caleb turned eighteen before I even considered bringing you two in on this. I didn't want him going off and trying to find answers on his own. We need to work together. I'll pay you both to help us, and we can all get what we want. Does that seem fair to both of you?"

I wasn't sure how I felt about this. "But you've known—suspected—that I would set off that detector?" I asked. Roman nodded with a sad expression as I made my way around Dominic. "For how long? What does that even mean? That I came from Perilous Island but don't remember it? Were there people living there ten years ago? Did you find anyone?"

Roman sighed as if he'd been dreading this entire conversation for the past decade. "There are abandoned structures—mostly along the coast—but nothing that's been livable for a very long time. I don't know where you came from or who your parents were, Caleb. I just think there's a possible connection to the island that might help you. Your memory never fully came back, did it?"

He was concerned about me—that seemed real—but he

was still holding back about something.

"Everything after Dominic rescued me is fine," I replied. "Everything before that...it's like that feeling when you know you've dreamed something but are too awake to recover any of it. I knew a lot more at first, but I just get frustrated when I try to recall any of it now."

"I kept his mom and dad's cell numbers in my contacts every time I changed phones—just in case," Dominic added. "We try them about once a year, but they're both disconnected at the moment." He took out his phone but then frowned at the display.

"What's wrong?" I asked.

"Just got a message from Dad's latest public defender. She's already on her way to the shop—thinks I'm there. I'll call and tell her it can wait until we get back. Can't be anything good, anyway..."

Roman nodded. "Our exploration permit from the city got delayed until Monday morning. If you feel comfortable leaving your gear here with us, I'll have Andy load it onto our boat with everything else. We have plenty of extra rooms if you want to stay here until then. If you need a day or two to take care of some family business first, you can meet us at the marina. We're planning to leave as early as legally possible—a minute past midnight."

"This shouldn't take long," Dominic replied. "Most of the other lawyers Dad scared off just emailed me any paperwork, but if it's something medical-related I suppose she needs it in person. I'll be back as soon as I can. You good with staying here, Caleb?"

I was about to offer to go with him when I noticed Adira standing in the office doorway. She smiled at me. I smiled back, and she didn't look away. "Good I am—with staying, I mean. I'm good with staying."

Dominic laughed. "All right, Yoda." He looked at Roman and relaxed his posture. "Thank you—and I'm sorry for the interruption. I'm normally more professional, and I promise it won't be like this for the entire trip...might actually get some peace if there's bad cell reception..."

Roman relaxed, too. "I understand. Would you like to

borrow a car to get there and back or—?"

Dominic shook his head. "Thanks, but I can fly there once I clear your security defenses as long as I'm not weighed down. Will probably take me about an hour total if it's something quick. I'll call Caleb if it's anything major."

Dominic called the lawyer back on his way down the stairs, but I didn't hear much of their conversation before he was out the front door.

Roman smiled at Adira. "Would you mind showing Caleb around the rest of the house and grounds? There's still a lot that needs to be done, even with the permit delay, and I don't want to bore him to death before we even leave."

"Sure, Dad. Are you hungry, Caleb? I just got back from bringing food for everyone—would have told your brother, too, but he bolted out of here before I could."

I nodded but started babbling nervously. "Dominic will be back soon and can reheat it—literally, with his laser vision. We don't even own a microwave. This place is so nice. This is the best set of clothes I own, and I still feel—"

I shuddered. This time, I physically saw everything going backwards.

"...but he bolted out of here before I could," Adira repeated, and then her eyebrows furrowed. "Caleb, are you okay?"

That was a first. Apparently, the visions also worked when I could potentially die of embarrassment.

"Oh, yeah," I replied, unsure if it would happen if I messed up again. "Thank you for the food. This place is amazing, and it was nice to finally meet your dad."

Her tone turned excited. "Thanks—and this isn't even everything. Our workshop is in a stand-alone garage behind the house. It's just for our personal equipment and suits, but I think you'll like it."

Roman came around his desk and clasped my shoulder, practically directing me out of the office and into the hallway where Adira was standing. "You two go have some fun. Thanks for the food, Sweetie. I'll tell Dominic where to find you if Andy brings him back here first."

"You're welcome, Dad." She shut the office door. "See, I

told you he's not who most people think he is."

"Yeah, I think I get it now. I wish things had been different for you, and I'm sorry your mom died and your dad got blamed for it. You probably would have been really popular at my school, though, so I doubt you would have even spoken to somebody like—"

I am an idiot.

I took a deep breath and concentrated, and I was able to go back to when I wanted with some degree of control. It was only a few seconds, but I had to focus on what I'd wanted to say in the first place. "Yeah, I think I get it now. I wish things had been different for you and your family. I can't even remember my parents anymore."

Adira seemed confused by this. "Because you were a baby when they were both imprisoned?"

Her response confused me, too—until I realized why she'd asked. "What? Oh, I'm not...sorry, I thought since your dad knew that you did, too. I'm kind of unofficially adopted. I've never even met Dominic's actual parents in person. We got to video chat with his mom once a few years ago. She was interesting..."

More like terrifying and insane, but I didn't want to get into any of that—not with someone I still barely knew and with Dominic not being there.

"So, Dominic isn't like Chaosis and Dara?" she asked in a reluctant tone. "You really do trust him as if he was your brother?"

I nodded. "If anything, he's spent his entire life trying to be the exact opposite of them. Saved my life when he could have looked the other way. Probably would have been an engineer or an instructor by now if he hadn't been hassled so much as a kid. He acts like it doesn't bother him anymore, but it does. Your dad giving him a chance with this job—giving us both a chance...he needs this."

Her tone turned skeptical. "You don't even care about the money, do you?"

I laughed. "I won't turn it down or anything. To be honest, two hundred thousand might as well be two billion to me. My mind hasn't fully let it sink in yet...that could be my entire college and a house if I'm smart about it. Could help Dominic get his business off the ground if we move to the same city—split costs. It would be a solid start. What about you? Your father is still being a little vague about what exactly you want us to salvage, but it must be important. If all the buildings there were destroyed decades ago, I'm not sure if there's anything we can do—whether I'm from the island or not."

"You're from there?" Her eyebrows rose. Roman must not have told her much of anything, at least about me. It seemed like an odd thing to keep from her.

I shrugged. "Your father believes I am—showed us the whole harmless radiation detector just before you got back here. It went off with me but not Dominic, so that's another weird mystery to add to my life."

Something went odd in her expression—enough for me to wish this was a vision and could change what I'd just said to her. For some reason, I couldn't this time. "Well, hopefully you'll get some answers out of this, too. Come on. The shop is this way."

EXTINGUISHED WORLDS: WHAT GOES AROUND

CYCAD COVE ARCHIVES: ACCESS GRANTED_LEVEL 1

'For just a moment, forget everything you think you know. Which is more plausible—that an alien discovered an environment and people compatible with his species by sheer luck, or that Fortis is human—just centuries farther down the timeline than the rest of us?'

'You're talking time travel?'

'I'm talking both time and space travel—the opening of one dimension into another when two versions of Earth were in close alignment. That's why we'll never find his spacecraft. There was never one in the first place. What we do have evidence of in 1908—mere days before Fortis was rescued—was a massive release of energy over Siberia, Russia. If that was his entry point into our world, he could have recovered and flown to where he wanted to be found.'

'Or maybe a meteor got caught in the trail of his ship by accident. He did claim he was in emergency stasis and didn't regain consciousness until he hit the water.'

'You believe him without question then?'

'No, but why lie? If he had any hostile intent, no one in 1908 could have stopped him. He seems content to be a retired grandfather now, and younger heroes in Cycad Cove run all day-to-day operations. If you had these concerns before, why bring them up now?'

'Because it still means he changed our timeline to suit his personal vision. From 1908-forward, we have no idea who or what he's manipulated...I'm sorry, I have to go...'

CCA File 00071_NG19940817_SWOI_IL_GFP

Interview transcript between reporter Irene Lawson and George Fredricks/Pacer.
Audio cassette recovered on Orchid Island, Southwest Quadrant.
Logged August 17th, 1994 by Nadia Greene

CHAPTER SIX

THEIR "STAND-ALONE GARAGE" TURNED OUT to be a freaking aircraft hangar. Once Adira opened its main doors, I just stood there gaping at everything for a solid ten seconds—armor-plated off-road vehicles...excavation equipment...all sorts of modular gear compatible with suits of various sizes.

The suits were made out of titanium alloys, carbon fiber, and a refined version of the fluorescent mineral—similar to what was embedded inside the meteorite near Roman's office. The general public would have assumed those sections were blue LEDs, but there was almost an organic quality to them once I got a closer look.

"Your parents built all of these?" I asked.

Adira shook her head. "Actually, your—I mean, Dominic's—grandmother did most of the design work, and I'm assuming she contracted out the manufacturing, too. My parents supplied all the raw materials and overall funding." She pointed to a small stamped logo on one of the suits. I recognized it as the same one we still used. "Mom and Dad always called her Maggie when they brought me to your shop, but I wasn't sure if that was her real name or not. She's always been nice to me—just seems kind of sad sometimes. I think it's good that she has you and Dominic around to protect her."

I smiled, considering it had always seemed like Grandma was the one protecting us. It was sometimes weird to think that most people saw her as just some frail old lady. Whoever she was before she found Dominic and me, I wouldn't have wanted to go against her. "When everything hit a dead end with finding my family, Grandma got me a fake ID—but it's all based around my actual name and what little I remembered. It allowed me to go to school, get my own bank account...all the things most people tend to take for granted with just existing. I'm grateful to her, but I think she wants Dominic and me to move out soon—very soon by the way she's been talking lately."

"My dad is the exact opposite—keeps trying to convince me to stay here and do online college courses for the next four years." Adira broke eye contact with me and stared at the floor. "He's protective. I get that with what happened with Mom, and I didn't have the best experience with normal schools soon after. It's been ten years, though, and I'd hope people would be more understanding about everything now. I don't know...people are just weird sometimes."

"Yeah, I understand that." I picked up a wrist gauntlet with a grappling hook. Its mineral edging lit up brighter, and the entire thing suddenly began to heat up in my hand.

Startled, I dropped it.

Its trigger engaged, and the hook launched into one of the off-road vehicle's front tires, flattening it.

Adira's eyes widened, but she didn't run or back away from me.

This was real, not a vision ahead I could repeat and redo. If it had landed at another angle, it could have easily been one of our ankles...or worse. "Yikes! Adira, I'm so sorry. I thought the thing was about to explode on me or something."

She snapped out of what was either fear or shock, maybe both. "You may not have been too far off..." She picked up the gauntlet with her bare hand, but it didn't light up with her. As she brought it closer to me, the edging brightened again.

She backed away a few steps and grabbed something else—a block of the refined mineral about the size of a cell phone battery. It lit up bright blue, too—almost white—as she placed it in my hand. I started to drop it on purpose, but it seemed a lot more stable and felt cool to the touch compared to the gauntlet.

"How—?" I asked.

She took the block back from me, but the light didn't

fade once she had it. "It took a lot of attempts to get things chemically stable—not your fault. I'd suggest you don't touch anything else on that side of the building, though—or this whole place could turn into one massive death trap." She gestured to the entire left side of the hangar and then laughed when I panicked and jumped over to the side where she was standing.

"Why did it react to me but not to you?"

"Normally, we can charge these battery packs with a converted generator and run everything a few hours at a time. You seem to have an ability to power things without them—and even charge the packs, too. That will be kind of handy on the trip—and I'll be sure to warn Dad and Andy not to bring any earlier-generation gear. You should be fine." She seemed calm as she explained, but it bothered me.

"But it doesn't scare you?" I asked.

She shrugged. "Don't see why it should. I mean, if you're from the island it makes sense. You could have been exposed to this mineral when you were very young and developed abilities connected to it. It has a name, but, please, don't laugh. Mom had it registered as Adiralite...knowing what she and Dad planned to name me when I was born a few years later. I still feel weird every time I say it, but it's sweet, too—one of the things I remembered that made her happy."

"I think it's beautiful..."

She smiled again—and then my cell rang and startled us both.

It was Dominic. If he'd been on his way back, he would have just texted.

Something hadn't gone well.

"Hello?"

"Hey, Caleb. Sorry, but I need you to come to the shop. I have to move something important I'm working on to Roman's place—don't want it falling into the wrong hands while we're gone, and it might be useful if he allows me to take it with us." His tone sounded cheerful, but I could tell it was forced and that he was upset. "Grandma left to talk with a contact who could possibly help with your visions, but she won't be back for at least a week. Even with the security measures here, I don't like the idea of leaving the place empty."

"Sure. So, you're okay, though?"

"I'll fill you in on everything the lawyer told me once you get here. If it all hits on your social media before then, call me back. I'd rather explain in person if I can."

This made me think it was something about his dad. Chaosis had tried to escape a few times over the years, but he'd always been stopped before he'd succeeded. If we were in any major danger, Dominic would have warned me before I left. "Okay. I'll be there in about thirty minutes."

"Don't rush and get yourself hurt. I'm fine. It's just something I still need to process, too. Getting away on this trip will probably be the best thing we can do. I'm glad Grandma won't be here to deal with it, either."

He ended the call, and I looked at Adira. "Dominic needs help with bringing something here he wants to keep safe, and we'll both be right back—an hour or two tops, if it's something heavy."

She gave me a sympathetic nod. "We have plenty of space here. Don't just try to fly off the property, though. Take one of the carts up to the gate. I'll let Dad and Andy know the situation."

It didn't take long to leave, and I oriented myself in the right direction once I was able to fly. I wasn't tempted to check my phone, but I wanted to look ahead for Dominic to tell me what had happened.

I wasn't sure if it was the energy drain from touching the equipment in the hangar or normal exhaustion from a long day, but I couldn't get anything clear—just short bursts of Dominic upset about something his dad had done.

I'd almost reached the city limits when something sideswiped me out of nowhere—and the ground began to get dangerously close.

"What the hell? Who are you?" At first, I thought it was someone in one of Roman's suits, but this one looked far more advanced than any of them—almost robotic. Whoever or whatever was inside it didn't reply as I recovered and got some distance from it.

Wondering if it was a genuine accident or just a misunderstanding, I started flying towards Cycad Cove again.

The thing came at me before I could react—and started forcing me toward the ground. Its voice sounded furious but also robotic, possibly modulated. "Stay away from Adira Greene and Perilous Island, or you will all die! It's not what they believe it is, and you can never save her—"

I tucked my legs in and then kicked it hard in the torso—not that it did much good with it being armored.

This also sent me toward the ground faster and at an angle. I skipped and tumbled through a field of grass for a good forty feet before I finally came to a stop.

Dirt had gotten into my mouth and nostrils, cutting off my air, and it took me a minute to get most of it out and calm down.

Robot Demon Guy had vanished. I was sore and bruised up from the landing, but I'd heal by morning—if nothing else insane happened.

I flew closer to ground level until I finally made it to the shop much later than I'd intended.

Dominic's eyes went wide when he opened the door. "Let me guess. You used a horribly lame line on Adira, and she threw you across their driving range?"

I laughed but then winced in pain. "No, Adira's great—think she actually likes me, too. This was some random guy—must have been watching me as I left their property. Threatened me to stay away from Adira and Perilous Island, but he made it sound like a warning—as if telling me I can't save her was doing me a favor."

Dominic glanced around the alley. "She has an ex-boyfriend? Stalker, maybe?"

I didn't think I'd been followed, but I was exhausted, too. "I don't know. She didn't mention she'd been dating anyone, and this thing sounded like an angry sentient robot. Roman and Adira have some incredible tech you really need to see, but this thing...I'm not even sure if it was a human inside there."

Dominic stepped back from the doorway. "Well, get

inside for now. It's getting dark, and if that thing's still out there we might have to wait until daybreak to move this. As long as we're at the marina on time Sunday night into Monday, Roman will understand—maybe send us some extra help. Before I forget, don't freak out when you get to the loading bay. My suit's in there, but it's empty."

"Your suit?" I followed him to the loading bay.

I'd seen Dominic sketch prototype suits for years—borrowing aspects from existing heroes and villains and integrating them into his own designs.

To be constructed from twenty years' worth of recovered tech, it was more streamlined than I expected. He'd stripped the paint from the older tech—chroming some parts and painting the rest a glossy dark blue. At certain angles, a portion of its helmet and chest plating transitioned to purple and black.

Even though Dominic could already fly, several retractable rocket boosters could increase his speed and maneuverability. If he ever needed to escape a situation, there were options for mounting tools and blast weapons at his wrists and shoulders.

"This is actually GRIFFIN 7.2," he explained. "Most of the previous versions were complete disasters that Grandma would've never let me live down if I'd showed you both." He paused. "So, what do you think?"

"I think if you tried to scavenge sites while wearing this, it would scare the crap out of a lot of heroes. The design's great, though—like the blue and chrome. What are you planning to do with it? I guess if Roman has the permit and we're the only group on the island, no one would say anything if you tested it out there."

"It's also space worthy—meaning all these investment companies wanting to mine asteroids will be lining up at our door. I'll even give all the heroes and villains their cuts so they won't sue me later, even though I found alternative ways to mimic most of their tech."

"This is your business idea?" I asked.

"Yeah. Sound crazy?"

"No, I'm in. Just wish I was tall enough to try it out, too.

Would have been handy a few minutes ago—defense-wise."

He smiled. "Well, I can build you one when we get back for say, two hundred grand? I'll even throw in anodizing it for free—and free shipping since I'll only be moving it a few feet from where I'll build it."

"Deal." I laughed. "College and having a new place to live are overrated."

"Oh, you can live in the suit, too. I'll just lift the helmet and throw you a slice of pizza and an energy drink every once in a while. You'll have to figure out the whole bathroom solution on your own, though. Most over-weaponized supervillains wouldn't instill the same amount of terror if people knew they wear astronaut Huggies for their longer days of heisting. Probably the same with any hero trying to save the day for twenty hours straight. Even with what we do, I'm not doing a catheter—will figure out an emergency eject system first...probably not the best idea in space, though..."

Toward the end of that, he started to sound depressed.

"So, how did it go with your dad's lawyer?" I asked.

He sighed. "She was kind, given the circumstances. A lot of lawyers wouldn't have even bothered or cared, and it would have been a lot worse finding out like everyone else. You already know everything by now, don't you? You don't have to humor me or dance around it."

"I didn't look ahead—honestly tried, but I think I'm too tired or something. I just know it's bad."

"Well, Dad tried to escape Brunel Heights—again. Tricked a guard who'd been decent to him for the past year or so. Just killed the guy after dozens of friendly conversations...like it was nothing." He turned away from me and started pacing. "The other guards had to protect themselves and prevent him from getting free. They had to kill him, Caleb."

"What?" I was stunned, too—I guess because of all the times the guards at Brunel had managed to recapture Chaosis without killing him.

"Yeah..." Dominic continued. "My dad's dead, and I can't feel anything right now except relief...and a lot of pain for all the innocent people he took out with him. Nothing I ever do with my life can make up for any of it. Logically, I know it's not my fault, but when total strangers look at me and just see him—are reminded of him. It makes me feel sick...always has...and I don't know if this really changes anything..."

"I'm sorry...not sure if that's the right thing to say. I know with everything you've been through because of him—"

He sighed. "Caleb, this will all hit the media feeds soon if it hasn't already—possibly at the national or global level because of who Dad was—and I don't want us to be easily found once it does. Nearly every hero and villain in this city keeps waiting for me to turn out just like him—for different reasons...and rejecting their expectations makes me a target to both sides. I hate that it carries over to you and Grandma, too. I never wanted any of this."

"Have they told your mom yet?"

"Don't know. I tried calling her facility after Dad's lawyer left—reached one of her docs, but he said he'd have to clear any communication from me through the warden now. Apparently, Mom's participating in some super-secret government-funded clinical trial. It's supposed to dampen her powers to where they're more manageable, but with side-effects and her never being quite stable to begin with...I'll try again before we leave if they don't get back to me. Right now, I'm just completely drained and want to go to bed. Go get cleaned up and try to get some rest, too. I'll update Roman on everything, and we'll probably meet up with them first thing tomorrow."

"Okay. If you need anything—"

He shook his head but then hugged me. "I'll be a hell of a lot better once this dies out in the news and most people forget that I exist again—hopefully in a month or two. I appreciate it, though. Seriously, go clean up and try to get some sleep—or Adira will think Grandma made you mow our lawn by eating it."

I took a shower and was about to go to my room when I heard something power up in the loading bay. It sounded like the Griffin suit's rockets.

"Dominic?" I shouted. "What the hell are you doing?"

His voice was amplified by the suit. "I think I just saw that metallic bastard who attacked you on our security feeds. It's trying to break in through the front doors. Stay here, and lock everything else down. I'll circle around and take care of it."

Before I could stop him or try to talk him out of it, he flew out of the open bay door.

"Hey, can you still hear me?" he asked, his voice coming from a couple of nearby speakers. "I haven't tested out this transmitter yet. You can talk back using the radio on my desk. Eventually, I'll find a way to link my phone to it."

I found the radio and tried the button attached to the microphone. "Yeah. I'm here. I can still see it on the security feeds. It's moved from the front to the side entrance on Crown Street. Not even sure what it could want there—"

An explosion rocked the building, causing all the small metallic parts on our shelves to rattle.

All the security feeds went dark. Robot Demon Guy somehow knew where the hub and cabling to the cameras were located.

I tried the radio again. "Dominic? Can you still hear me?"

"Yeah. It's just this thing seems to know what I want to do before I—"

A second explosion hit, more distant but louder than the first.

Dominic's signal went dead.

CYCAD COVE ARCHIVES: ACCESS GRANTED_LEVEL 1

The nightmare of this is I keep losing all of them over and over again—just in slightly different ways.

It all feels real to me. Every mistake I've ever made still lingers in my mind, even after I go back and fix things.

I don't know what it means.

I don't want to know what it means.

CCA File 9405600181_CA19881018_CH_SEOI

Hand-written message from Caleb Harrison
Dated April 8th, 2035.
Spiral notebook page recovered on Orchid Island, Southeast Quadrant
Logged October 18th, 1988 by Caleb Averelli

Log note by C.A.—This resembles my handwriting. If it's mine, I haven't written it yet.

CHAPTER SEVEN

I TRIED THE RADIO AGAIN. "DOMINIC, CAN you hear me? Do you need help?"

A low rumble explosion rattled the building, and a couple of our loose parts containers spilled onto the floor.

Dominic's signal still seemed dead—not even any static.

Unable to see ahead if he was okay or not, I grabbed a recently-repaired freeze ray from one of our storage lockers and stepped outside.

Everything went eerily quiet as I walked the building's perimeter. The shop's front windows were cracked and partially shattered. Smoke billowed from another building a few blocks away.

I took a deep breath and started walking toward the fire. My pulse was racing, but I wasn't going to cower and hide if Dominic had gotten hurt trying to protect me.

I started talking out loud to myself. "Just keep calm. You can do this..." I just wanted to stop the thing, not kill it. I never wanted to kill anybody, even if it probably wasn't alive in the first place.

Right behind me, something knocked over a trash can. Its lid hit the asphalt with a loud clang.

Startled, I fired off a shot from the freeze ray. A wall of ice began to develop along the brick and mortar. A gray tabby cat appeared from behind the trash can's base and hissed at me.

"Sorry!" I shouted. The cat meowed and edged away backwards until it felt safe enough to run. "And now I'm apologizing to a cat..."

A set of rocket boosters engaged right above me. I aimed

the freeze ray toward the sound but didn't fire.

It was someone in a metallic teal and purple suit, but I recognized it and lowered the ray gun to my side.

Adira still raised her hands for a moment as she touched down a few feet from me. "Sorry, Caleb! It's just me! I tried calling your shop number, but no one picked up. Dad and I heard about Dominic's father, and I came to help with whatever you needed to move. Are you okay?"

I pointed to the building that was on fire. "Somebody else has a suit that looks a lot like your tech—only it's more advanced...possibly even remote-piloted. It attacked me on my way back here and then tried to break into the shop. Dominic took after it in a prototype suit before I could stop him. I think they went that way."

She nodded. "You fly a little ahead, and I'll cover you. The police and heroes will probably be here soon, too. Be careful."

As we started toward the plume of smoke, a vision hit me—Dominic face-down on the pavement in the Griffin suit. He wasn't moving.

Standing over him was the Robot Demon Guy.

The thing seemed to be able to see me but said nothing—just creepily pointed its index finger up to the sky.

I recognized the intersection behind it—Crown and Fifth—and started flying faster. By the time Adira and I actually arrived, it had vanished.

"Dominic? Dominic?" I lightly shook him, but he didn't respond. I couldn't tell whether he was still breathing. "Can you help me get him turned over, Adira? The suit's too heavy..."

"Be careful about his neck. I have some diagnostic equipment built into my visor, too. He's alive—took a direct shot to the back with some sort of laser weapon, but I'm not seeing any major internal injuries. His suit dispersed most of the blast and probably saved his life."

Dominic groaned as we turned him over onto his back. "This isn't exactly what I had in mind to test it, and you two really shouldn't be here. Go back to the shop and wait for me there. They could still be close..."

"They?" I asked.

"That mirror-coated bastard wasn't alone—lured me out here and made me think I was winning while his buddy took a cheap shot from behind me. I didn't get a good look at either one of them."

"I'm not leaving you out here alone without backup," I replied and tried to look ahead again. "I think they're gone, anyway. I'm not seeing the Robot Demon Guy anymore...just a flatbed truck and the guards from Roman's house. They're going to help us."

This startled Adira. "I was just about to call Andy and Scott. If Dominic can get out of the suit, we'll transport and store it for him until we get back from the island. Both of you can stay with us on the *Kairos*, and we should be ready to leave by tomorrow night."

"I like that plan," Dominic replied, but he winced when police sirens blared in the distance. "Hate to ask this, but can you two help me back to the shop? Might be safer for your security guys to meet us there with the truck, Adira...and I'll need Caleb's help and a Jaws-of-Life-sized can opener to get out of this thing."

We managed to get him back to the lower level of the shop before the police reached us. There could have been questions when they saw the destruction to the shop's storefront, but we weren't the only building on the block with damage. That bought us some time, and I kept a lookout in case they arrived before the guards did.

"How exactly does your ability work, Caleb?" Adira asked in an uneasy tone. "You're living and interacting with us right now, but at the same time your mind is a little in the future, too?"

I nodded, hoping I wasn't scaring her. "It's kind of like skipping ahead a few minutes in a movie I'm experiencing—only I don't have full control over the remote. Sometimes I can change things in the present based on what I learn might happen. Sometimes I can't and have to watch everything play out twice. I don't quite know how to tell the difference yet. When I'm drained, there's no looking ahead at all. Right now, it's kind of sputtering out on me like an engine low on gas."

Dominic sounded like he was in pain but trying to downplay it. "We both need some actual rest, or we'll be useless on this trip." As he exited the suit, several gears grinded, and parts scattered across the floor. "That's better—oh, and I managed to swipe one of Tin Man's glow sticks...stored it here in one of my suit's empty rocket compartments."

He held up a small baton. As I got closer to it, it began to glow blue, then white—just like the tech at Roman's house.

"That's a little unsettling." Dominic said, and he laughed nervously. "Since when are you an orc from *Lord of the Rings*?" Then his tone turned serious. "Caleb? It was just a joke. You okay?"

I looked at him and then Adira, who had her visor up and was staring at me with a concerned expression. "If Roman's right about me, I might not be the only person in Cycad Cove from Perilous Island."

EXTINGUISHED WORLDS: WHAT GOES AROUND

CYCAD COVE ARCHIVES: ACCESS GRANTED_LEVEL 1

'What happened to my family—it's more than just some tragic set of accidents. It was literally never supposed to happen! Why won't you help me? Dad said to go to you if anything ever happened to him. I don't know what else to do...I'm scared...'

'I'm so sorry, Ms. Fredricks, but I really don't know what you mean. I've never heard of a hero named Pacer or interviewed him. Could it have been someone else at the station? I can try to get you in touch with—'

'Never mind. They've already gotten to you. I'll figure it out myself—until they kill me, too.'

'Ms. Fredricks—'

'Fortis, Fast Track, Terrashield, Rodoxian—they're all in on this somehow! If something happens to me, then you'll know. By then, it will probably be too late. Thanks for your time, Mrs. Lawson. I'm sorry I bothered you...'

CCA File 23095_IL20230317_IL_PA

Transcript of doorbell camera video dated March 17th, 2023

Connected log note from Irene Lawson—Young woman identifying herself as George Fredricks/Pacer's daughter showed up at my private residence. Seemed genuinely distraught and angry. I don't recall interviewing anyone by that name and can find no official record of him. Will contact Ben Wallace/Terrashield to be on the safe side. Bizarre situation.

CHAPTER EIGHT

ONCE ANDY AND SCOTT ARRIVED, we used one of the shop's cranes to lift what remained of the Griffin suit onto their truck's bed.

"We'll cover it with tarps and take things slow," Andy said. "You're both welcome to fly alongside us to Dr. Greene's house, but under the circumstances it may attract unwanted attention."

"The suit's just a big metal paperweight now if the heroes confiscate it, so don't risk yourselves over it," Dominic replied. He still seemed upset by all the police and firetruck sirens. "I didn't cause any of this damage—just defended myself after that thing and its friend fired at me first. That doesn't mean the heroes will believe me, though. Some of them have spent years looking for a reason to bring me in, and now they have it."

Adira shook her head. "My dad won't allow that to happen—not to either of you. We should go ahead to the marina. Dad's already waiting for us there."

I'd never had a reason to go to the marina before this, and we flew there slowly and at street-level—in part to avoid attention and because Dominic was injured. Despite being in obvious pain, he refused the offer for any medication Adira had on hand for emergencies.

"I'm basically cursed with an addictive personality from both parents. You can ask Caleb. I don't even like taking aspirin if I can avoid it. My back will heal up once I get some rest. Thank you, though."

Adira frowned. "I guess I should warn you there's a fully-stocked bar on the boat...not that my dad drinks a lot or anything. It's more for guests."

Dominic looked away from us. "I have no problem with other people doing their thing, and I won't be offended if your dad offers me anything. You don't have to warn him. I'll just let him know if it comes up—no worries."

We were about a half-mile from the marina when a woman in a hero uniform and yellow cape touched down and blocked our path.

She had dark hair and looked to be in her mid-twenties. It took me a moment to recognize that it was Samantha— Dominic's ex-girlfriend from a few years ago. I'd only seen her a few times when she'd come to the shop to meet him, and that had been back when I was in middle school.

Dominic went wide-eyed in shock. "Sam? What are you doing here? And since when the hell are you a hero?"

Samantha seemed agitated by the question, but she focused more on Adira and me than Dominic. "Look, it's a long story. Can I speak with you in private? I don't particularly trust the company you're keeping..."

Dominic glared at her. "I could probably say the same. You had no issues with Caleb before, and Adira here isn't exactly Public Enemy Number 1. I—"

"Give it a few more years," she interrupted, "especially with the way Roman is training her..."

Adira clenched her fists, and a reddish/orange glow began to build inside her hands. In response, Samantha suddenly teleported into Adira's personal space.

Even without seeing ahead, this wasn't going to end well. I stepped between them. "Whoa! Whoa! Hey! It's been a really long night for everybody, and none of us probably need this!"

Samantha backed away but wasn't happy about it.

Dominic got my attention, and he tried to keep his voice calm. "You and Adira go on to the marina, Caleb. I'll catch up."

Adira slowly relaxed her hands, and the glow inside them faded. "That new cell tower is just past it. You'll see the *Kairos* before you reach it. Call Dad if you have any trouble.

I'd suggest keeping your phone out and ready to dial—just in case. If there's a problem, we have your back. Our friends will, too."

Samantha glared but said nothing. Dominic nodded for me to follow Adira.

I was worried about him but listened.

Once we were out of sight, Adira's expression turned upset. "That woman is older than she looks, Caleb. When I was a kid, she was one of the heroes who tried to capture Dad."

That didn't make any sense. If Samantha had been there, she would have been a teenager, and there were age limits to who the heroes allowed into dangerous situations.

"What? Are you sure it wasn't her mom or something? Maybe her older sister?" It had been chaotic the day of that fight, but the yellow in Samantha's hero costume and cape did seem familiar. I hadn't gotten a good look at her at the time, but I supposed it was possible. "Or maybe she just didn't age...some sort of ability?" I didn't mention Ms. Watkins by name. "We've seen that before in someone recently—one of the teachers at my school. She's not entirely human, but I don't think she means anybody any harm. Maybe—"

Adira was adamant that she was right. "Caleb, I'm sure about Samantha. I don't know why she hates Dad so much, but it's personal—even more than the other heroes, in a way. Dad genuinely doesn't seem to know why, either. She hates me now, too. I can almost physically sense it—want to instinctively react even though it's not the most logical thing to do."

I started to fly back toward Samantha and Dominic. "I don't like this. We should go back—just keep watch at a distance. I really wish I could look ahead right now..."

Adira nodded in agreement, but then we saw Dominic coming toward us—alone.

When he got closer, he flew past us with a hardened expression. It took Adira and I a few seconds to catch up.

"Hey, what did she say to you?" I asked.

Dominic laughed bitterly. "She apologized—if you can

call it that."

This confused me. "For freaking out on you when you told her about your parents?"

"Oh, it's even better than that. Turns out, Samantha was only dating me as research for her dissertation—Insights into the Supervillain Mind from a Hereditary Perspective." His tone went quiet. "Once she realized I wasn't a total train wreck and cared about her, she started feeling guilty about the whole thing—waited for an excuse to exit and has been avoiding me until tonight."

"That's terrible!" Adira replied. "It doesn't matter who your parents were. Nobody deserves to be treated like that."

"Well, I would say I'm used to it, but Sam's caused another problem she claims she didn't intend." Dominic turned away from us. "Portions of her research predict I'll psychologically snap before I'm thirty—didn't use my name anywhere in the paper itself, but some other heroes recently put two and two together. Now I'm on some ultra-dangerous watch list, and the entire city is on edge after what Dad did. I don't know what to think of Sam right now, but she at least took the risk to warn me. I guess I'll get over the rest eventually—if I'm not captured and locked in a padded reinforced cell first."

That made me angry, too. "But you haven't done anything wrong—at all! At worst, you defended yourself against being attacked first."

Dominic gestured toward downtown. "I didn't have to chase after that robot thing in the first place, and it might have baited me into it. That could be enough. If any other businesses have the fight on camera, it'll be a problem for me. That's why I originally wanted you to stay clear, too."

"Let's just get to the boat as soon as possible." Adira got slightly ahead but waited for us to catch up. "Maybe Dad might have some ideas that can help."

By the time we reached the marina, everything about Dominic's father murdering the guard and being killed had hit most social media feeds. In part for our own safety, we had to read all of it.

Roman had his phone out when we approached him and

appeared relieved to see Adira was safe. "You boys can stay here with us on the boat. If there's any sign of trouble, we'll go out on the water early—technically not set foot on the island until Monday. If the heroes or media give you any hassle, they'll have to deal with me. I sadly have more than enough experience at it."

"Thanks," Dominic replied. "Again, I'm very sorry for the distraction—"

"You have nothing to apologize for." Roman walked over to the boat's railing and leaned on it, facing away from us. "I'm aware of your situation—the basics of it, anyway. For a temporary period following Nadia's death, I was detained in Brunel Heights where Chaosis was a few cells over. He and I never met, but I want to assure you that I'm nothing like him." He turned and faced Dominic. "I don't believe you are, either. Do you and Caleb still want to go forward with helping us? I won't boot you out today, even if you say no."

"I'm still in." Dominic replied and then looked at me. "Caleb?"

Based on Adira's expression, she seemed worried I'd say no. I probably looked terrible and sleep-deprived, and we hadn't even left yet.

"I'm in, but my ability isn't working properly right now—think it's tied to my sleep somehow. If there's somewhere I can rest for a few hours, I'm hoping it will come back so I can be useful."

"I can show you where the guest berths are down below," Adira offered. "Dad and I can keep watch so you can both get some rest before we leave tomorrow night. We have more friends on the way, too—just in case."

"What kind of friends?" Dominic asked in an uneasy tone.

"No offense to you or Caleb, but he'll likely be occupied with his abilities and you no longer have an operational suit." Roman brought up a series of profiles on his phone and showed them to us. I didn't recognize any of them. "These people are professionals I've vetted personally—all very stable—and they will be paid well to watch our backs. I want everyone to return from this alive."

I got a brief flash ahead of the four of us plus these new people sitting around a table later that night—eating and laughing about something.

It made me relax. "It's okay, Dominic. We'll be okay. Let's try to get some actual sleep."

CYCAD COVE ARCHIVES: ACCESS GRANTED_LEVEL 1

I spent my high school and college years in Washington, D.C. while my father was President and later a multiple-term senator, but I stayed at my grandparents' farm in Wyoming during the summers. I loved the animals—and started to use my abilities to help with chores when I thought no one was watching.

'How long have you been able to do that?' Terrashield's confused voice startled me, causing me to drop several gallons of water I had hovering above a trough. The splash hit my shoes and jeans. 'Sorry, Rachel. It's just me. I didn't mean to—'

'You're fine—just wasn't expecting any visitors,' I replied, purposely not answering his question. Once I regained my concentration, I pulled all the water up into the air again— including what had splashed me. 'Dad's not here. He's at some meeting with Fortis in D.C. this week. I'm kind of surprised you weren't invited.'

He shrugged it off but still had an upset expression. 'They've been keeping me out of the loop lately, but I assume it's for a good reason...' He started to leave. 'Sorry again for interrupting you.'

I decided to say something. 'Terra, wait—'

He laughed and gestured at the fields outside. 'There's no crowd out here. Ben is fine. What is it?'

I waited until he returned inside the barn. 'What do you know about the man in the metal suit?'

CCA File 17273_RMN19750417_RX_PA

Rachel McNabb/Rodoxian
Personal Archive
Original Event Date April 17th, 1975

CHAPTER NINE

DOMINIC AND I FOLLOWED ADIRA below deck. The guest beds weren't as cramped as I'd imagined, and right after Adira left I felt safe enough to fall asleep.

Until I was around fifteen, I never dreamed when I slept. No good dreams when I was little, but no nightmares, either. Until my abilities started to manifest, we just assumed it was because of my head injury. I've read that REM sleep is needed for survival, but I seemed to get by without it for years—or just failed to remember anything once I'd wake up.

The vision seemed real, but I also remained aware of the gentle rocking of the boat.

Directly in front of me was Perilous Island—the western side of it sometimes visible from the city. Something was off about it, though. The beachfront looked as if it was swelling up—like volcanoes will do just prior to an eruption.

As the surface cracked open and the surrounding water turned to steam, something small and metallic emerged from an opening.

Dozens of similar objects followed—like bees fleeing a hive and heading straight up to the sky. They all had blue and white lights—the alternating shift in colors similar to Robot Demon Guy's baton. They grouped into a larger hexagon formation, and then a burst of light stretched across the sky.

It was some sort of signal—and we were too late to stop it.

I started talking in my sleep. "We have to stop the

Messengers, or we're dead. We'll all be..." As I woke up, a wave rocked the boat and rolled me onto the floor. I groaned. "Oww..."

"I'll probably regret asking this..." Dominic sounded half-asleep himself. "What were you talking about?"

"What was I saying?"

"Something about 'messengers' trying to kill us...?" His tone turned concerned. "You didn't mean anybody coming with us to the island, did you?"

I shook my head. "No...this was tech...like glowing eggs the size of basketballs. Beautiful, in a way. Intricate designs on their shells—writing, maybe? We didn't understand what they were, and they all got away. Then everyone died. Everyone except for me. It felt like it was all my fault..."

An overwhelming wave of pain and guilt caused my chest to constrict—like I really had just lost everyone I'd ever known.

Dominic rose up on his bed. "Hey, we're all still here—alive. Nothing's happened yet, and now we'll avoid any gigantic glow-in-the-dark Easter eggs. I personally would have done that anyway because of all the *Alien* movies, but sometimes other people can be stupid. It would probably be better to warn everyone else tonight than dismiss it as a nightmare."

"I don't understand why I'm feeling this as if it's already happened—that there's nothing I can do about it. It sounds crazy, I know..."

"Look, I don't think you're crazy," Dominic replied. "I mean, I knew what my abilities would likely be ahead of time, and it still wasn't easy for me at first...almost burnt down the shop by accident a few times before I finally got it figured out. I kept expecting Grandma to kick me out, but she always did her thing—acted annoyed but told me I'd better stick around to work off all the damages. Maybe the island will turn out to be something that can help you learn."

Someone knocked on the door. It was Adira. "Caleb? Dominic? Are you awake?"

"See—she likes you," Dominic whispered. "You got top billing on the question."

"She can probably hear you," I whispered back then said in my normal tone. "Hey, Adira. Yeah, we're awake. Need to come in?"

The door squeaked open.

"Hey. Just wanted to let you both know we'll have company within the hour. Andy and Scott also called and said the Griffin suit is secured. Apparently, there was some sort of fire in our shop once they got there—but Dad said it was minor and not to worry about it. We have storage in our basement, too, so it should be safe."

Dominic nodded. "I'd like to talk to your dad about borrowing equipment to repair it after we get back—and some other things, too. Oh, Caleb had a vision and needs to catch you up on it."

He left before I could signal him to stay. I wasn't even certain those eggs existed—much less sure how I could describe them to Adira without sounding insane.

She looked concerned. "It's okay, Caleb. Whatever it is, you can trust me. You know that, right?"

"Oh, it's not that! It's not that at all. I—" I sighed. "In the vision, I saw these things that looked like probes or beacons coming from beneath the island. The weird thing is—and it could be something my mind just made up—they looked like giant eggs."

"Their exteriors were all uniform, but they looked like the meteorite Dad showed you?" She wasn't laughing. If anything, she looked almost terrified.

"Yeah...that's about as well as I could describe them. Have you seen them before then?"

She shook her head. "Not me. My mom found one, though—not long before she died. Come with me. I need to show you something."

She led me out of the guest section to her private cabin, which had a small bed, a desk with a laptop, and bookshelves with detachable rails to prevent the books from falling. I lingered at the room's doorway as she grabbed an oversized book from one of the lower shelves.

"It's okay. You can come in. Shut the door so it doesn't slam."

I did a quick look ahead, my imagination fearing I'd end up thrown overboard by Roman—minus a few vital limbs.

The only thing I kept getting was everyone at dinner later...nothing else past that. Then something else caught my attention—sketches and notes in the book once Adira opened it.

"Is that some sort of journal?"

"My mom's. She loved to draw—originally wanted to illustrate science textbooks when she went to college. Dad minored in art while he was studying archeology. They met in a class a few years before I was born."

Across two pages were dozens of carefully inked illustrations—all of the same object from different angles. It was one of the eggs.

"They're real..."

Adira nodded. "Mom never touched the one she found, but with the way the mineral reacts to you..."

I backed away toward the door. "Yeah...this is all starting to feel like a major mistake, Adira. If I activate one of those things by accident when we get there—or anything else that could be dangerous—"

"Dad isn't afraid of you. In fact, he's more afraid of what could happen if we don't bring you this time."

"Why? I don't understand."

She started to turn the page but then hesitated. "I don't feel right keeping anything from you and Dominic. Just don't freak out, okay? And don't tell Dad I told you anything."

"I don't know if I can make that promise if—"

She turned the page before I could finish. The right side was blank—making me think what was on the left was her mother's final entry.

The sketch looked like me, only older somehow...closer to Dominic's age. In the lower-left corner was the date and Nadia Greene's last hand-written words: 'Roman, please trust him no matter what else happens. I love you and Adira so much—always.'

"Adira, that can't be me! When your mother drew this, I was just a kid. Same as you."

"Meaning your father could have been—what, maybe

around thirty? I think he was on the island the same time my parents and I were—trying to warn us or protect us. It's just something went wrong, and Dad won't tell me what happened. Mom died. Your father may have, too. It would explain why no one ever came looking for you. If that's the case, maybe we can get them both…"

She trailed off like she'd almost said something she wasn't supposed to—something Roman didn't want Dominic and I to know yet.

"Can get them both—? Are you talking about recovering their bodies or something? To help clear your dad's name? It's not our typical job, but Dominic and I would understand why if that's the issue. Hey, you can trust me, too. I just want to help."

"It's going to sound insane…"

"I have psychic visions. My brother can shoot laser beams out of his eyes. Almost the entire world seems insane in one way or another right now. Try me."

"Dad believes that the island is some sort of multidimensional portal and time—"

She was interrupted by shouting above deck—sounded like Dominic and some other voices I didn't recognize arguing. That was followed by the freeze ray firing and other weapons fire.

By the time Adira and I got there, Roman had put himself between Dominic and three hired mercenaries. Dominic had the freeze ray I'd brought in his hand, and one of the mercenaries had a patch of frost on his armor.

"Everyone, this is Kaylor, Patterson, and Hackney." Roman said in a calm tone. "I didn't pay them any extra to make a surprise entrance, but we can give this whole introduction another try. You want to go first, Kaylor?"

Kaylor was still angry and had her electrical ability primed to use on Dominic. "Do you have any idea who that is, Roman? What his parents—"

Roman raised one of his hands, like he was willing to take the hit instead. "Dominic was a five-year-old kid when all of that happened, and he wasn't raised by them afterwards. Calm down—all of you—or nobody's getting paid.

I expected better out of you, Patterson. You have training your friends don't."

Patterson was still inspecting his armor. "He fired first! If I get frostbite out of this—"

"All three of you appeared out of nowhere right behind me—and I've already been shot in the back once today!" Dominic shouted. "What the hell was I supposed to do?"

The other guy spoke slower and with an odd accent. "Well, a little warning would have been nice is all I'm sayin', Roman...given his mum and pops were crazy mass murderers and all. It's not unreasonable for anyone to think the apple didn't fall too far from the psycho tree."

Dominic sneered at the man but then noticed Adira and me standing behind him. He relaxed his shoulders and handed the freeze ray over to Roman. "I apologize—I really do. Roman, do you have a bottle of whatever these three like that I can buy from you for a peace offering?"

"Probably. Remind me to take it out of your cut once we get back. That sound fair to the rest of you? I'd rather cook you all a meal than kick you off the expedition."

The mercenaries seemed to relax.

Dominic patted my shoulder as he passed me and Adira. "You're not drinking. Got it?"

"Wasn't planning on it. My visions lately are weird enough on their own."

"Well, I guess I'll be banished to the kids' table with good company this time," Adira said and smiled at me. "I'll meet you near the galley, Caleb—just want to put everything away in my room first."

Dominic waited until she was out of earshot. "At least things seem to be going well for one of us..."

I wanted to tell him what she'd shown me, but the mercenaries and Roman weren't far behind us. "Could have been worse. You kept cool and handled it. That's kind of impressive under the circumstances."

He laughed. "Only because you probably looked ahead and put yourself in my line of sight. I know I should appreciate it, but you and Adira shouldn't have to risk yourselves like that—ever. I need to do better, even when you're not around. It's just everything's hitting me at once right now. I can't sleep. I don't even really feel like eating..."

Roman placed a massive hand on Dominic's shoulder and then the other on mine, letting the mercenaries pass us and enter the dining area first. "Enjoy your food. Listen. Watch. Learn what you can. Laugh along with them as if you're plastered, too. It won't take long before they won't know the difference. Once they're out for the night, then we'll talk actual business."

"They're afraid of me—possibly even hate me for what my parents did," Dominic replied. "I'd be better off trying to sleep now while the rest of you eat."

Roman shook his head. "Where do you think they'll be sleeping later, too? Not to mention how things will be set up later at our base camp. Trust me—better to make friends now than have it be an issue for the entire trip."

CYCAD COVE ARCHIVES: ACCESS GRANTED_LEVEL 1

Shortly after the tragic death of his wife, Fortis came to me for advice about their two teenage children.

The marriage between Fortis and physicist Virginia Averelli had been kept secret from the general public for safety and security reasons. Both their children were born healthy, and legal documents only listed their mother's surname. They were also instructed from a young age never to mention their father at school or any public events.

Catherine [case update: Dr. Catherine Averelli-Serrano], age eighteen, handled this upbringing relatively well. She's intelligent, seems emotionally stable, and interested in pursuing a career in medicine. She's grieving but was open to talking about it. She admitted she was closer to her mother than her father but doesn't harbor any resentment toward Fortis or how she was raised.

During our introductory session, Dominic [case update: Dominic Averelli, Sr.], age fifteen, claimed his mother's death was Fortis's fault—that someone named Samantha murdered Virginia out of revenge and that Fortis later covered it up as a car accident. When I attempted to press him to elaborate, he refused, shouting that I work for his father and that there was no point. His official school records indicate a history of violent and erratic behavior, though his I.Q. tested at 156. He's at a vulnerable crossroads right now, and I'm very concerned for him.

When I contacted Fortis to follow-up this morning, he stated Dominic had ran away from home. His whereabouts are currently unknown.

CCA File 339940_KB19890914_KB_BHAA

Dr. Kimberly Brown
Brunel Heights Asylum and Correctional Facility
September 14th, 1989
[File last updated February 17th, 2019 for database search purposes]

CHAPTER TEN

OUT OF THE THREE MERCENARIES, I realized I'd seen one before. When I had gone up to the rooftop of Grandma's shop, she'd been the villain with electrical powers fighting the hero making the protective orange bubbles.

She'd survived their fight but appeared nervous to be on the boat—kept circling a small charge of energy in her open palm. I picked up that she was either married or dating Patterson—the armored guy who'd said Dominic had fired first.

"So, why do you really need the three of us plus those two?" she asked Roman. "I've seen you fight. If your daughter can control her powers to half your level, nothing on that island will want to mess with either of you. It's how you've survived previous trips, correct?"

"This is a bit more than simple survival," Roman replied. If I could do this on my own without involving the rest of you, especially Adira, I would."

"Hey, you want to spend a small fortune to play Indiana Jones for a week, I'm more than happy to accept it." Patterson seemed in a better mood once he'd calmed down, and the frost on his armor had melted away. "The good heroes of Cycad Cove don't seem to like it, though—tried to hassle us for intel on our way in, but there was nothing we could tell them. That was smart of you, Roman. I just don't want to end up shot with a bunch of poison darts or whatever the hell booby traps you're sending us into."

Roman laughed. "Real archeology is typically much safer than the movies...except for maybe the snakes. There are legitimately a lot of snakes..." He shuddered as if he'd remembered a bad previous experience.

"But Perilous Island ain't your typical vacation destination—or even archeological site." Hackney reminded me of a gruff old pirate and kind of talked like one. "I've done my homework. Radiation is the big one. Bizarre fluxes in the magnetic field. Compasses rendered useless within seconds of setting foot on the place. Entire flocks of birds dropping from the sky because their senses get scrambled up. Then you get into the real spooky non-scientific reports. Ghosts. An entire army of metal men who all look identical..."

"Hey, wait a sec—there are more than two of them?" I interrupted. Everyone looked at me at once. "Oh, sorry, hi. I'm Caleb."

Hackney put his fork down and held his hand out to me. I reluctantly shook it but remembered to keep my grip as solid as I could. Dominic had taught me that when I was a kid, too.

"Not sure if you heard Roman earlier, but I'm Hackney. The happy couple there are Kaylor and Patterson. So, you're Chaosis Junior's teenage psychic henchman?"

Dominic and his father shared the same legal first and last name—something he'd tried to face head-on instead of changing his to something else. His father's villain alias was a different story. Even I flinched when I heard it.

Dominic stood up. "Caleb isn't my henchman! I didn't help him just to use him later like some expendable pawn!"

Hackney smiled and took a drink of what I guessed was scotch. "Relax, Junior—or we'll end up drinking Roman dry before we even leave the dock. I'm just trying to sort out the dynamics here. Back when your father had some semblance of sanity, he had a lot of loyal followers...worked out rather conveniently that he and your mother were the only two to walk away in the end. You're not leading this expedition, but my gut is still giving me bad vibes about this entire situation."

Dominic glared back at him. "So is mine—but I'm not him. I don't even know any of you, but I wouldn't judge you based on who your parents were."

This upset Kaylor, and a crackle of electricity popped in her hand. "Well, you can't with mine—considering yours got them both killed!"

This was all going in the opposite direction of my earlier vision. No one was happy or laughing. I concentrated, and everything backed up to where Hackney started to introduce himself and the others.

"I'm Hackney. The happy couple there are Kaylor and Patterson. So, you're—"

"Psychic," I interrupted. "Yeah. It's all pretty weird right now. I haven't been able to guess the lottery yet, though. I'm still kind of limited to what I'm around to experience."

Kaylor stopped the electrical pulse in her hand and leaned her elbows on the table. "So, you're not a mind reader? I could think of a number between one and a hundred, but unless I say it out loud, you've got nothing."

"Yeah—that's pretty much how it works as far as I can tell."

"So, if I tell you the number forty-two out loud..."

I went back and demonstrated once reality caught up again.

"You said forty-two," I repeated.

Kaylor's eyes widened in shock, and then she said to Roman. "Now I get it. If he's like this now, imagine what he can do once he's older and can focus it. You'll never be caught off-guard again—by anyone."

That got everybody in on it—as if it was a magic trick or game to stump me somehow.

I was relieved this outcome was more positive than the previous one, but it started to get a little draining, too. Roman seemed to pick up on it and eventually escorted the mercenaries from the dining area to the guest berths.

"So, do you still remember everything that doesn't come true?" Adira asked once they were gone. "I'm sure that would get confusing after a while."

I shrugged. "Not really. Those visions sort of fade out on me after a while. It's not like amnesia, but I guess my brain sorts out what's useful from what isn't. It's hard to explain. I should probably start recording things on my phone or something—just in case I forget later."

Dominic laughed. "Caleb's *'Holy Crap We Almost Died*

But Didn't' Playlist—not my usual genre, but I can learn to like it if it keeps us alive. Adira, do you think your dad would mind if I used one of those lounge chairs on the deck? I'm probably not going to sleep, but I don't want any trouble with your bodyguard friends. I'm kind of glad they're around, and I think the money will be enough for them to look out for you and Caleb. That's what should matter."

"Dad won't mind. Other than our private rooms, you're all welcome to anywhere on the boat," she replied. "As far as the others, we're paying them to look out for you, too. The moment they seem like they won't or try to cause you problems, Dad will do something about it. I promise you that."

We left the marina at exactly a minute past midnight, and no heroes showed up to hassle us. I was honestly worried about getting seasick, but the *Kairos* was so huge the waves didn't affect it that much. I didn't feel like sleeping, so Adira and I walked around the upper deck.

"Have you ever traveled anywhere outside Cycad Cove before?" she asked me.

"Other than your house? Not really. A few school field trips—nothing longer than a week, and it was always with a tour group. It's not that I've never wanted to...just honestly couldn't afford it. Grandma kept us sheltered and from starving, but Dominic and I have had to take care of ourselves on everything else for as long as I can remember. Before I was old enough, he worked his ass off making sure I was taken care of, even before himself. He won't tell me if that's really why he never went to college, but I've always suspected it."

She nodded that she understood. "Dad and I have never struggled financially—at least not to the point I ever knew about it. After Mom died and Dad basically got blamed for it, he just shut down for a long time—threw himself into work and what remained of their research. I don't have any siblings obviously, and I didn't want to make things any harder for him than they already were. School became a bit of a nightmare, too, so I didn't mind being homeschooled by tutors and taking online classes. That's basically been my life for the past ten years—other than trips to the island every six months or so. I know it could have been a lot worse...it's just kind of nice to have you here with us. You're not like most guys I've tried to talk to around our age—in a good way."

We both went quiet and looked out at the water.

I took a deep breath. "So...I'm going to assume you don't have a boyfriend."

"That would be an accurate assumption." She smiled, but then her expression turned panicked. "Oh, wait—do you—?"

"No, no girlfriend. You're good...other than the fact I sometimes lose all ability to form sentences around you."

"You'll get over that once you really get to know me. If it makes you feel any better, you make me nervous, too. It's a good kind of nervous, though. I like you."

My ability suddenly flashed ahead, and I got this overwhelming sense that I loved her...but I was going to lose her, too.

Adira would die in my arms years from now—and it would be my fault. Just like the vision with the probes, it felt as if it had already happened.

I cringed, trying to force the vision out of my mind and ground myself back into the current moment.

Her eyebrows furrowed. "Caleb, what's wrong? You can tell me."

I didn't want to tell her or try to explain what I still didn't understand. "It's just something bad on the island that hasn't happened yet. I guess I wouldn't see it if there wasn't some way to avert it."

The sudden feeling as if I'd known her for years still lingered with me, and I definitely didn't want to freak her out by admitting it. It hadn't even been a week since we'd met.

"That can't be the easiest thing to deal with—seeing bad things before everyone else," she replied in a careful tone. "Even when you stop them, you still know what could have happened. You still have to live through it at least once."

I shuddered, thinking back to when I had saw Dominic die. It had seemed very real at the time, but that memory had faded after I went back and stopped it. "These visions aren't final. They're just possibilities or warnings. It's not the same thing as fully living it and then going back. It couldn't be. I'm definitely not powerful enough to make the entire universe go back in time or anything. I barely even understand what little I am able to do."

She forced a smile and made an effort to change the subject. "My mom didn't have any superpowers, but I inherited mine from Dad. Have you seen what he can do?"

"A little—the same day Dominic found me—but I saw more of it on video than in person."

"Let's move closer to the stern. I can show you."

She led me to the back of the boat and then charged up a burst of energy in her palms. When she released it, it exploded twenty feet above us in a reddish/orange burst—like an oblong firework. She followed it up with several others, able to control their color and shape to some degree.

"It's not seeing the future or laser bursts, but I can knock someone off their feet and give them a not-so-fun chest burn if I had to," she explained. "Dad could shoot a hole through somebody if he really wanted. Most of the heroes don't understand that when they've come at him. He's learned to be restrained, or he could have killed all of them a long time ago."

"Note to self—never break curfew bringing you home..." I mumbled.

She laughed and leaned on me. "We're eighteen!"

"And I'd personally like to make it to nineteen," I replied, and I wasn't entirely joking. "Seriously, though, I like your dad. I wish he'd been able to bring you to the shop more often when we were growing up. We could have met sooner, and I think Dominic could have used having somebody like him around for advice."

Her smile faded. "You're really worried about Dominic, aren't you?"

"Yeah, I am," I replied, but I didn't want her to get the wrong idea. "Not in a 'he could turn evil and go insane' kind of way. He's just struggling and depressed lately, and I don't know how to help him."

"You're here with him and didn't stay behind when you could have. That's something. I think he knows that—Crap, that was stupid of me..."

"What is it?" I asked.

"Those bursts I made probably looked like emergency flares from the mainland." She pointed out at the water. "The heroes saw them, and now they're coming."

CYCAD COVE ARCHIVES: ACCESS GRANTED_LEVEL 1

By the time I reached the blast's epicenter, I was starving and had very little water left. I honestly believed it would be a one-way trip, anyway.

Waiting for me, sitting on a tree stump, was a bald man about the same age as my father. He was unarmed, but his skin glowed blue and white in the middle of the day. There were patterns to it, almost like tattoos.

I rushed him—punched him in the head as hard as I could—and he allowed me to do it. Didn't fight back. Didn't say a thing while I cursed him with every word I knew.

'Fight me, or die already!' I finally yelled, and a wave of heat erupted from my palms. 'You killed my father!'

The blast sent him flying toward a pile of downed trees, and he landed in a broken slump.

I stared down at my hands—horrified—and then collapsed to my knees. Everything I'd held back since the funeral hit me at once, and I felt worse instead of better at how my father would have seen me.

'I didn't do this,' a firm voice said from behind me, and the same old man I thought I'd just killed placed a hand on my shoulder. When I checked again, his body near the trees had vanished. 'It's okay. Come with me. I need to show you something.'

CCA File 4200006_AG20211217_RG_PA

Recorded interview of Dr. Roman Greene
Conducted by Adira Greene, age 16
December 17th, 2021
Archive Access Restricted to Level 2 or Higher

CHAPTER ELEVEN

THE MOMENT ROMAN SPOTTED the heroes, he ordered everyone except him and Adira to get below deck. I found the first vantage point I could where I could watch and listen without being easily seen. He didn't seem upset with Adira—just didn't want to escalate the situation with us outnumbering the heroes almost two to one.

"As you can see, our permit is valid and everything else is in order." Roman handed one of the heroes—I'd learned his name was Terrashield from TV—a copy of the paperwork. "My daughter had full control over what she was showing her friend, and she apologized for accidentally wasting your time. For the record, those bursts were nothing compared to the displays some of you put on nightly in much more populated areas. Adira wasn't harming anything—not unless having fun is now illegal within the Cycad Cove city limits. It wouldn't surprise me at this point..."

Terrashield glanced at the permit then let his hand fall to his side. "I know you can't feel it out here in the water, but something within the past hour has caused the seismic activity on Perilous Island to increase dramatically. It's on the verge of affecting the city again—just like it did twenty years ago. I don't suppose you'd be willing to share why you're going there, would you?"

He handed the paperwork back to Roman, who folded it and stuck it in his jacket.

"That would be filed under 'none of your damn business', Terrashield—and I really don't appreciate the attempt to use my eighteen-year-old daughter as some probable cause excuse to set foot on my property. If this was one of your hero friend's kids, you'd have already left by now."

"If you and your daughter had actually been in trouble out here, Roman, we would have helped you—same as anybody else." Rodoxian, the hero I'd remembered trying to talk Roman down when I was a kid, put her hand on Terrashield shoulder. "Let's go, Terra. Our call list is already five-deep again. We've got civilians trapped in multiple locations, and Cyndero said his main visor is still missing. His backup works but takes longer to cut through metal."

I cringed. They were helping civilians who were trapped—good thing—but it also made me wonder why they didn't find me before Dominic had ten years earlier. Had they even tried?

Terrashield's tone turned frustrated. "Tell Cyndero we're on our way."

They started to leave, but then one of the heroes behind them stepped forward. It was Samantha. "What about your daughter's friend, Dr. Greene? How do we know they're not injured?" Her tone was so smug that even Terrashield and Rodoxian seemed annoyed by it.

Terrashield shook his head. "That really won't be necessary. We'll go. We've had our disagreements, but I know Roman wouldn't hide something like—"

Roman's tone turned dry and sarcastic. "Oh, I insist at this point." He looked in my general direction and shouted. "Caleb, could you kindly come out here for a moment so we can satisfy these f—ine heroic protectors of the city?" His teeth were gritted.

I swallowed and froze for a moment before making my way to a door. Dominic was nearby and started to follow me for backup, but I shook my head. Even without a vision, I knew the heroes would have a worse response if they recognized him.

I opened the door outside, and it creaked.

The heroes' reaction when they saw that I was uninjured was, well...bizarre. None of them said anything, but Terrashield and Rodoxian exchanged glances and then flew off back toward the city. Samantha pretended as if she hadn't recognized me and followed after them.

"Okay...what the hell was that all about?" I asked Roman after they were gone.

He seemed like he didn't want to tell me. "They have you mistaken for someone else, but we'll deal with it when they come back. I give it maybe a day before the city has a change of heart and revokes our permit. We'll need to work more quickly than I'd originally planned."

Adira seemed upset by this. "Dad, I'm sorry. I wasn't even thinking about how that would look to them."

"They were likely watching us anyway and just looking for an excuse," Roman replied. "It's not your fault. I'm just sick of them constantly doing this to us. I need to get back to the helm before we go off-course. We'll talk later."

Once we made landfall, most of our focus went into setting up a base camp on the beach. The periodic earthquakes didn't help with this, but at least there was nothing massive that could land on us.

As we were putting up tents, Dominic and I noticed ruins of a lighthouse and a few other structures. They didn't appear ancient—more as if they'd been destroyed in a fight within the past twenty years but never cleared.

"Well, the place isn't as ominous as I expected," Dominic said. "My phone even still works. Must be pinging off the tower near the marina."

"Up until this year, we had to rely on satellite-based equipment to relay our data." Adira checked her phone, too. "This is going to make things a lot easier—which has Dad concerned for other reasons."

I looked back at the cell tower, which was distant but still visible. "Pretty expensive project, and the island would be the only major gain in coverage area. Someone else in the city getting ready to compete with you?"

Adira nodded. "Someone with a lot of pull behind-the-scenes, and the heroes have been watching us for years. Chances are that once we get close to anything, they'll step in and try to shut us down. We need to be ready for that. Dad's not asking either of you to fight alongside him, but he doesn't want you taken off-guard and getting caught in the middle, either. If anything happens here, we're all supposed to get clear and not engage. That's personally going to be difficult for me..."

Dominic grabbed a bin of supplies and brought them underneath the tent. "The heroes quit harassing me over salvaging a long time ago, but if it comes down to them trying to hurt your dad—or any of you—I'll have your backs."

"Same here," I agreed. "Maybe I can give everyone a warning before they even arrive. We'll be prepared for them."

Dominic had an upset reaction to this but said nothing. I was eighteen, and he'd been the one to teach me to stand up whenever anyone was being bullied. Given, that hadn't been too many people—and I'd gotten my ass kicked in every instance.

I guess it was the principle of it that mattered.

Roman had overheard and approached us. "I appreciate that—all of you—but I'd prefer it if you all stayed clear if they show up. Their problem is with me. They won't bother with the rest of you unless you give them a reason. I'll handle it. Caleb, Dominic—come with me for a moment. There's something I need to show you. It won't take but maybe ten minutes."

He started walking on a path into the woods, and we followed in what felt like a straight line. A few minutes later however, we reached water again. Dominic checked his phone and shook his head, which caused me to bring up a map on mine.

We were on the eastern side of the island—a distance that should have taken us at least an hour at our walking pace.

"Whoa!" I said. "Did we just teleport or something? I didn't even feel it."

Roman didn't seem startled or surprised. "This is part of the reason I need your help, Caleb. We need to find some pattern or scenario that gets us into the island's interior. As best as I can tell, this is some sort of protection against that."

"Like magic?" Dominic asked in a skeptical tone.

"I'm holding out for a more technical explanation." Roman replied. "In twenty years, I've never come across another ancient site like this. Whoever or whatever put all of these safeguards in place, they're more advanced than us. In terms of the tech my team has already developed, it's been more of a process of rediscovery and reverse engineering than inventing anything new."

"And you want me to look ahead to us finding what's in the island's center?" I asked.

Roman nodded. "If you can. I hate to put you in a time crunch and make things worse, but it's what we have to deal with now."

"Okay...let's see if this works." I tried to concentrate—and found myself standing face-to-face with a glowing red-eyed robot demon.

Its voice was modulated and sounded similar to the one that had attacked me before. "Roman believes he can save Nadia from dying, but he can't. Neither can you—but of course you'll try, anyway. It's who you are. Can't change that, either..."

I had no idea whether it was the same guy from the city or not. We were near the base camp, and there was nowhere to run or hide.

"Who are you?" My voice came out shaking and terrified. "What do you want?"

It laughed, which sounded hollow and distorted. "You'll find out soon enough—if you don't get yourself killed first."

It stepped closer, and I screamed.

The next thing I knew, Dominic had his hands on my shoulders. "Whoa! Hey! You're okay! You didn't even move. What the hell did you see?"

"Robot Demon Guy." My pulse was racing, and my chest hurt again. "I think it can track me through the visions somehow. I don't know if I can find a way around it."

CYCAD COVE ARCHIVES: ACCESS GRANTED_LEVEL 1

'I want to remind you that you're under oath, Mr. Brant...'

'And I want to remind you that Dr. Greene didn't kill his wife. He loved her—and all the money on this planet couldn't have motivated him to cause their daughter pain. What is wrong with you people?'

'We just want the truth.'

'No, you don't. You want us out of the way, no matter how you have to do it. Orchid Island isn't what you think it—'

'Then enlighten us. If Roman Greene cared so much about his family's safety, why keep bringing them and your team to such a dangerous place?'

'Because it's more than a dangerous place—and averting its original purpose could save billions! I'm not your enemy. Dr. Greene isn't your enemy—and Nadia Greene died to protect us and buy the entire planet more time. That's the truth—and that's all I have left to say. If you want to place me in jail for contempt, have at it.'

'That won't be necessary. One last question—how did you and Scott McDonald come to meet the Greenes? You both obviously have a strong degree of loyalty to them.'

'Ask your friend—Fast Track. He introduced us.'

'That's impossible. Fast Track has been dead for years. How—?'

'You'll figure it all out eventually, Terrashield. We did.'

CCA File 1072893_AB20130711_AB_FGA

Witness deposition of Andy Brant
July 11th, 2013

CHAPTER TWELVE

WE STARTED BACK TOWARD the island's western side again. Roman let me borrow one of his compasses along the way, but it started spinning wildly about midway there. I showed it to Dominic.

"This isn't exactly Star Trek teleportation, is it?" he asked Roman. "We're aware the entire time we're walking—not getting broken into atoms and being put back together again on the other side...not unless it keeps happening so fast our brains aren't processing it."

"I thought Star Trek teleporters murdered you and then recreated your exact copy on the alien planet—then killed that copy on its way back," I said.

Roman seemed confused by both of us. "I only watched the one with Kirk, so I'm probably a little behind on some things. Just be careful about flying here, or you'll overshoot. Going west to east, you'll end up over the Atlantic and have over an hour-long flight back. Nadia and I learned that twenty years ago."

"What about going east to west?" I asked.

"The last time I tried that, I crash-landed in the middle of Cycad Cove's downtown. It was right after my lawyers got me released from custody following Nadia's death, and I came back here hoping to find proof of what happened. The heroes thought the destruction was intentional—that I was upset about the accusations and went off out of revenge. The worst part was they kept pushing me until they seemed right. Even after I explained later, they never believed me."

Dominic's tone went uneasy. "So, that's what was going on between you and the heroes the day I found Caleb?"

"Yeah. I ended up defending myself but didn't intentionally harm anyone. The overall damage to the buildings was from both sides...and I'm sorry for my part in that."

Dominic nodded, but I wasn't sure where he was heading with this. "But you flew through where we're walking right now at a fast speed just before that?"

"Above the tree line, of course, but it was basically along this path," Roman replied. "Why?"

Dominic handed the compass back to me and slowed his pace. "What if you somehow pulled Caleb through to the city with you and just didn't know it at the time? Grandma and I never found anything on him—at all. It was as if he'd never existed until that day, but he still seemed to know details about his family and the city. It's just none of it ever panned out whenever we followed up, and we never understood why."

I laughed nervously. "Wait—so, now you think I'm from some alternate dimension? One where we all still spoke English and had the same exact breakfast cereals? It's more likely I just got my family's phone numbers mixed up after I got hurt. If you hadn't saved them in your phone, I don't know if I'd remember them now."

Dominic and Roman both still seemed to be seriously considering the possibility. As we reached the western side of the island again and had the base camp within sight, Adira's voice came over Roman's radio.

She sounded panicked. "Dad, I'm on the *Kairos*. There are heroes coming—at least twenty of them showing on the tracker. Not sure how many others could be cloaked somehow."

Roman cringed. "Dammit...okay, Sweetie, just stay on the boat. Tell Kaylor and Patterson to stay in case you need backup. Send Hackney to us. Don't use any of the boat's weaponry systems unless the heroes do something first. Don't go with them, either—no matter what they tell you. Got it?"

"Copy. Dad, be careful. I love you."

"I love you, too. Everything will be all right. I promise." Roman's expression fell as he clipped the radio back to his belt. "I don't want a fight, boys, but they evidently do. If things go south, fly to the *Kairos* and get the hell out of here. Let me and Hackney handle them. Adira will make sure you both still get your money, with or without me."

"Sir, this isn't just about the money for us—" I started.

"I know. That's why I'm telling you to leave with my daughter." He looked from me to Dominic. "I trust you—both of you."

"Let's just hope it doesn't come down to that..." Dominic replied.

As we reached the base camp, the two heroes from earlier—Terrashield and Redoxian—bypassed everyone on the boat and touched down on the beach a few yards from us.

"I'm sorry, Roman, but we can't allow you to do this." Terrashield said. "You know why."

Roman kept his tone calm and gestured to Dominic and me. "Last time I checked, everyone on this expedition is here at their own free will. Our permit is legal. Trying to intimidate me won't work this time—and you know why on that."

Redoxian's attention kept alternating between Roman and me. She wasn't exactly terrified, but she kept staring at me as if I had three heads or something. I thought back to that drawing in Nadia Greene's journal—about the possibility that these heroes may have known my father but had kept it from me. Would they have left me to die if Dominic hadn't found me? It didn't make a lot of sense, but it bothered me.

"Caleb, we need you and Dominic to please come with us," she said in a pleading tone. "It's just to talk. We're not here to hurt anyone. We're here to help you. There's a lot we need to explain."

Dominic stepped forward. "Other than seeing you on the news, we don't know either of you. I don't want your help or need an explanation of why you're here, and you've had almost a decade to find us if you ever gave a damn about Caleb. You try to take him off this beach, and you'll have to go through me."

"And me." Roman added in a harder tone, nodding for Dominic to head toward the boat.

Then Hackney flew in to join us, using a loud jetpack instead of an ability. "Hell, I'd fight the whole lot of you for a Klondike bar—but Roman's money is right and nice, too. Leave, and tell your little hero army to turn tail if they know what's good for them. If you want a war, we're geared for one."

"We don't want a fight—at all!" Terrashield replied. "There's someone trying to turn us against each other. Distract us from what's really—"

The explosion happened so fast my mind didn't want to comprehend it. One minute the *Kairos* was there—Adira, Kaylor, and Patterson calmly standing on its upper-deck. They had laid their weapons on the planks in front of them. Short of having a white surrender flag on the mast, there was nothing else they could have done to show they weren't a threat...and then they were just gone.

Several concussive waves hit us on the shore soon after— and I could feel them to my bones. Closest thing I could compare it to was standing directly beneath a fireworks show.

They were dead.

Adira was dead.

Shock and then pure fury hit Roman's expression. Building up energy in both hands, he yelled and began to unleash attacks on Terrashield and Redoxian.

More heroes I didn't recognize began to converge on us. Hackney opened fire on them with some sort of pulse rifle, then tossed two pistol-sized versions to Dominic and me. I caught mine, but my hands were shaking.

"If you didn't see this coming, at least make yourself useful! And remember whose side you're on, Junior."

Dominic glared at him and then fired—causing a hero behind Hackney to redirect the blast and then retreat towards the trees. Hackney gave a mildly impressed nod and then flew off to fight someone else.

I aimed my pistol at Terrashield—then Rodoxian—and

then back to Terrashield again. Neither of them were attacking Roman or fighting back, just trying to dodge his blasts.

Roman was shouting and barely understandable. "All you had to do was just leave us alone, and I could have fixed everything!"

A stinging pain hit my ribcage, and I turned to look at Dominic. He'd tried to block someone from shooting me, but the blast had still hit us both. My side was bleeding, but when I placed my hand over the wound it felt like it was on fire.

"Dominic?" It was hard to breathe, and I could barely talk.

"It was Sam, but something's wrong with her." He seemed confused. "I don't know why she'd warn us then do this..."

Samantha appeared in a blur of yellow behind him, shot Dominic in the back and through his chest, and then teleported again before I could fire back at her. Dominic dropped his pistol and collapsed a couple of feet from me.

He was gone.

Before I could even process this, I felt something pressed against the back of my head.

"You can't save them, Fast Track. You can't even save yourself."

Samantha fired before I could face her.

I thought I was dead. Everything—the beach, all the fighting, the *Kairos* in flames—became a rapid blur of movement and color. I caught glimpses—maybe visions—of my life, but not all of them made sense.

In some of them, I was much older than eighteen. In others, it was when I was younger than the day Dominic found me. I couldn't latch on to any one thing long enough to understand it.

Everything was scrambled, and then it went dark.

***

I wasn't sure how much time had passed, but I became

aware of a hospital monitor beeping.

"This shouldn't be possible." Terrashield said in a stunned tone. "Where did you find him?"

"Exactly where his message told me to look." Rodoxian replied. "You know what this means, right?"

"Yeah, but my brain is still trying to wrap around it."

I groaned and tried to open my eyes. "You're alive...we have to stop Samantha. I think she set this up on both sides. We're all going to die on the island, and she's going to get whatever Roman was after once we're gone."

Terrashield laughed, and his tone turned humoring. "We don't know who that is, buddy. Get some rest, and we'll talk about it later."

I shot up in the hospital bed, confused by how I'd gotten there and back to Cycad Cove in general. Terrashield and Redoxian seemed startled but didn't try to attack me.

They looked different, too, but the lighting in the room was dimmed.

"We don't have time for this!" I shouted. "Where's my brother? Where are Adira and Roman? Are they alive?"

Again, both heroes seemed confused and exchanged glances as if they genuinely had no idea who I meant.

Terrashield walked over to the window to open the blinds and let some light into the room. His facial features seemed younger than they had on the island. Redoxian's did, too.

Now I was confused. "So, can you two make yourselves age backwards?" I asked. "Some sort of ability?"

"That would be handy, but no." Rodoxian replied. "You didn't come back here on purpose this time, did you? You told us it wasn't controllable when you were younger."

"I don't remember telling you anything." I was beginning to think if I wasn't crazy, they were.

"That's because you haven't yet—at least on your side of things." Terrashield replied. "If you're confused on that, imagine how we feel."

Still somewhat disoriented, my attention darted to the skyline behind him.

All the skyscrapers that Roman and the heroes had

destroyed right before Dominic found me were intact.

Somehow, I'd gone back in time at least ten years.

EXTINGUISHED WORLDS: WHAT GOES AROUND

CYCAD COVE ARCHIVES: ACCESS GRANTED_LEVEL 1

'So, this man in a metallic suit just shows up out of nowhere in Cycad Cove, and Fortis just automatically trusts him?'

'They're apparently related—four generations apart, even though they look around the same age.'

'So, he's Fortis's great-great-grandfather?'

'Close, but other way around.'

'Fortis's great-great-grandson? From an earlier marriage before Virginia Averelli then? Their original planet? Have they told Catherine yet? Dominic should probably know, too, if they can ever find him.'

'Look, it's a family issue—and really awkward right now at headquarters. I'm honestly trying to stay out of it while they catch up.'

'This is a good thing, though, right? It means more of their people may have survived the evacuation—that they can find each other again.'

'Maybe...'

'Seriously, what's bothering you, Ben? You can tell me.'

'I don't understand why, but Fortis and your father both seem kind of afraid of him—and that scares me.'

CCA File 17274_RMN19750417_RX_PA

Rachel McNabb/Rodoxian's Personal Archive
Original Event Date April 17th, 1975

CHAPTER THIRTEEN

BEFORE I COULD ASK TERRASHIELD and Rodoxian what year it was, I spotted a calendar hanging on the hospital room wall.

It was worse than I'd first thought.

I still seemed to be eighteen and hadn't aged backwards, but I'd somehow time-traveled past the point when I should have been born.

This meant Adira hadn't been born yet, either. Roman and his wife were likely in college. Dominic would have been five...the age he was taken from his parents right after they—oh no...

I scrambled out of the bed, detaching some monitoring equipment and knocking my IV pole to the floor. "I have to get out of here—now! We need to warn everyone in the city before it's too late!"

Terrashield blocked the exit to the hallway. "Caleb, listen to me. I know this has to be really crazy from your perspective, but you shouldn't leave and go off alone. You've been in a coma for almost three weeks, and our team has been watching over you. For Rodoxian and me, we met you years ago—when you're older than us. We're your friends, and we're worried and trying to protect you. Do you understand that?"

"I'm trying, but this isn't just about me. A lot of innocent people are about to die. I don't think it's happened yet. Both of you are way too calm right now, and I need you to believe me. What day is this?"

"It's the 4th of July," Rodoxian replied. "Cyndero, Jhett, and Fortis are already leading patrols of the city parade and fairgrounds, and we told them to call us if they need any backup. It's been relatively quiet."

"Yeah...too quiet." Terrashield at least seemed to believe me. "Caleb, if there's something you came back to warn us about that we missed before, we'll try our best to avert it. Just tell us what you can. We'll handle it—I promise."

I was going to sound insane either way, but I tried to think it out first. "For me, this already happened two years before I was born. My brother told me what he remembered, and I read about it later in school. Your hero friends...a lot of them died or got hurt...and just as many villains did, too...like it was a set-up against both sides. I don't know if it will change anything if I tell you how it—"

A vision hit me before I could finish the sentence.

It was the city fairgrounds—seemed more like the past than the future based on the bright neon clothing and everyone carrying around those old disposable film cameras. A handful of people had cell phones, but they looked like something the military would use to call in an airstrike.

One man was dressed in a magician's suit, only his tux and top hat were dark red instead of black. A young woman in an assistant's outfit handed him objects to juggle—bowling pins...carving knives...then sticks with one end lit on fire with his laser vision.

A small crowd gathered around them and applauded. When the man bowed and removed his hat to gather tips, he looked a lot like Dominic. After a few minutes, the spectators moved on, leaving the couple alone.

They were Dominic's parents—Chaosis and Dara.

"It's not crowded enough yet," Chaosis said. "We'll wait until tonight—just before the fireworks start."

Dara gave a reluctant nod. "If the heroes find any of the devices before then, they'll shut everything down and evacuate everyone. Every second that passes is a missed opportunity."

"Yeah, I'm counting on it." Chaosis replied, and then his

tone turned concerned. "Where's that boy wandered off to now?"

Dara sighed. "He was just here a minute ago. Probably trying to win that stuffed lion again. I keep telling him it's a scam, but he won't listen. I'm not even sure how he's finding money to play. I'm not giving it to him. Are you?"

"No—and nothing's missing from my wallet, so he didn't pickpocket me. I'll go find him. We'll eat and wait things out. Just keep a lookout for anyone who could spoil the show later."

I followed Chaosis until he reached a target practice booth. Dominic sat on a wobbly stool, his feet dangling. Instead of interfering, his father watched and waited.

Using his faint laser vision as a sight, Dominic hit ten metal targets in a row with a pellet rifle and then grinned...until the man operating the booth handed him a small stuffed dog.

Dominic seemed upset instead of happy. "Wait! You said if I traded you back all those little puzzles and won again that I could have a griffin!"

The booth attendant shook his head. "I'm so sorry. You're so little you must have thought I was pointing to the top row. I was gesturing here to the middle one. See, to earn something that big you'll have to trade me three of these dogs back. Puzzles for puppy dogs. Then dogs in exchange for dragons or griffins. Do you understand now?"

Dominic calmed down but still sounded irritated. "But that will be a hundred and fifty dollars, even if I win every time! I don't have that much money. Will you be back again for the fall carnival? I'll hang on to this dog—keep it like new so I can trade it back to you. If you'll be back, I'll try to win the second one tonight. I just have to figure out how."

The attendant smiled and nodded. "You'll have to keep them both absolutely spotless to trade them back next time, but that seems reasonable." He spotted Chaosis watching them. "Hey, looks like your dad might be willing to help you out a little, too. How are you, sir? You've got quite the little sharpshooter here."

Chaosis's tone was dry. "I'm prouder of him for being

able to do math in his head. He just needs some practical negotiation experience. I'll give you fifty bucks for a griffin, and my son keeps the dog so it can have a little snack-sized friend. That sound fair? I know what these things go for in bulk on eBay."

The attendant laughed. "Well, then maybe you should buy him a bulk griffin army and wait half a year for them to ship. A hundred and fifty keeps food on my own kid's plate and a roof over our heads. You should know how it is. I wouldn't try to short-change you on whatever discount Houdini act you're pushing."

Chaosis didn't respond but took off his top hat and gave it to Dominic. "Nic, can you do me a big favor and run this to your mother? She should be near the food trucks by now, and there's enough money hidden inside the brim for our dinner. Just no stopping for any other games on the way, or we don't eat. Understand?"

Dominic nodded as if he was embarrassed that he'd been ripped off. "Yes, sir."

Chaosis waited until he'd left before facing the booth attendant again.

The attendant started packing up to leave. "If this is where you go all tough-guy and try to scare me, you picked the wrong outfit for it. I'm just disappointed there isn't a parade of elephants following behind you."

Chaosis laughed. "Good one." He approached and leaned forward on the booth. "Look, I can't afford one-fifty for some ten-dollar toy. You've already squeezed fifty out of my kid for something that probably cost you less than a buck. Work with me here. He'll even parade the thing around all night and send more people your way. It will send the message that it's possible for a kindergartener to win—and that's all some people need to try for it."

"You look—it's either one-fifty or—" The attendant yelled in pain from Chaosis blasting him in the eyes with his laser vision. "What the hell did you just do to me? I can't see! Somebody help me!"

Chaosis blasted him again, and he fell to the ground screaming. "Oops, I thought I was aiming at that top row just above your head. Turns out I was aiming for the middle one. My mistake." He continued until the man stopped screaming. "Eew, that's gross. Let's see...wonder what color griffin the kid wanted..."

While Chaosis searched, several small children without their parents climbed up on the stools in front of the booth.

I couldn't warn them.

I couldn't do anything.

One of the kids hit a metal target, causing it to ping.

Chaosis was startled but recovered quickly, mimicking the booth attendant's voice. "Oh, hey there, kids. Sorry, but this game is broken. Who wants a free dragon or fluffy dog to go away and play a different one? Here's one for you and one for you..." He cringed as one kid's mother spotted the attendant's body and screamed. "Gotta go! Help yourselves!"

Then he ran right past me as if I wasn't there, laughing maniacally the entire time.

CYCAD COVE ARCHIVES: ACCESS GRANTED_LEVEL 1

All official records regarding Dara McDonald-Averelli have been sealed, but I've pieced some things together.

She has a younger brother—Scott McDonald—who works as a security guard for Dr. Roman Greene. Scott spoke with me but stated he hadn't seen his sister since childhood. Dominic Averelli, Jr. is unaware that Scott is his uncle, and Scott requested that I didn't disclose this publicly. The current consensus between all parties involved is that Dominic, Jr. and a younger boy named Caleb Gregory are safest under the care of Margaret Serrano. Under the circumstances, I agree and won't interfere.

Similar to Dominic Averilli, Sr./Chaosis, Dara demonstrated genius-level intelligence at a young age. Scott stated that their home life was stable. Their parents worked in engineering fields, but they took regular vacations and seemed to have a balanced family life. When Dara disappeared at age seventeen, it was initially believed to be a kidnapping. Her behavior up until that point showed no indication she was motivated to run away.

I asked Scott if he'd be willing to set up a meeting with their parents, but he declined and stated the situation would just upset them and not provide anything relevant.

My requests to directly interview Dara have been declined, but I'll keep trying. The overall timeline of events means it's possible Chaosis and Dara targeted your family over a year prior to their attack at the fairgrounds. Just give me some more time to prove it, and I'll help you as much as I—

CCA File 23095405960_IL20230329_IL_PA

Email from Reporter Irene Lawson to Samantha Fredricks.

Lawson's body and laptop were recovered inside her car, which she appeared to have driven off a bridge and into a river the following morning.

CHAPTER FOURTEEN

"FAST TRACK? CALEB, can you hear me?" Terrashield snapped his fingers in front of my face three times. I could see and hear him but couldn't respond.

"Great job, Terra." A younger hero said from the corner of the room. I didn't recognize him or the woman standing next to him. "You've just destroyed seven-eighths of all life in the cosmos in less than three seconds."

"What are you talking about? I'm trying to get him out of a vision without killing him in the process. He told me the sound helps." Terrashield snapped a few more times. "Apparently not this time, though..."

"Rox? Jhett? Anybody?" The younger hero sounded annoyed. "Come on, one of you has to read actual comic books! That settles it. I joined the wrong team..."

"There was a movie, too...a bunch of them, actually," I groaned. "Who are all the rest of you? How long have you been here?"

The hero seemed startled by my reply and looked around at the others. "Whoa, we're in trouble, aren't we? As much as part of me wants to know the future, he really shouldn't be telling us, should he? He must not know any better yet..." Then he approached my hospital bed and held out his hand. "Um, hi. My name's Cyndero—and that's my girlfriend, Jhett. We know you're Fast Track, but it's really weird seeing you as a teenager. You were more like the dad of the team before you...disappeared. Anyway, it's nice to have you back again. We could definitely use your help."

Rodoxian gave him a warning look and seemed uneasy. "We have to be extremely careful about all of this, or we'll just make things worse. Once he's cleared medically, Caleb needs to be brought up to speed on everything—no different than what he did for us."

Jhett nodded in agreement but looked worried. "Talk about terrible timing...we need the other guy."

This confused me. "What other guy?" I asked.

"It's a long story, and I'll try to explain as soon as I can make sense of it," Terrashield replied quickly. "The main concern right now is if you're okay."

All things considered, I felt fine. "Don't worry about me. There's a villain named Chaosis who's about to murder a booth worker at the carnival—and do a whole lot worse by the end of the night. We have to stop him." I recapped as much of the vision as I could remember, but none of them scrambled away once I was finished. "That's all I saw—really. Go on! Do whatever hero rescue thing you're all supposed to do! Then we can work on stopping Samantha when you get done. I'll help you...then hopefully find some way to return to my own time."

"We've already prepared for some things today based on other intel," Terrashield explained, but he didn't elaborate. "Does the booth worker die? I mean, do you remember him dying in the time you came from? Or reading about it? It's important, or I wouldn't ask. Knowing the original timeline of certain events helps us keep things stable."

"I don't know. Why? If you can prevent something terrible from happening, shouldn't you at least try? It would make the future better, right? Yeah, the booth worker seems like a jerk, but he said he has a kid he's trying to provide for."

Rodoxian shook her head. "It's not that simple, Caleb. Tampering with the overall timeline has consequences—even if it's with good intentions. You were extremely clear about that the first time we met you."

To be heroes, they still seemed really apathetic. "So, we're supposed to do what?" I asked. "Stay where we are? Just let hundreds of people die tonight? My brother is at that carnival right now. Dominic is..." I hesitated, wondering if they already knew or not. "He's Chaosis and Dara's biological son, but he grows up to be a decent person. He saves my life ten years after he's adopted and helps me, too. Villains like Chaosis and Dara are just as dangerous to us as they are to you."

"We know, and we want to help," Terrashield replied. "It's a bit of an adjustment being on the other side of things, and I know it's frustrating. We'll do everything we can."

I sat up in the hospital bed. "Can I get out of here and go with you? If you need to leave now, I'll find a way to catch up."

Cyndero gestured for me to not get up. "I might be able to solve this without a fight, but I'll have to go alone. It's a long story, but Chaosis won't hurt me. He's my uncle. I haven't exactly seen him at any family gatherings for years, but he should still know me. I might be able to talk him down from murdering the booth worker. If I find out anything else about his overall plans, I'll tell you as soon as I can. I just have to ditch this uniform but will keep my radio. Keep everyone else clear of us—especially my grandfather."

"Does Fortis know he's involved in this?" Terrashield asked. "Did you know prior to Caleb having the vision?"

Cyndero frowned. "Look, I didn't even know I had a cousin until now. My family life is messy—part of the reason I'm working with you and Rox instead of them. We can talk about it later—and I'm sorry I never brought it up before, Jhett. It's embarrassing and sad, and I don't want you dragged into it if it all ever goes public."

"It's okay," Jhett replied. "I understand, and I love you. Just be safe. If it seems like Chaosis is about to turn on you, get out of there. We'll figure out another way to bring him in."

"You're the best. You know that, right?" Cyndero kissed her. "I gotta go."

Rodoxian looked at Terrashield. "In the meantime, Jhett and I can warn Fortis and his team to stay clear and try to get word to everyone about the evacuation routes being potential traps."

He nodded. "I'll get Caleb checked out of here, and we'll keep watch on Dara and the kid at a distance. We'll meet up with Cyndero later if everything goes well. If not, we'll regroup near headquarters. Everybody, be careful."

After everyone but Terrashield left, he spoke with one of the hospital's doctors and found my clothes so I could change. They were what I'd had on when Samantha had shot me on Perilous Island, and the blood stains at my ribs and back hadn't completely washed out of the t-shirt.

"Where did you find me?" I asked.

"The marina. Older you left us a hint, and we followed it. You still almost died. It was a close call."

"Meaning I interfered with my own life? Isn't that a bad thing—according to what you said earlier?"

He shrugged. "It's a fixed time loop. If we hadn't found you, you wouldn't have lived to tell us where to find you. You do stuff like this to us all the time. It honestly gets a little dizzying."

"I don't even understand how I did it," I replied. "One moment I was on Perilous Island—knowing Samantha was about to shoot and kill me. Then I woke up here. If you hadn't told me, I would have thought you or someone else had saved me."

Terrashield seemed confused, too. "You've never mentioned anyone named Samantha to us before. I'm not sure why you would have kept that from us. Same goes with your adoptive brother. You never talked about your family—at all. I always got the impression something terrible had happened to them but never wanted to press you for details."

"Do I ever remember where I came from?" I asked. "Where I was born, I mean. Can you even tell me that if you know?"

The conversation was making him uncomfortable. "Let's get to the fairgrounds and handle this situation first. I need to think this out before I say anything else. I just don't want to screw anything up for you or anybody who could be affected. I hope I'm making some sense."

Once we left the hospital, we didn't have to fly far to reach the fairgrounds. I'd never been to an event there, but Terrashield seemed to know his way around. I was starving, and the whole place smelled like buttered popcorn and funnel cake. I still had a little cash in my pocket, but

Terrashield stopped me and paid for everything.

"Keep all of that until you get back to your own time, or people will think you're a counterfeiter. Look at the dates on the bills. Even the oldest one is five years from now."

"Oh—sorry. I'm just glad my clothes and what I had in my pockets came back with me. Guess this is more like *Bill and Ted* than *Terminator*. You've seen both of those, right? Am I ever able to bring other people with me, or is the ability's range more of a personal bubble?"

He frowned, either worried or irritated by all the questions. Maybe a little of both. "I want to help you, Caleb—I really do—but this is getting into territory where I don't know what I should tell you and what I shouldn't. I'm sorry."

I decided to let up, at least until a better moment. "It's okay. I get it. Thank you and Rodoxian for looking out for me—and sorry in advance for being weirded out and not knowing I can trust you in the future."

He pointed ahead of us. "There are most of the food trucks. Do you see them?"

I nodded. "Yeah, Dara is the red-head waiting at the picnic table. Dominic has black hair like his dad and was wearing a blue and green striped shirt in the vision. He should be here soon. I wonder if Cyndero is having any luck with Chaosis."

"He'll have to radio me to update us. If I contact him, it could get him killed. From what I've heard, Chaosis doesn't need an amplifier for his laser vision like Cyndero does."

I was about to ask him why nothing had been done about Chaosis before now when another vision hit.

Almost everything played out the same until Dominic left to find his mother. Then Cyndero stepped up and greeted Chaosis before he and the booth attendant could start to argue. "Hey! I thought that was you! Long time, no see. I heard you got married and moved back here. How you been?"

Chaosis didn't seem to recognize Cyndero and seemed caught off-guard. "I'm fine. How do you know me exactly?"

Cyndero kept smiling. "It's me—David. I've probably had a growth spurt since the last time you saw me, but you haven't changed that much. I've missed you. You were a fun uncle from what I can remember."

Chaosis laughed. "Wow. You did grow up, didn't you? I'm surprised your mother and grandfather didn't warn you about me. They've never liked Dara, and I doubt they even know or care about our son. We haven't exactly been hiding over the past five years. It's just to the rest of the family, we no longer exist to tarnish the perfect hero dynasty. I thought you might have been avoiding us, too."

"Actually, I ran away when I was fifteen and ended up coming back last year because of my girlfriend. I caught a lot of hell from Grandpa, and I don't know how long I'm going to stay around. It's not the same as your situation, but I think I get what happened. I'm sorry for how you've been treated, and I'd like to catch up sometime. How much more money do you need to get that griffin for your son? I'd like to help—could consider it a birthday gift to make up for all the ones I've missed with him. I know you would have done the same for me when I was his age."

Chaosis seemed to calm down and looked almost sad. "I'm a long way from who I was, kid, but that's generous of you. I'll introduce you to Nic and let you give him the griffin. He reminds me a lot of you. Soft-hearted. A little gullible, but what kid isn't? Sharp as hell on almost everything else, though. It wouldn't be the worst thing to have you around—just as long as you don't pressure him into becoming a hero or turn him against us."

"You're still my family, too. I wouldn't do that to you."

Chaosis's posture relaxed, and they shook hands.

The booth worker cleared his throat. "If you two are just going to stand there and chat, could you at least move out of the way so the booth isn't blocked? It's almost to the point you're costing me money now."

Cyndero scrambled to salvage the situation. "Here—here's two hundred. Keep the change. Just let my uncle pick out what my cousin wanted, and we'll leave."

The booth worker grinned and then looked at Chaosis. "That's more like it. See, you could learn a thing or two about how to deal with people from your nephew here. He—"

Chaosis blasted the booth worker, anyway—and he didn't let up. The attendant screamed, and the booth caught on fire.

Chaosis sounded calm again. "Huh, those cheap wooden puzzles and stuffed dogs caught fire more rapidly than they should have. You and the rest of the spandex brigade should probably check into that. Let me grab one of these griffins, and we'll go find Nic and my wife. You hungry?" He asked Cyndero and then laughed at his shock and disgust. "I'm talking pizza—not barbecue. There's a quiet place a few blocks from here where we can have a nice family conversation. With what's about to happen here, the smart thing would be to walk away while you still can—trust me."

Cyndero wasn't much older than me in this time—maybe nineteen—and he seemed frozen in shock. "Y-You killed him. I didn't want to believe you actually would, but Fast Track was right...guy's always right..."

Chaosis seemed annoyed—and apparently knew about me. "Oh, you've been consulting with the great time traveler from the future again? He's not a god, David. Just because you can see a little ahead on the ride doesn't mean you can change where all the tracks lead. I can prove that to you."

Chaosis reached for something in his jacket pocket. Cyndero reacted and managed to tackle him to the ground, but it was too late.

It wasn't a gun.

It was a transmitter.

CYCAD COVE ARCHIVES: ACCESS GRANTED_LEVEL 1

'You're the last known person to talk to that reporter, and it slipped your mind to tell me she died under mysterious circumstances? You're a person-of-interest, Scott—and Terrashield and Rodoxian are trying to tie everything to me.'

'Look, Irene Lawson didn't ask me a single question about you or Adira. It was about my sister. I thought if I told her about Dara, she'd drop it and move on.'

'The Cycad Cove paper must have been really desperate for a story to send her this far...'

'I don't think it was a project for them. She had more of a private investigator vibe. Maybe some side-project?'

'Did she mention anyone else?'

'Just my nephew, the old woman who adopted him, and some kid named Caleb Gregory. I swear she wasn't with the heroes or the cops, Roman. This was something else.'

'I'll still contact Maggie and warn her, anyway.'

'Maybe I should offer to stay at her shop for a while—explain to Dominic who I am. He grew up to be a good person, Roman. If there's any way I can help him—'

'Maggie can protect him—just trust me. The best thing we can do for now is stay out of the way and keep attention off of them for as long as possible.'

'I really hope you're right...'

CCA File 203948040500_RG19940902_SBFOI

Security footage, Greene residence. Dated March 31st 2023
Small playback display recovered on Orchid Island, Southern Beachfront by Dr. Roman Greene. September 2nd, 1994.

CHAPTER FIFTEEN

ALL OF THE RIDES SLOWED to a stop, and their lights and music shut off in a wave—the Ferris wheel, the carousel, the teacups, the tilt-a-whirl, the swings...

Nearly every pendulum-based ride had people hanging upside-down by their safety belts.

Nearby screaming knocked me out of the vision.

I was back near the food trucks—closest to a pirate ship ride and a tunnel that held in riders through centrifugal force. Both were slowing down, meaning the vision wasn't too far ahead of real time.

"Caleb, what did you see?" Terrashield asked.

"Chaosis still killed the booth attendant. It happened too fast for Cyndero to stop him. It wasn't his fault."

"And the rides losing power all at once?" he asked.

I tried to recall anything I thought would be helpful. "It's from a shut-down signal sent from a handheld transmitter. Chaosis still has it. I remember reading each ride was sabotaged with an independent receiver. Dominic taught me a few things about them...said Dara originally designed them for a space station project, but then she allowed Chaosis to use them for this. I can help you remove them. We just need to convince the ride operators to let me."

Terrashield nodded. "You focus on that. I need to help Cyndero and the others capture Chaosis. Hopefully we're not too late..."

"What about Dominic?" I asked. "We can't let Dara leave with him. She didn't push the button, but she knows everything. She helped Chaosis set all of this up!"

"Don't take Dominic away from her tonight, Caleb. Don't even let them or Chaosis see you. I'll explain once we're able to regroup. Just get those rides out of Chaosis's control. Got it?"

"Yeah, but—"

Terrashield flew off, and I hoped he and the others were as informed about the situation as they had made themselves sound.

I approached the operator of the pirate ship ride first. He already had its control panel open and was trying to restart the ride.

"Hi. I know you don't know me, but I know what's wrong and how to fix it. Can I just—"

He gave me a skeptical glare. "If I even let you touch that panel door, I'll be fired. Thank you for the offer to help, but I've got this. See. Just needed to turn it off and back on again...it's fine."

The ride's lights came back on, followed by the music. As the ship gently glided back and forth from being upside-down, people began to clap and cheer.

The pace of the music started to increase, and the ride operator scrambled to his microphone. "Everyone, please stay in your restraints! I'm going to try the emergency shutdown!"

A boom from behind us caught my attention. Someone had triggered the fireworks display a few minutes early. Silhouetted against the bursts, several heroes and villains fought in the distance. I didn't recognize any of them. Forks of red and yellow lightning streaked across the night sky, and a low bass rumble shook the ground.

Closer to us, the centrifuge tunnel had sped up to a dangerous and terrifying speed. There was no way to rescue anybody on it without potentially hurting or killing someone.

I turned back to the pirate ship ride operator. "Listen to me—these aren't accidental malfunctions! Someone did this on purpose. Is there any way you can warn the other operators to not restart them? I think if you can just cut the power at a safe point, a group of us can fly and get people free one at a time."

"I have some numbers—can text them. Who are you again?"

I lied—claiming to be a hero-in-training on Terrashield and Rodoxian's team so he would let me help. He recognized their names and finally stepped aside.

The receivers weren't large—maybe slightly bigger than the ones used for Bluetooth at the time. They had a much longer range however, and it would take at least an hour to remove them all and evacuate anyone stuck on each ride. Locating Chaosis and the transmitter would have been the faster solution, and I couldn't blame Terrashield for taking it.

Unfortunately, the sabotaged rides weren't our only problem.

Chaosis had sold nearly every villain in the region on his idea—attack the heroes once they were in rescue mode and wipe them all out in one night. He and Dara had provided the bait. All the rest of them had to do was wait until the right moment to strike.

Each ride had several villains watching it. Since I was helping at the pirate ship—and they had no idea who I was—it made me a target just like the heroes. While I was working, three large guys attempted to attack me from behind.

The first villain resembled Kaylor and might have been her dad. He tried to use his electrical powers on me. "Anyone in the mood for fried shrimp?"

I saw this coming and managed to go back in time a few seconds.

"Anyone in the mood for—hey, where'd he go?" The man with electrical powers couldn't fly, so I got out of his attack range.

I doubted reasoning with them would do any good, but I did try. "This is a trap for all of you, too! Chaosis and Dara don't care if any of you die tonight. The heroes are their enemies. You're their competition. Think it out on who wins once this clears."

"How did you know about their plan?" The second man asked, but he tried to freeze me before I could answer.

I rewound time again, beginning to feel like I was getting the hang of it.

"Anyone in the mood for—what the hell?" Kaylor's father asked.

I had timed his attempt to electrocute me and circled around, knocking the other guy with ice powers into his path—where I had been standing in front of the ride's control panel. The shock wasn't enough to kill Ice Guy, but it did piss him off.

"Whose side are you on?" Ice Guy asked, and then he tried to freeze Kaylor's father.

The two of them started fighting each other—leaving one villain left to focus on me.

I wish I could say it made it a fairer fight, but this guy could have been Roman's bigger monster brother. He had reddish/purple skin and yellow hair that went all the way down his back, almost like a horse's mane.

"Uh, hi—I'm not exactly a hero." I explained. "I just wanted to stop the ride. So, there's not a lot of gain in killing me or beating me up."

"You lied to me?" The ride operator started. "You said you were with—"

I'd forgotten he was still nearby. I gritted my teeth. "Please, stop talking…oh, I'll just go back and try this again."

I tried, but this time it barely worked—and it wasn't enough.

"You lied to me?" The operator repeated. "You said you were with Terrashield and Rodoxian. Now I'm going to be fired…"

"And I'm going to be killed!" I freaked out and gestured to the third villain. "Does the Jolly Maroon Giant here look like a ride inspector to you?"

The villain looked offended, almost hurt. "I could be—if I wanted. I heard you were dead, Fast Track. Must have been a long vacation because you look younger and scrawnier without your suit. You should have stayed gone…"

He lumbered past the other two villains—who were still blasting electricity and ice at each other—and lifted the entire control panel from its base and above his head.

I flinched and closed my eyes, expecting him to crush me to death with it.

CYCAD COVE ARCHIVES: ACCESS GRANTED_LEVEL 1

It was Dominic's idea to start recovering the meteorite fragments ourselves, but I went along with it.

We sold off the raw mineral to anyone who wanted it until word got back to Roman. When he showed up at the island and confronted us, Dominic started a fight and blasted him with his laser vision. Roman shot a blast of energy from his palms and killed Dominic in one hit. I freaked out—which somehow sent me back in time about an hour.

It took multiple tries, but I warned Dominic about Roman's movements until he finally won out. He'd never killed anyone before, but we had no other options.

I keep having visions of Roman with a family and being our friend. He never had children, but there's this girl, too. His daughter somehow? Any attempt to go back farther than the fight doesn't work for me anymore. It's like the island put up a barrier, and I can't get past it.

Exposure to the meteorites has enhanced Dominic's laser vision, but he's becoming paranoid and agitated. I've had to avert several outbursts of him nearly killing me, but he doesn't seem to remember anything afterwards.

The heroes in Cycad Cove will be coming for us soon.

I still don't fully understand how this place works, but I need help. I've screwed up here, and I don't know if I'm already too late.

I'm so sorry.

CCA File 930473_CSAS20250701_CW_NEOI

Hand-written note by Caleb Warner, no date listed.
Recovered on Orchid Island, Northeast Quadrant by Caleb and Adira Serrano, July 1st, 2025.

CHAPTER SIXTEEN

AFTER A FEW SECONDS, nothing happened. I opened my eyes again and stood. Fortis—a hero I'd never met before but had grown up hearing about—had taken the control panel and was flying several feet above the gigantic man's head.

"If I drop this, it's going to hurt, Goliath. Go home. Take your friends with you. You look as if you don't want to be here, anyway. Did they talk you into it?"

Goliath nodded. "Chaosis did. Made it sound like this would be easy. He said we'd have more help, too, but I haven't seen anyone besides us...I don't like liars..."

I sighed in relief as Goliath picked up the other two villains—who were still fighting—by their shirt collars and started to walk away.

Fortis touched down and dropped the control panel. The pirate ship ride had eased to the right stopping position, and the ride operator was getting everyone out safely.

A similar scene was playing out at the centrifuge tunnel. With the receivers removed, the heroes could focus more on the villains than saving people from the rides. The overall fight had turned in their favor.

Closer to the food trucks, Terrashield and Rodoxian were fending off eight villains surrounding them. Terrashield sent up several walls of dirt, and Rodoxian used her abilities to add superheated water to the mix. The end-result was a radial burst of mud and steam that knocked the villains unconscious. They both nodded to Fortis and me and then flew off to help someone else.

I held out my hand to Fortis. "Hi, I'm Caleb. Nice to meet

you—and thanks for the save. I know there are probably other people you could be helping right now. I'm okay—just so drained now I can't see anything else that's coming. I'm sorry."

He seemed amused. "Don't be. I need to catch my breath a little myself. If it wasn't for you, this could have been ten times worse. I hope you realize that. Anything else you see tonight—the things that haven't gone so well...you're not to blame for it, Caleb. Chaosis is..."

I was still confused by a lot of what I'd seen in the visions. "Are you really his father?" I asked. "What happened?"

His smile faded, and the question upset him. "Anything resembling my son died ten years ago. This murderer—this psychopath—he's nothing like who he was supposed to become."

We both heard a noise behind us and turned to face it.

Chaosis appeared from behind us, slow clapping while holding a stuffed griffin tucked underneath his arm.

Clipped to his jacket was Cyndero's radio. It was covered in blood. He pushed the call button. "I want every single one of you who's still alive to know I tried to be reasonable about this. All my father had to do was tell the truth—to a news reporter, the police—even one of you who wasn't taken in by his so-called perfect persona. His public reputation mattered more to him than any of your lives—and all the innocent people we had to kill just to lure him out onto the field with you. I'm sorry, and I asked my associates to be as quick about it as possible. There's only one person who needs to suffer tonight, and I'm going to handle this myself."

Fortis looked at me with a pleading expression. "Caleb, get out of here! You can't do anything else to help me!"

Chaosis laughed. "Isn't that noble of him? He already knows how you die, Fast Track—and you're not my problem. I'm still not quite sure what you are, but I've been informed that killing you now could harm my wife and son's futures. So, you get a pass—at least for tonight. Go. Stay. Time is locked, so it doesn't really matter what you do. You're still trapped on the same ride as the rest of us—just have the ability to move seats while you're on it. That's a curse—not a gift."

A laser blast fired.

Fortis used the opportunity to fire at Chaosis's chest. It was hot enough to melt the plastic in Cyndero's radio, but Chaosis didn't react as if he was in any pain.

Fortis looked weakened, though. "She used you, Son—manipulated you! Turned you against your own family and our team. Your mother and sister loved you. I loved—"

Chaosis glared at him. "The only thing you have ever loved is the sound of your own voice. Dara accepted me for who I was after the rest of you abandoned me. Everything else has been you escalating everything again and again and again—trying to erase history and the fact that I'm so messed up because of you. You think I started out wanting this? You made me into this, and now I'm putting an end to it."

I stepped forward, terrified but unable to just walk away. "No! Don't do it. If you do this, you'll never see your wife and son again. You can leave right now. Walk away. I'll even go with you—warn you so you can keep running. No one else has to die."

Chaosis hesitated. "You really do mean it, don't you? See, the problem with that is you'll never be rescued by my son. One day, however many years from now, you'll just vanish in a paradox—and then everything in our known existence will unravel in very spectacular fashion. Don't get me wrong. You're very important, Fast Track—but more like a stopper in a tub drain kind of way. Twenty years from now, it won't even matter. We're all just buying time against the inevitable—even you. Excuse me for a moment."

He yelled and blasted Fortis with his laser vision.

Fortis didn't even fight back or run.

I know it was probably futile, but I ran toward Chaosis anyway—only to be blocked by another robot demon. I punched it in the head, but it grabbed my fist and twisted my wrist until I was on the ground in pain.

"You've tried this before, Caleb—and it doesn't end well for anyone." The modulated voice said. "How about we bypass the lesson about choosing your battles, shall we?"

"He's going to kill him! Let me go! I can—"

"What? Get yourself killed, too?" It mocked. "You're not ready for something like this. Chaosis left you a way out. I suggest you take it while you still can. Understand? If I wanted you dead, it would have happened already."

"Who the hell are you?" I asked. "Do you work for Samantha?"

It shook its head. "I'm a Messenger. So is she. You want a real opportunity to change the future? Live to fight another day."

It kept twisting my arm, and the pain got so intense that I blacked out.

CYCAD COVE ARCHIVES: ACCESS GRANTED_LEVEL 1

'You keep mentioning these 'Messengers' as if I should know who you mean. I don't. We've never spoken before today.'

'Oh, yeah—I forgot. That was a different Dr. Brown. Okay, short version: Messengers are beings capable of manipulating space-time and can cross over into neighboring dimensions. The originals were aliens, but some humans were later abducted and altered by them.'

'Including you?'

'Technically, I'm defective—mind control didn't quite take the way they planned. Now they just want me wiped out.'

'So, you're on our side?'

'I'm trying to be. Can't do a lot of good sitting here, though.'

'I'm dampening your so-called time-traveling abilities?'

'Or I'm just crazy. If you'd like to go across the street and get yourself a sandwich, I'll just wait right here—promise.'

'I'm not going anywhere.'

'I knew you'd say that. Do you have a Chaosis here? Real name Dominic Averelli—Senior, not Junior.'

'I've never heard of Chaosis, and I doubt Griffin will want to waste his time on this.'

'Call him. Then I'll tell you whatever you want to know.'

CCA File 594830483_KB20010318_KB_BHAA

Brunel Heights Asylum and Corrections Facility Archive
Interview by Dr. Kimberly Brown
Male patient approximately thirty years old, refused to identify self during intake process; DNA and fingerprint results are pending.

CHAPTER SEVENTEEN

I WOKE UP TO THE SMELL of smoke. I rose up on my elbows, put weight on my right arm wrong, and almost passed out again.

Chaosis had set everything around us on fire. Police, ambulances, and fire trucks had started to arrive, and the flashing lights started to give me a headache. I managed to get to my feet but stumbled when I tried to walk. Rodoxian spotted me and touched down to help.

I was relieved to see her. "Rodoxian, Chaosis killed Fortis, and I—"

She held her hands out in a calming gesture, but she was upset. "The police just blocked off where it happened. There's nothing else you could have done, Caleb. Chaosis would have killed you, too..."

It made me nauseated that she and Robot Demon Guy were in agreement, even though Rodoxian had no way of knowing it. "I thought the rest of you might have been dead, too...only Chaosis said something about the future being fixed?" I continued when she didn't seem to know what I meant. "He somehow knew how some things turned out in the future. I didn't tell him anything, but that means you had to survive this...and Terrashield...and who else? Are Cyndero and Jhett okay?"

"They're both missing...Dara and your brother, too," she replied and then sighed. "This wasn't how tonight was supposed to happen, Caleb. Something's off-track now in the timeline, and you've never been wrong or lied to us before. Withheld things, maybe, but not to do us harm. I don't know what to do...other than find Terra and meet back at headquarters. We need a plan."

"What about Chaosis? Was he captured?"

She nodded. "Yes, but we won't be able to get access or interrogate him until he's been processed. That won't be until morning at the earliest. Did he do that to your arm? We need to get you to a first-aid tent, or it will heal incorrectly. It will be more painful if they have to break it again..."

My arm hurt like hell, but I had bigger worries. "I understand why you and Terrashield can't tell me everything at once, but since I've woken up I've gotten more answers from a psychopath and bone-breaking robot than I have either of you. If something's wrong—and I possibly caused it by coming back here—I'd like to know enough to at least not make things worse. Please."

She nodded. "We'll talk but not here. I'll be right back. Just need to find Terra."

An EMT set my arm back into place and splinted it temporarily. I didn't have as rapid of a heal rate as some people, but I estimated from past experience that I'd be fine in a few days. That still bothered me, given everything that had happened.

Another low rumble shook the first-aid tent—and my arm—and I flinched and stood up from my seat as Rodoxian returned with Terrashield. He was hurt, too—had burns and damage to portions of his suit.

"Are these aftershocks from where you were fighting earlier?" I asked.

"No," Terrashield replied. "I never pull from any layer deep enough to affect that. These are earthquakes. First one this evening was maybe a 1.5 on the Richter scale. Most people can't even feel those, but I sense them all the time—usually ignore them unless there's a pattern. There were two others while we were fighting—then this one was maybe a three...three and a quarter. It's not the severity that's bothering me. It's the origin point."

"Perilous Island?" I guessed.

He nodded with an uneasy expression. "Yeah. I wish I could say it was coincidence, but they're pairing up with you regaining consciousness. We're aware you have some connection to the island—to the point you practically ordered us to stay away from it...and to keep other people clear of it, too."

I laughed. "I ordered you—and all of you actually listened to me?"

Rodoxian was about to reply when she got a call on the radio to meet someone at the target practice booth. I didn't recognize the voice.

When we got there, we were relieved to see Cyndero alive. He was holding a young girl and then passed her over to a police officer. He waited until they left before he explained. "Booth operator's kid—was sleeping in their camper. I don't know exactly how much she saw and heard, but I didn't want to take off and leave her. Sad story—told me her mom and younger brother died in a car crash a few years ago, and then something happened recently where she and her father had to abandon their apartment. He must have been desperate to get them back on their feet and stable again...and now this happens...I heard my uncle was captured. Any word from Jhett? I keep trying her radio and cell, but nothing yet..."

Cyndero still had his radio—meaning the one Chaosis used earlier hadn't been his.

Rodoxian looked at her phone. "I can't even get a signal right now, and Jhett has the same provider as me. Try not to worry."

"What's Jhett's real name?" I asked. "Textbooks in the future are really weird about listing aliases, and I honestly can't remember all the details of who survived. A lot probably got glossed over, too. My history teacher was in a rush to move on to the next chapter at the time. I know how horrible that must sound right now, and I'm sorry I don't know more that could help you."

Cyndero frowned. "Wow...never imagined the worst day of my life could get boiled down to a multiple-choice quiz. So, how many people tragically died today because I didn't want to hurt my uncle and screwed up? Is it A)..."

"I'm sorry. I shouldn't have even brought it up."

"Jhett's real name is Jenny Weiland. Do you know if she made it or not?"

The name didn't sound familiar. "I don't remember either way. That could be a good thing, though."

Cyndero started to walk away from us. "Well, I'm not leaving until I find her. The three of you are hurt, so I'll understand if you need to go back to headquarters. Let me know if you hear anything or if Fast Track manages to have a vision about—"

Another earthquake hit, noticeably worse than the previous one. Chips of brick and stone from the nearby buildings started to fall, and I noticed faint cracks developing in the sidewalks.

"That was a six." Terrashield said. "The next one could do some major damage if we don't figure this out soon."

"I'll take Caleb to the island—tell him what I can on the way? You stay here with Cyndero and search for Jhett?" Rodoxian phrased the plan more like a question—looking at Terrashield and then me.

"I don't think we have much of a choice right now." Terrashield replied. "As soon as we find Jhett, I'll catch up with you."

"I'll come, too." Cyndero added. "I just need to know she's all right. I still want to help. For the life of me I don't know why, but I can't walk away from this. I know she wouldn't want me to just give up..."

I got a brief flash of Adira...and of Roman's boat exploding again. Then there was something else.

Something impossible.

"Do you want to hold her, Caleb?"

It was Adira's voice—clear in my brain. Happy. Relieved. Alive. It had been real once. She had said those words to me, and I had looked down at a baby.

Our daughter.

Adira and I had a daughter.

"Caleb?" Rodoxian said, knocking me out of the vision. "Caleb, I'm sorry. We need to go. Are you okay?"

"Yeah, I'm fine," I lied. "Let's go."

What the hell had I done?

CYCAD COVE ARCHIVES: ACCESS GRANTED_LEVEL 1

Long story, Rox, but I'm face-down in the water at the Cycad Cove Marina and could use a bit of help. Take care of that before you read the rest of this. Dr. Serrano knows and will meet you at the hospital. If you have this note, I should be fine in a couple of weeks.

Keep the rest of this limited to you and Terra for now. I trust Cyndero and Jhett but want to keep them safe for as long as possible.

This isn't me coming back from the dead or anything. Those events happened in your past—my personal future—and I couldn't tell you about this part without making things worse. I tested a few alternatives, but the rest of you can't remember those scenarios. I've accepted what I need to do and am at peace with it.

Going forward, this note and any other messages you receive from me were all written prior to my death and are being delivered by younger versions of myself at specific times. They may or may not know as much as you do.

This particular kid—my eighteen-year-old self—knows almost nothing. I can remember being confused by everything and not knowing who I could trust. Just be patient and give me some time—pun intended—to get to know the team. I'll catch on soon enough.

Thank you—for everything. I'm so proud of you. I hope you both knew that before, too.

Take care,

F.T.

CCA File 4700303301_RMN20030614_FT_CCM_PA

Logged by Rachel McNabb/Rodoxian June 14th, 2003

CHAPTER EIGHTEEN

SINCE CHARTERING A BOAT would have taken too long, Rodoxian and I flew directly toward Perilous Island. Its lighthouse was operational, and the beam circled about once every twenty seconds. Before we got above its range, I had to turn away or shut my eyes so I wasn't blinded.

Near its base were several stone buildings. We were too far away to see any signs of people, but it wasn't morning yet, either.

"I don't know if it's an issue right now, but I was warned by a friend not to fly there too fast," I said, deciding not to mention Roman by name yet. "The island's defenses will teleport us over the ocean, and it will take us even longer to get back."

Rodoxian nodded as if she already knew and then pointed ahead of us. "The general public doesn't know why they're there, but there's a line of buoys that mark where we need to slow down. We got tired of finding confused jet skiers in the middle of downtown, too, so the buoys on the eastern side have radioactivity warnings. It's technically true and keeps most people away. We rarely have incidents like that anymore."

This made me wonder about the heroes fighting Roman in about another decade from that point. If they knew it was an accident, they didn't act like it. "So, if the island launched someone with powers through a few buildings—not their fault—what would you do about it?"

This seemed to upset her, like she thought I was getting a vision about an upcoming threat. "Why? Did you see something?"

I changed the subject, not wanting to cause Roman any problems. "No, nothing like that. Just wondering about the possibility. Who's running the lighthouse?"

Her posture relaxed. "It's automated—other than a city maintenance crew inspecting it a few times a year or making repairs if something goes wrong. You...the older you...used to live there and operated it until..." She trailed off and eased to a stop a few feet above the water. The lighthouse's beam now passed over her head.

I flew down to get eye-level with her and hovered a few feet away. "Until what?"

She started to answer but hesitated. "I'm sorry. We really need to get to the island before I tell you any of that. There are some things I need to give back to you, too. I just don't want to accidentally drop them over water right now."

Based on her reaction, I had a guess. "I'm dead, aren't I? Not me, but the older me who you knew before? That's why you're all acting so weird. One of the villains at the pirate ship ride mentioned it, and Chaosis basically confirmed it before he killed Fortis. You don't have to lie to me. I'd rather be freaked out than clueless on what's going on."

She sighed but nodded. "We went through all kinds of other scenarios while you were in a coma—cloning, shape shifters...even you possibly being the original Fast Track's son. Your DNA is an exact match, though...same mannerisms are there. You're just really young right now, and we never expected to see you again. You were like family to us, Caleb. Do you understand that?"

This caused me to think about Dominic still being in danger...and the impossible memory of Adira and our newborn daughter. I needed help. Despite their conflict with Roman later, these heroes seemed like decent people. Older me had trusted them, anyway.

"I won't know you when we meet again in another couple of decades, so be patient with me." I explained. "Time travel is crazy. The only things I have for reference are TV shows and movies Dominic and I used to watch when we had downtime at the shop. Couldn't afford to do much else. I don't know what I'm doing, Rodoxian—not really. What happened back there with Chaosis and the booth worker...and later with Fortis—I'm sorry."

"It's not your fault. You did everything you could. Sometimes bad things still happen—no matter how much warning you give us. That's not on you."

"I still hope Jhett's okay and that Terrashield and Cyndero find her soon. If you can give me instructions on what to do to stop the earthquakes, you can go help them. I'll be okay."

"You have a broken arm and just got out of the hospital. I'm not abandoning you here without backup."

We reached the shore, and she headed for a small cottage with a keypad on the door. She knew the passcode—1-0-1-6—and opened it.

"Huh, that's Grandma's birthday. Did older me ever tell you about her? She adopts Dominic soon and then me about ten years from now. I'd like to talk to her once we fix this, but that might mess something else up..."

"Or that code is a clue to help you out," she replied and then smiled. "You did that a lot—hints instead of directly telling us what to do. Used to annoy the hell out of us when Terra and I were in training—but in an affectionate sort of way. I've missed you. The rest of the team has, too, but this is a lot to process right now on top of everything else."

"How big is your team?" I asked. "Is there anyone I haven't met yet?"

"We're a branch off of Fortis's original team—Terra and I have been co-leaders for about three years. You were in charge before that."

I found that hard to believe. "I was an actual hero? Spandex uniform, cape—the whole deal?"

She laughed. "More like if we didn't know you were a nice person, you'd give us all nightmares. Your suit is in storage back at headquarters. We'll show it to you after we get clear of all of this. Once you get healed up, you're probably going to need it."

"Hey, I can be pretty intimidating for five-foot-eight and a quarter."

She smiled again, but then her expression turned concerned. She made a gesture underneath her nose, and I wiped beneath mine with my good hand. When I brought it forward again, it was covered in blood—the worst sudden nosebleed I'd ever had, and I'd thought it was just a trail of sweat earlier. Great...

"Are you okay?"

I was terrified but tried to downplay it. "Yeah, I'm fine—no migraine or anything. Maybe it's just a minor side-effect—like time travel jet lag. Give me a minute. Don't want to bleed all over the place, even if it used to be mine."

I located a wrapped package of toilet paper in the cottage's bathroom and grabbed an entire roll. The nosebleed appeared to be slowing, but I held a rolled-up piece underneath my nose and sat down in a dusty leather chair. Nothing here was familiar. No visions triggered. This could have been a stranger's house who hadn't cleaned in years.

"Here—this hasn't expired yet." Rodoxian held a water bottle out to me. "We've rotated a small stock of emergency supplies for the past three years—your instructions. Guess now we know why."

The bottle was cold and covered in condensation. The cottage's fridge was working, and the place had lights.

"Where's the power coming from? I didn't see any solar panels, and we're really far out from the grid."

"Combination of a geothermal system you and Terra installed and a battery backup you designed. The lighthouse and cottage are—"

Something roared outside.

We both heard it and looked at each other for an answer. It sounded like the same creature hidden away near the guard shack at Roman and Adira's house. Andy had called it Ziggy. I never saw the thing, but the fact he'd mentioned it was capable of eating intruders wasn't exactly comforting.

Rodoxian's tone turned uneasy. "If you had a pet velociraptor and didn't tell us to check on it for the past three years, I'm going to be a little upset with you."

I shook my head. "I don't know what that is, but Roman

ends up with it later. I don't know how he got it off the island without someone noticing."

"We haven't run into anyone named Roman yet. Friend or threat?"

I didn't exactly want to lie to her, but I hoped I could explain and smooth out the situation. "Both. If you're staying, I guess I need to tell you enough for when you do meet him. Maybe that will help somehow."

The monster—whatever it was—roared again.

"Hold that thought," Rodoxian said. "I'm going outside—just long enough to see if I can spot what's out there before it gets any closer. Better to know now than when it's tearing off the roof. Stay here. I'll be fine—have plenty of sand and water to work with if it tries anything...maybe even magma if I have to..."

She quietly eased opened the front door, and I stood and followed until I reached the doorway. She was out-of-sight by the time I got there, but I assumed she'd flown up for a better vantage point.

I waited a few minutes in silence. The monster didn't roar again. It was just the sounds of seagulls and the waves crashing onto the beach. "Rodoxian? Rox? Where are you?"

Nothing. I took a chance and stepped outside the cottage to see if she was hovering above the roof.

She'd disappeared. Across the bay—where there should have been a distant line of buildings—there was nothing but a natural line of trees and what appeared to be another beach.

The entire city of Cycad Cove had vanished, too.

I was alone.

The monster roared a third time.

Almost.

CYCAD COVE ARCHIVES: ACCESS GRANTED_LEVEL 1

I know at some point you'll have questions, Adira, and I want you to hear this from me.

Even at the risk of losing his future with you, Caleb tried everything he could to save me—went back in time and warned us as our friend years before you were born.

After he finally told us the entire truth, Roman and I asked him to stop. The repetitive time loops were hurting him—killing him— and he can't change what will happen to me.

In the time I have left, your father and I are going to help him map the island and find some answers. The vision Caleb fears the most hasn't happened here yet, and we still have time to avert it— to save you, him, and your future daughter.

The monster who will murder me will receive justice in due time. Never allow vengeance to poison your heart and the best of who you are.

All my love to you.

CCA File 300098742003_RG20210722_NG_WBOI

Message recovered July 22nd, 2021 by Dr. Roman Greene and Andy Brant Western Beach, Orchid Island

Note by R.G.—We now have two seemingly identical copies of Nadia's message and camera.

Note by A.B.—Nearby fragments of wreckage indicate there was a recent explosion and/or fire of a boat. The *Kairos* is perfectly fine and intact on the eastern side of the island, but the similarities concern me. We need to prepare for a future attack.

CHAPTER NINETEEN

MOVEMENT NEAR THE TREE LINE caught my attention. The creature was as tall as a horse but looked more like a cross between a brindle-colored hyena and a gigantic wolf.

Definitely a predator, and I was injured prey.

It had spotted me at the same time, and it dashed toward me in several rapid bounds. I made it back inside the cottage and locked the door just in time.

The creature roared and began scratching on the door.

Then it started whining.

"Whatever you are, I'm not falling for that!" There were a few windows that were possible escape options, but I'd need enough clearance to fly before the thing caught up to me. The lighthouse was a better place to hide, but it may not have been as supplied as the cottage...

The prehistoric monster broke the door down and made eye contact with me. There was no time to think things out. I made a run for the bedroom, but the thing pounced on me and pinned me to the floor. I landed hard on my arm and screamed. Barely able to stay conscious, I scrambled for any last-ditch weapon and only found a pile of old papers.

Then it started licking my face.

It knew me—recognized me.

It wasn't there to kill me.

"Ziggy? Uh, down boy? Sit?"

It listened—backing away from me until I managed to sit up. Then it stood and wagged its tail—knocking down and breaking a lamp in the process.

I tried talking to it like a dog. "Let's go back outside. You know 'outside'? I'll go, too."

In the early morning daylight, the only thing that made Ziggy less terrifying was his demeanor toward me. If he'd wanted, he could have torn me to shreds. As it was, I felt as if I was about to fall over, anyway.

He whined again.

"I know—stay awake," I replied. "You wouldn't happen to know where my friend went, would you?"

I wasn't really expecting an intelligent response, but he took a few steps toward the woods and then looked back for me to follow. When I didn't, he bounded back and then headed toward the woods again.

"Sorry—long night, and I'm moving a little slow right now," I said. "Could use some painkillers, too, if you know where to find any."

Ziggy dashed through the already-broken door and returned with a drool-covered pill bottle. It had my name on it but was expired by about five years.

I couldn't exactly fault him for not being able to read dates, and it made me trust him about Rodoxian. "Thanks. You're a good whatever-you-are."

I followed him through the woods. There were orchids blooming everywhere—the vivid yellow, red, and blue popping in color against the green of everything else. The air smelled sweet and was more humid than I'd remembered the last time I was there.

I stepped in one of the muddy paw prints Ziggy had left, and it was longer than my shoe print and about twice as wide. It made me wonder what time he'd come from...or more likely what time I'd ended up stuck in...

When I started to look around, there were signs of things that were possibly even bigger than Ziggy—broken branches...fallen trees...a half-buried skull of something that had to be as large as an elephant. Something else roared in the distance, and Ziggy roared in response. They were possibly the same species of animal, but I'd never seen one before—even in a textbook.

A few minutes later, we came to an open area with flowing water. I was relieved to see a tent—and a woman with a portable easel set up in front of her. She didn't seem startled by Ziggy or me and just continued concentrating on a small painting and a rough sketch beside it.

"Um, hi," I stammered. "Sorry to bother you, but have you seen anyone else pass through here recently?"

Her tone was friendly, but she seemed distracted. "Give me just a second, Caleb—the humidity changes are wreaking havoc on these canvases. Painting on-site seemed like a great idea at the time, but I'll probably just wait until we get home before I do any others. Roman will be back soon if you're looking for him. With everything you gave us, he thinks he's narrowed down when the *Kairos* will appear again so we can transport the meteorite safely."

She resembled Adira enough that she had to be her mom, but I had no idea what to say to her. Nadia Greene shouldn't have known me. She had died weeks before Dominic had found me when I was eight. This didn't make any sense.

"Are you Nadia Greene?"

She laughed. "I will be in a few months. If Roman hasn't invited you to the wedding for helping us, you have it from me. Are you feeling okay? You sound different." She finally looked at me—then at Ziggy—and then back to me again. "Ziggy was here with someone else about an hour ago, but he looked about ten years older and didn't have a broken arm. Is Caleb your older brother or—"

"No, I'm Caleb, too—just having a harder week than the other me, I guess..."

She gave a reluctant nod. "Here, we have extra chairs. Are you hungry? We have plenty of MREs."

"I'm mostly thirsty but haven't finished this bottle yet...thank you, though."

The moment I sat down, Ziggy bolted off into the woods again.

Nadia gave me a canteen anyway and began to rummage through one of their storage bins inside the tent. "I could be wrong, but I'm going to assume you didn't find the fountain of youth in a 24-pack of bottled water. You knew my name and that Roman and I are getting married. What are you doing here?"

I had no idea how to explain—or if telling her would make things worse. If she hadn't already known my name, I would have found some excuse to leave.

Some older version of me had already spoken to her and Roman, though—which I hadn't known about before Roman had sent Adira to talk to Dominic and me. I needed answers, and it was possible I wouldn't get another chance to ask Nadia anything. I just had to be careful about it.

"A friend of mine and I just came here to stop some earthquakes originating from the island. We got separated. Either she disappeared—or possibly I did."

Nadia seemed skeptical but amused. "To stop some earthquakes? You can do that, too?"

"I know it sounds crazy," I replied. "You said Roman found a way to get back to your boat? When you get the opportunity, you should both leave. I would say never come back, but I can't stop you from it."

"We're aware of the risks. We have equipment to avoid the areas with higher radioactivity—and the sinkholes. There's so much we can learn here—biology, physics, chemistry, geology...this place could keep the scientific community busy for years, and most of the world believes it's nothing but a death trap."

"It can be," I replied. "I just wish there was some way to prove it to all of you."

EXTINGUISHED WORLDS: WHAT GOES AROUND

CYCAD COVE ARCHIVES: ACCESS GRANTED_LEVEL 1

Irene Lawson is dead. Apparently erasing the memory of her interview with Dad wasn't enough. She got too close to something.

They made it look like a car accident, of course—just like what happened with Mom and my brother. Terrashield and Rodoxian are at least acting like they're investigating this time, but they're still not bringing in Roman or his lackeys. Not enough evidence—as if a time traveler would ever allow them to find anything useful.

Because of Fast Track changing the timeline so much, I can't trust any of them anymore. I don't know if Irene believed me or ever remembered anything, but she still tried to help me.

This is my fault, and I won't try to convince anyone else.

Dominic Averelli, Jr. is the key to Chaosis and Dara, and I know when and where to find him without Fast Track being able to interfere. I don't know how all of the island works yet, but I know enough.

As soon as I have proof, I'm going after everyone responsible for this.

I don't care who they are.

CCA File 11839204787__DSCJSJ20240215_CC_319DGS

Personal log of Samantha Fredricks/Pacer
Recovered from Apartment 419D Gregory Street, Cycad Cove by David Serrano/Cyndero and Jenny Serrano/Jhett

Note by J.S.—Looked like someone had been here before us. David found this on a flash drive hidden inside a fake receptacle. This apartment is one floor above 319D, which had some significance to Caleb/Fast Track.

CHAPTER TWENTY

I DIDN'T INTEND TO, but I dozed off. When I woke up, I was on the ground and wrapped up in a sleeping bag. It was dark again, but someone had started a fire and was cooking some sort of meat.

I was panicked and disoriented. "How long have I—"

"It's all right," Roman replied in a calm tone. "You're safe. You looked as if you've been through hell, so we let you get some rest. We'll take you back to Cycad in the morning. I'm sure your hero friends are worried—or are they your babysitters at this point?"

He meant it as a jab, but there was nothing malicious about it—more like an old friend trying to get a reaction out of me.

"We're already friends, too?" I asked. "You know me?"

He laughed. "I should hope so. You have us paid up with enough grant funding for the next five decades. It's okay. Nadia and I are both good with secrets. I just didn't expect you back within an hour of saying goodbye—and your aging being all over the place. It's all linear for you, though, right? I'm an archeologist—not a physicist—but I think I'm catching on. I remembered what you said—when you're not on the island, don't even tell you anything. Seems simple enough. A little confusing, I admit, but you're not the craziest investor I've ever met."

I wasn't sure how to respond to that. "Well, we're going to meet again—a long time from now. I won't know you yet. You're part of the reason I'm here in the first place."

Roman looked at Nadia and forced a smile at her, but his eyes were sad.

Older me had apparently told him a lot more than I'd realized.

"You could have lied about everything, Caleb, but you didn't. That means something to me. As long as you try when the time comes, we're good. You never know—something might come to you this round...and you at least seem to be pretty stubborn about not giving up if it doesn't."

I assumed he meant Nadia's death—which wasn't supposed to happen for ten more years. With what had happened at the fairgrounds, it made me worry that Roman and Nadia were both targets—or at least still in danger if the timeline had been knocked off-course. If either of them died sooner, Adira wouldn't be born.

It would be another major event I possibly couldn't repair no matter what I did.

Adira had been the first target during the attack on the beach—and the heroes had nothing to do with it. Samantha had wanted her dead...and she'd wanted me to be last out of some sort of revenge I still didn't understand.

Only I wouldn't have technically been last if she'd killed me.

Roman would have been.

"Weird question, but humor me. Do either of you know someone named Samantha?" I asked.

Both of them seemed confused and shook their heads. They had no reason to lie to me.

"Never mind," I said. "Worth a shot."

We ate dinner, and my arm started to feel somewhat better. The nosebleed had stopped, too.

Because Roman had anchored the *Kairos* on the eastern side of the island, I decided to make one more attempt to find Rodoxian. "If I don't immediately come back, don't try to search for me. I'm just trying to work this place out."

Roman nodded and began searching the campsite. "Do you have a piece of scrap paper, Nadia? Not from your sketchbook. I'm just going to draw out the patterns I know about for him—hopefully give him a way back here if he needs it."

She ripped a piece from her sketchbook anyway. "It's

okay. This one didn't turn out quite right. You can use it." She also handed me a pack with water and MREs.

Roman gave me the rough map and one of his machetes. "Keep this with you, even when you don't think you'll need it. We've seen snakes here the size of telephone poles. The hatchlings are about the diameter of your arm. I know you could probably back things up if one attacked you, but just in case..."

Roman shuddered—and this was a guy in his early twenties who was built like a gun safe. I tried to get the knife's holster onto my belt without looking as if it was any big deal. I probably failed, but they humored me.

"Thanks...for everything."

"You, too...see you later, I guess." Roman replied in an awkward tone. "I suppose you would never be older if one of the snakes got you or something else happened, right?"

I hoped I didn't have to find out.

Using the combination of the map Roman had made me and tracing back my steps where I'd followed Ziggy, I ended up on the beach again.

Cycad Cove was back in place, but there was no sign of Rodoxian. I wasn't sure if I'd time traveled again or if this was some trait of the island—like different paths led to different times, too.

"You don't need any of them, Caleb. If you want to fix this, all you have to do is ask me how." Samantha had either appeared out of nowhere or had followed me from Roman and Nadia's camp.

In her hands was the same laser gun she'd use to shoot Dominic and me. I raised my hands and left the machete in its holster. My reaction time wouldn't have been quick enough, even if I could do anything with it.

I tried to go back for at least some sort of edge, but all it bought me was a couple of seconds to not seem startled she was there.

It made a slight difference in that she let the laser gun rest to her side. "You're getting better at that again. If you try anything, though, I'm still much faster."

All I could keep seeing in my head was the *Kairos*

exploding and then Dominic dying in front of me. "You set up and murdered nearly everyone I've ever cared about. Why? Other than you being Dominic's ex-girlfriend, I have no idea who you are or what you want! That's the truth."

"I'm like you—was sent to this world against my own will...only I still remember everything that happened when and where I came from," she replied. "You apparently don't—not anymore. If I try to kill you again, you'll just keep coming back more confused than your last loop. I'm tired, Caleb. I just want this to be over and done with, but you keep getting in the way. All of you do—the heroes, the Greenes, your little adoptive family who won't tell you the entire truth because they think they can save you."

"Save me from what?" I asked. "You and your robot demon army?"

She laughed bitterly. "From yourself. If you think all the changes you've caused out of ignorance are a problem now, just wait until it all comes back to you—if it ever does. When you're ready to end this, you'll know where to find me. Unfortunately, I can't do it without you."

A low growl came from the woods behind her, but she teleported again before Ziggy reached her. He snarled, and then his attention darted to someone behind me.

Rodoxian and Cyndero were on the beach. They saw me and then Ziggy, and I realized from their horrified expressions that they thought I was about to be attacked or eaten. Rodoxian started to pull up some sand and saltwater with her abilities.

"Wait!" I shouted. "It's friendly! It won't hurt me!"

Apparently not as familiar with Rodoxian and Cyndero, Ziggy put himself between them and me and continued snarling.

Cyndero nodded but sounded nervous. "My mom had a poodle like that—only it just believed it was as big as that thing. When and where have you been? The Ice Age?"

"It helped me find some other friends—Roman and his wife Nadia—when they were younger," I explained. "Seems a bit protective of me, too. Did you two see Samantha before she disappeared? Dark-haired woman in a yellow suit and cape with the futuristic laser gun?"

Rodoxian shook her head. "No, we just got here...got your message that the current you probably didn't send."

"How long have I been gone on your end of things?" I asked.

"Two days," Rodoxian replied. "You disappeared, and I tried to search for you. All this place does is send me to the other side of the island and back again. It's bizarre. Where did you go?"

"I followed Ziggy here. I guess he knows the right trails. Got a rough map from Roman, too, so that's something I didn't have before." I cautiously stepped around Ziggy to show them. "It's okay, boy. They won't hurt you."

Ziggy didn't approach them—just made a sneeze-like sound and then bounded toward the woods again. He seemed to wait for me for a moment but then left when he realized I wasn't going to follow. Once he was gone, Rodoxian and Cyndero seemed to genuinely relax.

"Okay, I get that you have Earth's entire timeline of wildlife to choose a pet from, but that's one of the most terrifying animals I've ever seen," Cyndero said. "How did you even tame it?"

"I honestly don't remember. I need you to catch me up on everything. Have the earthquakes stopped? Is Jhett okay?"

"The earthquakes did stop, and Terrashield hasn't sensed anything unusual since you returned here." Rodoxian replied. "Jhett..."

Cyndero was anxious and relayed everything faster. "Dara has her hostage, but we don't know where. I got a lead—security footage from a bank across from the pizza shop my uncle mentioned. I don't know if Jhett was being threatened or coerced, but they ate there—my little cousin, too. He had the stuffed Griffin with him."

"Meaning Chaosis made contact with them before he was captured?" I asked.

Cyndero nodded. "Oh, he's gloating enough to make me think he allowed himself to be captured on purpose. Terrashield and the police are trying to negotiate Jhett's release, but he's given them nothing useful...says he wants to talk to you. He mentioned the name Samantha, too. She wasn't around my uncle when my grandfather was killed, was she?"

I shook my head. "I didn't see her at the fairgrounds at all, but I was occupied with having my arm broken by one of her minions. Cyndero, it's like I told Rodoxian—I don't know what I'm doing. The fact that my vision caused you to confront Chaosis alone may have been the wrong call. I just thought that saving the booth worker's life—any life—"

"Hey, you didn't exactly hold a gun to my head and tell me to try talking him down. I've been beating myself up over this, too—not being there for Jhett...or for my grandfather. Hindsight is probably a lot harder on someone like you, but I get it. I just want to find Jhett. I know you can't have visions on command, but if there's anything you see ahead that can help us..."

"I think that's going to mean talking to your uncle," I replied. "Maybe if Chaosis says the right things, I can get a lead on Dara and where she might have taken her. I want to get Dominic out of there, too...while he still has a chance."

Rodoxian nodded but seemed distracted with the map Roman had given me. "Who sketched the orchids? They're talented—and they just ripped off this page as if it was a doodle?"

"Nadia—Roman's soon-to-be wife at this point. I'm not sure what her last name was before they met. I wasn't in the mindset to ask last night...really lucked out that Ziggy led me to their camp. Do either of you need water or food?"

"No, I'm fine..." Rodoxian replied, but she seemed confused. "You're not upset that they were here when the island is supposed to be off-limits to the public?"

I shrugged. "Roman and older me have some sort of understanding. I was apparently paying him and Nadia to explore here...and I know from past experience that I must not have ever told you or Terrashield about it."

"Why would you do that?" Cyndero asked. "Why hide that from us?"

Even though it technically wasn't my decision—yet—I

still felt bad about it. "I don't know. It kind of bothers me, too, so I get it if you're upset. I don't think I ever intentionally wanted you to be against each other. It just worked out that way."

"I'll keep that in mind in the future—try to reason with Roman and Nadia if there's ever a conflict." Rodoxian offered. "Terrashield will, too."

Even though I didn't really know them at the time, everything about how Rodoxian and Terrashield behaved in the future basically lined up with this. It was just Roman still didn't trust them for some reason—and then losing Adira had sent him over the edge at the worst moment possible.

Roman had lost his wife and daughter trying to do the right thing, and nothing else in the universe mattered anymore.

And I knew exactly how that felt...and the weight of all that anger and hatred fell on me so suddenly that I struggled to keep myself grounded on when and where I was.

"Caleb?" Cyndero asked. "You okay, bud?"

"I don't know...something's wrong..." My eyesight physically blurred and shook until Rodoxian and Cyndero were nothing more than blurs of color with the trees behind them—red, blue, and yellow against the green.

I could snap them in half like orchids, too...no, no, no, no—I didn't want to do that.

What the hell was wrong with me?

"Leave now—both of you!" I shouted, realizing my nose was bleeding again. "Just make sure Chaosis is ready to talk in about an hour. If I stay in Cycad Cove too long, the earthquakes may start up again."

"We can bring Doctor Serrano here if—" Rodoxian started.

I gritted my teeth. "Don't. There's nothing any of you can do about this. I just need you and Cyndero to get clear of me for a while. I don't want to hurt you. I don't want to hurt or kill anyone...not anymore. Guess I'm a little tired, too..."

Cyndero possibly thought I was joking and tried to humor me. "I think we'll be okay. Hell, we came all this way to make sure you were protected."

The energy in me released before I could rein it back in again.

All the stone buildings along the island's coast—including the lighthouse—toppled with the force of an explosion...my location being its origin point.

Cyndero and Rodoxian had been knocked unconscious and hit the water hard.

They needed help, but I was frozen in place. Everything was—for a moment.

The day Dominic had found me when I was eight, Roman hadn't been the cause of the skyscraper imploding. He just took the public blame for me—either as my friend or because the older version of me had made a deal with him.

That area of the city had been cleared of civilians ahead of time—something about a gas leak earlier that morning. No one else had gotten seriously injured—just me.

I had done that to myself.

What kind of insane time traveler drops a skyscraper on their own younger self's head—on purpose?

I collapsed onto the sand and blacked out.

CYCAD COVE ARCHIVES: ACCESS GRANTED_LEVEL 1

As I followed the old man, he offered me water in a thin clear bottle—what I later learned was plastic—and a piece of cooked meat wrapped in reflective foil. I kept both in case he needed them back, but he didn't seem concerned about their value.

'If you didn't do this, why did you wait for me?' I asked.

He gestured ahead. Morning fog over the fallen trees looked iridescent as we passed through it. 'I had this conversation with your father a few times. He asked me to help you in any scenario where you survived the blast instead of him. I'm honoring that.'

This made no sense to me. 'How could you have ever met him if he's dead? I've never seen you before in our village.'

His expression turned sad. 'Time doesn't work for me the same way it does for most people. Oh, watch your step.'

My foot slipped into deep mud. Startled, I looked up at a new canopy of trees—palms, not evergreens. The air turned sweet with the smells of fruit and flowers.

I'd regained my balance by bracing against a scaly, long-necked creature. A dinosaur—over twenty times the size of a reindeer—adjusted its footing and continued eating leaves.

'What magic is this?' I stammered and backed away. 'Where are we?'

'It's not magic—though the portals are a much faster travel method than boat.' The old man explained and then smiled. 'Welcome to Perilous Island. I'm Fast Track.'

CCA File 4200007_AG20211217_RG_PA

Recorded interview of Dr. Roman Greene
Conducted by Adira Greene, age 16
December 17th, 2021
Archive Access Restricted to Level 2 or Higher

CHAPTER TWENTY-ONE

"DON'T TAKE HIM! Don't take my baby!"

I couldn't see my mother's face, but I knew her voice.

Multiple laser guns blasted. They sounded similar to Samantha's gun.

The Messengers killed my mother right in front of me, and there was nothing I could do to stop them or fight them off.

I was barely old enough to walk at the time.

Then I heard what sounded like the Robot Demon Guy. "To truly conquer a planet and its people, you must do it in totality—its past, present, future, and all parallel branches. Remove all seeds of hope. Erase any potential obstructions and resistance before they ever develop. Only then can we begin to mold it to our will..."

"Caleb?" Cyndero asked, jarring me out of the vision. "Fast Track? Rox, he's breathing, but I'm not sure what else to do." He snapped his fingers several times. "Yeah, I'm beginning to think he told Terra that just to give him something to do."

I was relieved they were alive, but I couldn't respond. It was as if my entire body had gone catatonic.

"Give him a few minutes." Rodoxian said. "That blast wave probably took a lot out of him..."

"It almost took a lot out of us, too!" Cyndero replied. "I know he didn't mean to do it, but he could have killed us. What's wrong with him?"

"I don't know. On the way here, he seemed worried that he'd tampered with the timeline too many times. It could be the instability of the island and his abilities are linked somehow."

"So, it's possibly either 'fix the island to fix him' or 'fix him to fix the island.' Fifty-fifty chance is better than some other things we've gone up against."

"If you want to go back, I'll understand," Rodoxian replied. "I just don't want him to wake up alone and think we're dead. That would just make things worse."

"Stable or not, I still think he's our best chance at finding Jhett alive," Cyndero replied. "Plus, he's always done right by me—other than this whole island-leveling explosion thing. Even I've had bad days, so I guess I should cut him a break."

I struggled to say something. "I'm sorry...couldn't control it..." I opened my eyes to find them standing over me—both of them looking as if they'd just been through a hurricane.

Rodoxian reached into her uniform pocket. Crouching next to me, she placed what felt like a small pouch in my good hand. "We don't have all the answers, Caleb, but I think I know why you came back—and keep looping back over and over again."

I rose up on my elbows and looked in my hand. It was a baby's sock. Tucked inside it was a man's wedding band with an inscription. "Love you always—Adira. This was mine...but how?"

"I don't believe you came back to help us—not originally," Rodoxian explained. "This was personal—saving your wife or daughter...maybe both."

Cyndero apparently wasn't aware of this. "You're saying Fast Track lied to us—maybe not this one, but the older guy who knew more from the start?"

Rodoxian's tone turned defensive. "He gave these to me right before he saved all of our asses and the entire planet—so, no, I'm not saying that. He just didn't have time to fully explain, and he may have had his reasons."

"What did I do?" I asked.

"You bought us more time," she replied.

"Time for what?"

She looked up at the sky. "To prepare against something terrible that we're still not ready to face."

EXTINGUISHED WORLDS: WHAT GOES AROUND

CYCAD COVE ARCHIVES: ACCESS GRANTED_LEVEL 1

We sent our daughter and son-in-law into hiding over two years ago, but it wasn't enough.

As soon as Caleb was born, it was as if the Messengers knew exactly when and where to find him. They tracked down and abducted him—murdered [name illegible]—just like Caleb said he remembered. He warned us decades ago but said some events can't be averted or changed without destabilizing an entire timeline.

[Name illegible] disappeared but left behind a note saying he'd rescue Caleb or die trying. We don't know his final outcome. If Caleb ever met his father at any point in our timeline, he never told us.

Jhett and I don't have a lot of time left here, but if you get this— Caleb is a key to unlocking Perilous Island's full potential.

That's why the Messengers targeted him.

If they can't gain full control over Caleb and his abilities, they'll kill him—and our timeline and Earth will be eradicated.

He needs our help to stop both possibilities.

CCA File 957693049441_BWTSRMNRX20230104_FT_M

Message by David Serrano/Cyndero, date unknown.
Laser-etched media is only visible under a microscope.
Plate composed of Adiralite and several unidentified metals.
Discovered in Fortis's office by Ben Wallace/Terrashield and Rachel McNabb/Rodoxian.

Note by R.M.—Illegible areas appear to be lasered off using a cruder technical method compared to the text.

CHAPTER TWENTY-TWO

I KEPT WAITING FOR THEM to leave, but Rodoxian and Cyndero stayed with me on the beach for almost thirty minutes. Cyndero was anxious—alternating between flying a few feet above the sand and pacing. Rodoxian recovered some medical supplies from the rubble I'd created and focused on my nosebleed.

"Did the hospital's doctors run other tests on me while I was in a coma? MRI or that sort of thing?" I asked. "I felt okay when we first got here, but now my head feels like it's splitting. My ears are ringing, too—very high pitch in the background, and it's not going away."

"A specialized team examined you—people we've all trusted for years," Rodoxian replied. "If there was anything abnormal for you, they would have told us."

"Abnormal for me?"

"Didn't you have a doctor when you were a kid?" Cyndero asked.

"Not exactly—long story, and I know you have more important things to deal with right now."

He seemed concerned for me, too. "I want to find Jhett, but I don't want you harming yourself just to get a lead that may or may not pan out. If you don't feel like talking to my uncle, I'll do it."

"No, I'll go with you. I just wish I knew if the earthquakes are over."

"Terra can keep everything monitored from the mainland." Rodoxian replied. "If they start again, we'll have enough time to get you back here while they're mild."

They both seemed calm and rational, considering I'd

almost accidentally killed them. It reminded me of when I'd first woken up at the hospital and had tried to warn them about everything.

Maybe their everyday life was so insane that this was normal to them.

I tested hovering off the ground a few inches. "I think I'll be able to fly back to Cycad Cove. Just keep watch in case I pass out."

"The holding facility is called Brunel Heights." Cyndero said. This didn't surprise me, but Dominic and I had never gone there. "It's actually several miles north of the city, and there's an enforced perimeter where they don't want anyone flying or using certain other powers. I'll have to leave my visor behind, too. I'm thinking we stop at headquarters first—take a car and check-in with Terra. It won't take long to drive there after that."

"I'll stay at headquarters and recap Terra on everything." Rodoxian said. "I think there's a visitor limit, anyway."

"I'm sorry again for what happened here. If either of you are hurt and acting like you're not—"

"We're fine. To be honest, I'm more worried about you right now. If you have a vision or just a bad gut feeling once you're there, turn back. There's something bizarre about this entire situation, and I don't like it."

Stopping off at their downtown headquarters didn't take as long as I expected. They had a small 2-door sedan waiting for us next to the building. Cyndero took the driver's seat and passed off his visor to Terrashield.

"We'll give you the grand tour once you get back, Caleb— and you're welcome to stay with us if the earthquakes have stopped," Terrashield said.

"You trust me that much after what just happened?" I asked Rodoxian. "In the middle of a city overnight? I'm even a little worried about being in a car right now."

"Whatever comes, we'll handle it—same as if it was any of the rest of us," she replied. "It's not as if you did it on purpose."

I wanted to tell them what I thought I remembered, but it still didn't even seem real to me.

Cyndero went quiet for the first few minutes of the drive, and I almost dozed off out of exhaustion.

"Just for the sake of me trying to understand the overall timeline, my little cousin survives this and turns out okay?" he asked. "He rescues you when he's older and you're younger?"

I laughed at how crazy it all seemed. "Yeah—about ten years from now. You, Terrashield, and Rodoxian were there that day, too, but you didn't see me at the time. I'll be eight, but I was small for my age then, too. Dominic admitted to me later he thought I was closer to four or five until I calmed down and started talking."

"But you're not ageing backwards—just bouncing and looping all over the timeline. From our perspective, it's like even though you died three years ago, you're still around—living out your earlier life until you reach that point in your future and our past. That has to be weird for you. Could you ever meet with your older self who is maybe twenty-five or thirty? Sit down at a restaurant and have a nice you-to-you conversation about what you learned the hard way the first time? Who would pay for the check—assuming all the paradoxes don't kill us first?"

"I haven't had time to fully sit down and think about it. I really want to return to my present, but not until we find a way to save everyone. With twenty years of lead time, there has to be a way..."

"Yeah, I hope so, Fast Track...I really do." An impatient driver cut him off, and he had to slam the brakes and honked the car horn. "Damn it! This is why I'd rather fly everywhere...no red lights...no hassles—"

This gave me an idea. "Hey, I know Jhett can fly—but can Dara? Dominic said it took him until he was about ten to learn how—and he wasn't sure whether it would happen for him or not."

"I'm not even sure if Dara has powers at all. I've never met her. I could make some calls—see if there's anything connecting her name to a vehicle registration and address. Dominic never talked about where he grew up before my uncle and Dara were both sentenced, did he?"

"I think he remembered. He just never talked about it. They weren't abusive in the sense of hitting or yelling at him, but how they lived...neither of them were ever stable people, and it wasn't good for any kid to be in that."

He gave an uneasy nod. "If I knew it wouldn't make things worse, I'd adopt my cousin in a heartbeat once we find him. The team could keep him safe—rescue you and keep you safe, too, when you pop up again in ten years. Why can't we do that?"

It didn't seem like a terrible idea, but I wasn't sure what else it could change. "I don't know. Maybe something to do with Grandma adopting Dominic and me? Before I destroyed the cottage, her birthday was the password to its front door. Rodoxian seemed to think it was important."

Cyndero seemed ready to ask another question, but we'd reached the gates of Brunel Heights—part maximum security prison for superpowered criminals, part asylum for anyone just as dangerous before they ever became a problem. That line was blurry enough that it terrified Dominic into never visiting his father in person—believing he'd never make it out of the facility if he did.

Even in full hero uniform, Cyndero shuddered. Until then, I'd had an irrational fear he was secretly there to drop me off and had tricked me into it. This wasn't the case. He and the other heroes still trusted me—or at the very least still wanted to help me. I was willing to do the same for them.

As we shut our doors, thunder rumbled overhead.

"The sky was perfectly clear when we left, and now this place looks like the set for a horror movie," Cyndero said, holding out his hand as a few raindrops fell. "There has to be someone in there manipulating the weather—may not be able to fully suppress it or something."

I nodded in agreement. "You know that bad gut feeling Rodoxian mentioned? I'm totally fine if you want to turn around and go back to your headquarters. I still want to help you with Jhett, but this place is creepy..."

Of all the times for a vision to hit me, I didn't want it to be now.

I saw Cyndero ahead of me on a set of stairs inside the

building. Something had convinced us to go ahead with it.

Cyndero's cell rang—bumping me out of the vision—and he answered it. "How did you get this number? No, wait—please! Just let me talk to her. I need to know—Jhett? I'm so sorry. I'll—Please, don't hurt her. Just tell me what you want. All right. All right. We're really close to him now. Just give us fifteen minutes to get through security, and we'll let you talk to him with my phone." Cyndero pulled the phone away from his ear to make sure the call had ended. "Dara said she'll give us two hours to negotiate my uncle's release in exchange for Jhett."

"What?"

"If they still refuse to let him go, she's going to kill her. Caleb, I need you on this. I don't care what else you have to change about the timeline, Jhett can't die! Please."

CYCAD COVE ARCHIVES: ACCESS GRANTED_LEVEL 1

I've seen this invasion in visions dozens of times.

I can't save Earth. I can't even save everyone I care about personally. Nearly everything I've tried just seems to make things worse, and it's not as simple as going back and resetting our timeline to some sort of default.

To be honest, I don't even know what 'default' was here before I showed up in Cycad Cove. Compared to other versions of Earth, a lot of major events are different. If I'm the only cause of this, I haven't figured out how.

If I push my powers to their limit, I could maybe run and save myself—just to see everything eventually play out again for some other dimension.

I can't do that. I won't leave everyone else here to die.

There has to be another way...

CCA File 47382950435__RGNG18990408_CA_FT_OI7C

Audio file by Caleb Averelli/Fast Track
Recovered on Orchid Island Grid 7C by Roman and Nadia Greene

Note by R.G.—Nadia and I showed this to our Caleb. He doesn't remember recording it yet. Averelli is his adoptive brother's last name, but Caleb was advised never to use it as an alias. He didn't tell us why.

CHAPTER TWENTY-THREE

CYNDERO WAS DESPERATE and overestimating what I could do, but altering the timeline to save Jhett wasn't anything beyond what I'd be willing to do to save Adira.

I understood where he was coming from—and it wasn't as if I'd be changing anything original. Major events had already been tampered with before—possibly multiple times—and I had been at least one of the causes. Any of my past or future mistakes weren't Jhett's fault, and she didn't deserve to die because of them.

I couldn't save Fortis, but maybe I could save her. "I'll do everything I can—could repeat conversations until we find the right way to get your uncle released into your team's custody. How well do you know the people who operate this place?"

"Not that well," Cyndero replied. "They had a good relationship with my grandfather, but I don't know how this will play out in the first round. Just be ready to do the rewind thing. I'll sense when it happens and follow your cues on what to do differently."

This confused me. "You can sense when I do that? Remember it?" It also made me wonder if Dominic could, too—that he just hadn't told me.

Cyndero shrugged. "Sort of—if I'm nearby when it happens. My grandfather was a lot more perceptive to it, but I've inherited it to an extent. You at least know about that, right? If you don't, wait until we can talk privately. I'm not sure how much my grandfather told other people—especially here."

The first set of guards near the gate were nicer than I

expected. One offered his condolences about Fortis and knew Cyndero by name. My identification however posed a problem.

He suddenly seemed irritated. "If this is a joke, it's not a good one. I knew Fast Track, and the guy definitely wasn't a teenager."

"Have you ever seen him outside of his suit?" Cyndero asked.

"No, but—"

Cyndero clasped my shoulder and shook it. Other than straightening my posture, there wasn't exactly much I could do to seem more intimidating. "Well, now you know why. Go ahead and rewind, Buddy. He's not buying it."

I rewound time by a few seconds.

"If this is a joke, it's not a good one. I knew Fast Track, and the guy—"

I interrupted him, and sounding nervous wasn't completely fake. "I'm Fast Track's son—in training. Not in training to be his son, but to be a hero—and take over for my father who has been very dead for three years. Interrogation techniques are important, right?"

Cyndero seemed amused. "Exactly what he said—just more coherent. Look, I just want some answers from a family standpoint. Caleb is here to make sure I don't go too far off-base. I need him with me as someone objective. There are lives in the balance on this, and we don't believe we have a lot of time."

The guard sighed. "Okay. Give me a few minutes to run this through my supervisor. I'll be right back."

"Sure." Cyndero said and then looked at me once the guard had left. "What gave you that idea?"

"Combination of a drawing Adira showed me and Rodoxian telling me all the scenarios your team brainstormed when you found me at the marina," I explained. "Do you know anything about my actual parents?"

He didn't like the question and tried to dodge it. "You told us a little—not sure how much I'm supposed to tell you now, but—hold up a sec."

The guard returned and waved at us. "You're both

cleared. Keep these badges on at all times. Doctor Brown will meet you inside the lobby."

I almost laughed. "Doctor Brown? As in Doc—"

"She's a psychiatrist—has an ability to neutralize the powers of the people around her," Cyndero said. "Doesn't drive a DeLorean. She went to med school with my mom and might be able to help us out, though. At least it's someone I sort of know…"

After Cyndero parked, we were searched for weapons and warned with a list of powers not to use on the premises. Time travel wasn't on that list, but neither was uncontrollably flattening everything to ground level within a 30-yard radius. I felt exhausted but was afraid something would surprise me and happen outside of my full control again."

Cyndero looked concerned. "Try to relax. Stressing out isn't going to help Jhett or my cousin. I don't want to get kicked out of here before we even see my uncle."

He didn't want to get kicked out.

I didn't want to get thrown into the nearest empty padded cell.

Doctor Kim Brown was in her mid-fifties and wore a dark blue lab coat. She didn't seem surprised to see us. When she got closer, I tested to see if I could rewind time a few seconds. I couldn't.

"Don't worry, Caleb. Let me introduce you, and then I'll make sure you can talk to my uncle before we do." There wasn't time for me to ask Cyndero how he planned to do that—or any other questions—but he seemed confident about what he was doing. "Nice to see you again, Doctor—just wish it was under better circumstances. Mom was just talking about you the other day."

Doctor Brown seemed glad to see him. "I know…and she just messaged me, David. She doesn't want you to be the one to interrogate him. I'm inclined to agree. I know Rodoxian and Terrashield were likely close with Fortis, too, but for all of this to have happened within the past 72 hours…"

"My uncle's wife kidnapped Jhett during the attack at the fairgrounds and is still at-large with my five-year-old cousin.

I'm not going into this expecting him to tell me any details outright. I want him to gloat and slip up on something—a word, a phrase—anything. My friend Caleb just needs a safe place to observe. I'd prefer it if my uncle doesn't even know he's here."

Her attention went to me. It was no exaggeration that I felt as if she was analyzing me on sight—that she may have had other powers that helped her. "You're not with the police or the Cycad Cove hero team, but I've seen you around other cases before. Always hanging back at a distance. Never speaking to anyone. It was smart to leave your suit behind. We couldn't have allowed you in here with it."

I just went along with it and nodded. She led us to an observation room. A glass window divided it from another room roughly the same size.

"Both of you will stay here once Chaosis has been moved. I'll ask him any question you want, David, but you and him shouldn't be in direct contact right now. I'm trying to look out for you, and it's the best I can offer. He can't hurt me. I'll be fine."

"All right, but it's a lot of questions. Do you want me to write them down first?"

She nodded. "You can even record them, if you want. Come with me. I have a digital recorder in my office. It will take a while to move him from his cell to this side of the building, anyway."

EXTINGUISHED WORLDS: WHAT GOES AROUND

CYCAD COVE ARCHIVES: ACCESS GRANTED_LEVEL 1

'It doesn't bother you that Fast Track has tampered with your entire lifetime?'

'The way it sounds, I could have ended up becoming a horrible person and hurt a lot of people. I guess that part bothers me—who I would have been without some sort of intervention. Caleb's a good person, Sam. Time traveler or not, I'm thankful he didn't let me turn out like my parents. Yeah, it's weird, but I don't mind helping him now in return.'

'What if I told you he helped you out of guilt? That Chaosis and Dara turned out evil because of him—along with what happened to my family. That's why I'm here.'

'If that's true, I'd really like to hear it from him.'

'He doesn't know anything. He's still just a kid. The events in our past haven't happened from his perspective yet.'

'Then why are you trying so hard to turn me against him?'

'You know what? Never mind. If Fast Track can make people forget entire conversations, I can find a way, too.'

'Samantha, wait—'

CCA File 77482003__CS17841016_SFP_DAJr_8DPI

Audio recording recovered from cell phone by Caleb Serrano.
Grid 8D on updated map, Perilous Island

Note by C.S.—Phone looks brand new, approximately from 2012-2013 timeframe. There's blood on the case. I suspect it belonged to Samantha Fredricks/Pacer but currently have no way to confirm. Will regroup with Roman and Nadia as soon as possible.

CHAPTER TWENTY-FOUR

A FEW MINUTES LATER, Chaosis was escorted into the interrogation room by two massive guards. Neither of them acknowledged me being in the next room, which made me realize the glass looked like a wall-length mirror on their side.

Chaosis looked drugged—eyes somewhat vacant—but he complied and slumped into one of the chairs. Once the guards exited and bolted the door, his whole demeanor changed. He was alert—sitting upright—and then looked right at me.

I shuddered.

Chaosis laughed, and I heard him on a slight delay from the observation room's speakers. I coughed to clear my throat, and there was an echo to it.

That meant he could hear me, too.

"No security cameras—no one to get upset if anyone 'accidently' decides to wipe the floor with me after the good doctor steps out of the room. It's a shame, too, considering I did all of you a *big* favor. My father was a fraud. You're not too far from one yourself, Fast Track. You just believe what they want you to know."

I stood and approached the glass barrier. Maybe it was something about how his laser vision worked, but Chaosis could see me well enough to maintain eye contact. I glared at him, but he grinned as if it amused him

I found a microphone in my room and approached it. "Where's Jhett? Why are you doing all of this to your own nephew? Cyndero didn't even hate you before the attack!"

He made a tsk-tsk click with his tongue "Not so fast,

Track Boy. You've always been so impatient—impulsive. The only reason you're not where I'm sitting is your powers afford you all the second or third or thousandth futile chances you'll ever want. The rest of us poor souls are pawns being played over and over again in slightly different ways—or maybe you are now, too...trapped at the mercy of your much *better* and *wiser* self. Personally, I'd rather be stuck in here than have that kind of hell looming over me for the rest of my life. You failed your family and the entire planet, and you didn't gain a damn thing from sacrificing yourself. That's actually pretty tragic. I might even shed a few tears before this is all over..."

He was trying to get to me—and it was working. If I had managed to blast those rooms on any level of what had happened at Perilous Island, he probably would have escaped.

Instead, a small trickle of blood ran down my nose and hit my shirt. It was enough to startle Chaosis, and something resembling genuine concern hit his expression.

No, not exactly concern...more like surprise...or fear.

I laughed, even though I was scared. "Guess I'm not even much of a pawn—even to you. Was this your big plan on getting out of here? Me doing it for you?"

With Doctor Brown being distracted and kept out-of-range by Cyndero, my ability worked again. I focused—not giving Chaosis time to answer my question—and then rewound time back to the guards bringing him into the interrogation room.

He did the same act of pretending to be drugged until they left. Once they were gone however, he said nothing—just stared at me.

"What? No commentary about the security cameras?" I asked. "Crap, my nose is still bleeding...could you ask them to bring me a tissue? I have my t-shirt, but—"

He seemed borderline between being horrified and skeptical. "Are you dying or something? I know that can't happen—not when you're eighteen. Our entire timeline would unravel on itself, and we'll all be dead."

I shrugged. "I honestly have no idea at this point. I

thought you said at the fairgrounds that time was fixed—but then you act as if I can keep changing everything at will without any real consequences. Can't be both, right? I don't think you actually know anything about me or what I can and can't do. You're going off of what you were told by someone else. Samantha?"

This got a reaction out of him—just not one I was expecting. He and Samantha weren't allies. If anything, he seemed to hate her more than he did me. "The messenger you're calling Samantha murdered my mother, Fast Track—and my father stood by and allowed it to happen. That's how much influence she held over him—for years. What you saw me do at the fairgrounds couldn't have happened if *The Great Fortis* didn't allow it. I've never been as powerful as him, and I never will be. Both of you are making some really desperate and weird plays lately. I'm not quite following where you're heading with it all, but at least it's something new."

"Fortis let you kill him? Why?"

"To help you save the world—I suppose until we all loop back around and do this again. I've lost count how many times we've had this conversation...makes me wish you'd drop a skyscraper on my head, too. You're an ignorant teenager now but seem a lot happier...at least better than the mopey 'Oh no! I've lost my family trying to save everybody else...' Small piece of advice, Fast Track—just forget the world next time. You're never going to find a solution that allows both sides of what you want—and believe me, you have tried beyond all reason to find one. Anyone dumb enough to put themselves between my family's survival and me—they're dead. Problem solved. If this world wasn't meant to change, dinosaurs would be having this conversation instead of us. Think about it."

Chaosis slumped back in his chair again as Doctor Brown opened the door and entered. As she sat down across the table from him, he was acting drugged again—or at least more affected by whatever they'd given him than he actually was.

Cyndero entered the room next. He'd managed to

convince Doctor Brown to let him ask the questions as long as he kept his distance in the corner of the room.

"There aren't any cameras in here, Uncle. You can speak freely."

"Huh...hadn't even noticed. Who are you again? Oh, yeah...David. Almost didn't recognize you in that getup. Did Jhett let you borrow her bedazzler, or does everyone on the team get issued their own?"

Cyndero took several steps forward—looking ready to hit him—but Doctor Brown stood between them. Cyndero sighed and forced himself back to the same corner.

"Look, I have Dara's phone number. She wanted me to call back once I got here. Do you want to talk to her or not?"

Dr. Brown shook her head. "That's not a good idea, David—and I really wish you'd cleared it with me out there first before—"

"Relax...both of you," Chaosis interrupted. "Get Dara on the line. We always let the girl go, Doc. Hell, she's pregnant with David's kid. How else would you expect a nineteen-year-old to react to that? We apparently found out before she had a chance to tell him."

Doctor Brown's eyebrows furrowed. "What do you mean by you *always* let her go? Miss Weiland has never had contact with you or your wife prior to the attack at the fairgrounds."

Chaosis laughed. "Which came first? The insanity or the time travel? I'm the wrong person to ask. You need to have a little therapy session with Marty McAcne Face on the other side of that mirror. Maybe that will solve all our problems."

"You can see through two-way mirrors?" Doctor Brown asked.

"And normal ones—but that's boring because there's usually a wall on the other side of them. Totally ruins funhouses for me, too. Anyway, how's that phone call coming along, David? I have all day, but you seem to be in a hurry. You have what—maybe an hour and a half before something important happens? Dara will keep her word as long as you keep yours."

Cyndero started to panic. "She's not answering. Why the

hell would she not answer?"

Chaosis sighed. "Here—just give me the damn phone. I'll text her a code word so she'll know it's me and try again."

Doctor Brown shook her head. "Do not give him that phone!"

Chaosis seemed irritated. "Have you even seen his phone? Unless I'm planning to use it as a brick, there's nothing on it I can use to get out of here. Oh, maybe that Snake game will give me an escape path idea. Better watch out."

"You have absolutely no remorse for what you've done, do you?" Doctor Brown asked. "The lives you've taken? The hundreds of innocent men, women, and children who all are hurting right now because of your actions?"

Chaosis smiled and gestured to Cyndero. "I used to be more like him—cared quite a bit, actually. If some psychotic murderer had told me that all those civilians from the fairgrounds aren't dead—hypothetically—that we're all trapped in an increasingly unstable series of time loops, I would have thought they were crazy, too. Originally, I was on *your* side of the table—and then something in my past was altered...and that change rippled through my entire life. By the time I figured it out, there wasn't much I could do about it."

She wasn't buying it. "So, you blame this person for your current circumstances? For who you've become as a person? Even with awareness of this altered event, you now have no desire to fight against what it did to you?"

"I tried—maybe the first hundred times or so. You ever see *Groundhog Day,* Doc? Well, it turns out I'm not Bill Murray. I'm just one of the background saps who remembers all the overall outcomes but has no power to release us. That doesn't make me a psychic—and it sure as hell doesn't make me a hero. All of you have placed our lives, this city, and the entire future into the hands of someone who has no idea what he's doing anymore—if he ever did to begin with! That's insane to me. What if Fast Track just believes he's the answer to all of this when he's really not? Someone or something a lot more powerful than any of us is pulling the Messengers' strings—and they're getting tighter by the second. Tick-tock, Doc. You two won't even remember any of this, but at least he might. My offer from last time still stands once you're tired of this, too."

Chaosis looked toward me, and both Cyndero and Doctor Brown went quiet. I cautiously approached the microphone again.

"What offer was that?" I asked. "I honestly don't remember."

"Doesn't matter now," Chaosis replied and then focused on Cyndero. "Still no luck with that number, David? Dara always picked up before. Things are so strange this round..."

Cyndero tried Dara's number again, keeping the phone in his hand. He switched it to speaker, and I could hear it ringing.

"Hello?" It was a kid's voice...Dominic. "Who is this?"

"Hey, Kiddo. It's me," Chaosis replied in a friendly tone. "Where's your mother? It's kind of important."

"Dad? Mom's not here. She dropped me off at home after the fireworks and said she and the hero lady had to go on a trip. They're not back yet. I still have some leftover pizza and cereal—spilled some milk yesterday, but I cleaned it up. I tried to call you a bunch of times, but you never answered your phone. Are you okay? When are you coming home?"

This actually affected Chaosis, and his sadness seemed genuine. "I...I'm okay, but your mother and I may be busy for a while. It's an emergency, and she didn't mean to leave you alone for so long. I'm going to send a couple of friends to take you somewhere safe. Ask for the code word before you go with them. Understand? I'll talk to you soon, but I'm going to make sure you're safe first. I love you, Son."

"Love you, too...I miss you. See you soon."

"Yeah...see you soon," Chaosis replied, and he pushed the phone back to Cyndero.

EXTINGUISHED WORLDS: WHAT GOES AROUND

CYCAD COVE ARCHIVES: ACCESS GRANTED_LEVEL 1

'Why help me escape? I'm not seeing a goatee, so I take it you're not Fast Track's evil doppelganger?'

'It's me. I want to know how your mother really died. I spoke to Fortis before, but Samantha found a way to reset a few timelines. None of that affects you apparently.'

'So, you're finally believe me over Mr. Perfect Hero?'

'I didn't say that—but I am sorry for my part in all of this. I didn't understand everything at the time. Neither did the others on your father's team.'

'You ever wonder if your brain-damaged ignorance is a feature, not a bug? You already know more than I can ever tell you, but it terrifies you to prod your own memories.'

'Humor me.'

'Samantha Fredricks teleported inside our house—yellow suit and cape covered in her own blood. She shot my mother with a laser gun and then disappeared before Dad or I could react. Dad later covered it up as a car accident and told me not to say a word to anyone—not even my sister away at college. He wanted to handle the situation without the rest of you being involved—especially you.'

'Samantha was already wounded? Was she dying?'

'Not sure, but my personal theory—what if Dad's revenge triggered her revenge, and neither of them knows who started it first. It all just loops, repeating over and over again, Fast Track. It's like poetry in the chaos...'

CCA File 577302839932__BWTS20230405_DASR_FT

Interview of Dominic Averelli Sr./Chaosis by Fast Track
Storage card delivered to Ben Wallace/Terrashield
Envelope contained no postage or other delivery markings

CHAPTER TWENTY-FIVE

DOMINIC ENDED THE CALL, and Cyndero slipped the phone into his jacket pocket.

"Did your wife redirect her number somehow?" Doctor Brown asked Chaosis. "Where's your son? With what I heard, he's scared and about to run out of food. Even if you have money at home, a five-year-old child shouldn't be wandering the city on his own..."

Chaosis glared at her. "I'm not telling you, Doc. My son is off-limits. No matter what Dara and I do, he's still innocent—not your opportunity to win some psychiatry awards at the expense of his life and well-being. I've seen that path play out a few too many times, too. My nephew isn't an idiot—and Fast Track already has everything they need. He just has to have the incentive to recall it. They'll find him in time. They always do."

Dr. Brown stood. "Then I guess we're finished here. It's not an extensive list, David, but I do have a list of previous addresses I can give you without a warrant being necessary. Your uncle is right that your cousin should be off-limits, but I'm not the kind of person he thinks I am. I just want to do the right thing."

"Don't we all?" Chaosis said in a sarcastic tone.

Doctor Brown notified the guards outside, and they took Chaosis back to his cell. I met Cyndero in the hallway, but Doctor Brown wasn't with him and had gone back to her office to locate Chaosis's entire file.

"Does she know about me?" I asked. "Time travel? Samantha and the messengers? Everything? She didn't exactly seem surprised by anything your uncle said."

Cyndero seemed hesitant to answer. "Well, she thinks

he's insane. Even if he fully believes what he's saying, she'll never completely believe it. He almost convinced me on a few things, though. How many loops have you done trying to solve all of this—total? Do you even know?"

"I haven't experienced any of that yet," I explained. "Before you found me at the marina, that was the first time I'd ever gone back more than a few minutes. Even with my visions, I thought I was just looking ahead at possibilities—not seeing an actual outcome that must have happened at least once before."

"Once we have the addresses, it would help a lot if you can narrow them down before we physically travel to them. Rox and Terra can help us, too, but it's dangerous to be split up so thin that we're by ourselves. Dara and my uncle aren't stupid, either. All of this is just a little too convenient to me."

"You think this is some sort of trap? That Jhett and Dominic are bait for something bigger?"

He nodded. "If my uncle does have some idea of what we'll do before we actually do it, that gives him an edge—no different than how older you used your abilities to help us when we first met you."

Doctor Brown returned and gave Cyndero photocopies from a portion of Chaosis's file.

"Thanks for letting us in here—and for this. We'll keep you posted."

"It was no problem, David. Be careful—both of you. It was nice meeting you, Caleb."

I still felt uneasy around her. "You, too."

There was nothing obviously odd or creepy about Doctor Brown personally, but I felt a sense of relief once we made it back to the car.

Cyndero handed me the photocopies. There was a total of ten addresses—eight of them within the city limits—but nothing stood out to me from a memory standpoint.

"This sort of makes sense. Dara wasn't from Cycad Cove originally. Chaosis left the city at least five years ago and just recently returned with her and Dominic."

Cyndero cringed. "You're saying they may not even be in the city anymore? We can pull in outside help at the regional level, but most other city heroes have their own problems to deal with. Unless we have a solid lead, there's not much they can do."

I was beginning to feel drained and exhausted again. "I know. Give me a minute. I'll probably feel a lot better once we get away from..."

Another vision hit before I could finish talking.

I was back inside Brunel Heights—this time inside the interrogation room with Doctor Brown and Chaosis.

They were sitting on the same side of the table—opposite of me. Chaosis was wearing a hero uniform with a stylized Griffin logo on his chest. I could see myself in the mirror, and I looked older—late 20s or early 30s.

I was wearing an inmate uniform and looked as if I hadn't shaved or had a haircut in months. The facility had let me keep my wedding ring, but it felt loose on my finger where I hadn't been eating and was bone thin. My daughter's socks were in my pants pocket. I kept compulsively checking for them—afraid I'd lose them. They were my only connection left that my daughter had ever existed—that Adira and I had been happy and safe once.

I'd lost that life trying to avert the egg-like probes from ever launching from Perilous Island—accidentally changing our entire timeline in the process.

By the time I'd fully realized what I'd done, it had gained me nothing except a world full of strangers I still wanted to protect but who thought I was crazy.

Chaosis looked annoyed to be there, like it was a waste of his time. "So, you're a time traveler? Huh, that's actually a new one for me, Shaggy. My dad's an alien and my mom is practically an immortal superhuman, so forgive me for being a little skeptical of something neither of them have encountered before." He leaned forward. "The only reason I'm here is that they and my sister all have better things to do. So do I, and you're holding me up from helping people who actually need it. Do you get why I'm annoyed?"

I shrugged, and my voice came out flat. "It doesn't matter if you believe me or not. A hostile force will invade Earth a little over two decades from now. Anyone who could get in their way will be neutralized long before they arrive—one way or another. Their scout teams abduct children and then send them into the pasts of their own worlds—turn them into weapons to pave the way for conquering a planet sooner and sooner. Your parents will be targets. So will you, your siblings, and any of your family's descendants between now and then."

He glared at me. "Is that a threat?"

"It's a warning. These scouts—Messengers—want to destroy our original timeline and override it with what they want our planet and people to be before their larger force arrives. Most people will never know what changed, but you and I will—eventually. I might be able to delay things—maybe even stop them—but I can't do it alone."

Doctor Brown maintained a calm expression and handed Chaosis a file...my file. "The reason I originally contacted your father is that Caleb does have some similar markers in his genetic code to your family, but I didn't want to get into that over the phone. I thought you should know, and I have no plans to tell anyone else until there's a decision on how to proceed."

Chaosis sounded distracted, reading over my file as he spoke. "Dad was a refugee from a dying world. He got lucky that his escape pod found Earth before it ran out of resources and shut down. If his people had the ability to time travel, they would have solved their problems there and then—and he never would have ended up here. Just because this guy might have similar DNA to us doesn't mean we're connected or owe him anything."

"Genetically, Caleb appears to be either your great-grandson or the grandson of your nephew. I could narrow that down more accurately if you would be willing to bring David and Dominic here for testing—though it's also possible he may be connected to a child in your family who hasn't been born yet."

He seemed appalled. "We're not bringing them anywhere near this place! This is some sort of trick, Doc. It has to be."

At the time, all of this began to feel pointless to me. Chaosis—apparently a hero named Griffin in this timeline—

didn't believe me. Maybe if I went back farther, his parents would. "If you don't protect our family, there are already Messengers willing to kill all of you to ensure I never exist in the future. If you won't help me, at the very least stay out of my way—for the sake of our family and the entire planet. I'll still handle what I can once I've fully recovered. It cost me almost everything just to get here, and I'm not giving up until I've either stopped them or die trying." I coughed, and my voice strained. "Hopefully not for a while..."

I covered my mouth, but I'd coughed up blood.

Doctor Brown stepped away and brought back a large handful of tissues. She wasn't afraid of me. Whether she believed me or not, she'd felt sorry for me from the moment I'd told her about Adira and our daughter.

Chaosis's expression went a little terrified. He crossed his arms and looked over at Doctor Brown when she returned to her chair. "Are you really buying all of this? I'm not telling you how to do your job, but this is really out-there—even for me."

She seemed reluctant to answer. "I don't know, but I can sense he believes it's true. He's not a danger to other people, but he keeps having hallucinations—visions of the future. The scary part is he hasn't been wrong about anything in the past five days—since he was found in the ocean and brought here."

"The ocean?" Chaosis asked.

She nodded. "About a hundred miles east of Perilous Island. He claims the island 'launched' him back in time—that his powers are connected to it."

Cyndero shook my shoulder, startling me.

I was eighteen again and sitting in the sedan's passenger seat. I checked my reflection in the side-mirror to be sure and then started to calm down. We'd almost reached downtown.

"Sorry. I didn't want to interrupt whatever you were seeing, but you started to look as if you were in pain. Is Jhett?"

"No—I mean, the vision wasn't about Jhett...or even the future." I don't know if it was denial or just flat-out fear, but

I didn't want to tell him everything I'd seen. I didn't want to believe it myself, and the only thing it could have accomplished would have been me getting placed back in Brunel Heights. I couldn't help anybody from inside there—and Jhett and Dominic were both running out of time.

"What was it then?"

"I saw myself older, but I was here again—around this time, I mean. Everything is just really confusing right now. I know who I am, but all of these different loops I've done...I think maybe they've changed me, too. Maybe your uncle is right. Maybe I'm just along for the ride now like everybody else."

He sighed. "I know what it's like—everybody putting pressure on you before you're ready. I ran away from this city and everybody I cared about because my grandfather decided to dump the entire future of the planet on me when I was fifteen. He was powerful, and he knew how to leverage being in the spotlight. I'll never be quite like him...but how you operated your branch of the team with Terra and Rox was different. It was Jhett who convinced me to come back here and try again, but everything you put into place made me want to stay and keep trying to make things better. You did that—for everyone in Cycad Cove and for our team. That's the Fast Track I knew—and you're still him. Don't let my uncle or anybody else ever make you doubt that."

I looked over the list of addresses again, hoping something would prompt where either Jhett or Dominic had been taken. "It's a weird feeling—trying to live up to myself...or at least how the rest of you saw me before. I hate to say this, but it's none of these addresses. I'm not getting anything. Maybe something's wrong with me..."

Cyndero frowned and pulled into a reserved space in front of their headquarters. "I believe you. It's just...hey, when you were growing up, did Dominic have a favorite pizza restaurant? Maybe mention which ones he ate at as a kid?"

"He used to talk about an Al's on Baxter Street that closed when he was a kid. Sometimes they ate inside the building. Other times his parents ordered it delivered to their place. That one wasn't near the fairgrounds or Grandma's shop, but that's still a lot of places to search within their delivery radius."

"Well, it's not closed yet. Give me a second…"

He looked up the location and called the number. When the pizza place employee answered, he placed an order doing a decent impersonation of Chaosis. "Hey, it's me…yeah, the usual is fine…make that three of the usual. Listen, I don't know how the hell it happened, but last time the delivery kid showed up at my neighbor's instead. Did something change in your system? No, that's right. 114B Royal Grove. My nephew will be standing outside to pick them up and pay." He cleared his throat, nearly using his normal voice. "Okay, goodbye." After he ended the call, he laughed. "Well, let's go pick up some pizzas and my cousin. Maybe there's something in their house or apartment that can help us find Jhett, too. We still have time, especially if Dara and my uncle think we're following what Doctor Brown gave us."

I got a brief flash ahead that Cyndero was right.

Dominic would open the door for him while I stayed out-of-sight to avoid any potential interference problems. I still wasn't sure how Dominic would end up being adopted by Grandma, but at least he'd be safe until hopefully Dara was captured.

This lined up with what I remembered and had been told by Dominic, but Jhett was never mentioned…I didn't know what had happened to her either way.

"Once you get Dominic clear, I want to take a look around the place," I said. "That okay?"

Cyndero gave me a confused look. "Of course. Why wouldn't it be? I'll call Terrashield. He has contacts with the police and social services—can at least come up with a temporary solution that hopefully won't tamper too much with my cousin's life or yours. I'll park a block away, and you can stay with the car. I'll find you once my cousin leaves."

CYCAD COVE ARCHIVES: ACCESS GRANTED_LEVEL 1

Two months after the fairgrounds attack, I found a five-year-old boy huddled in the alley behind my shop.

His clothes were filthy, and his hair looked greasy and unwashed for at least a week. 'Stay back, Grandma! I'm dangerous.'

I calmly tossed a trash bag into the dumpster. 'I'm sure you are...' Then two police cruisers with their sirens on drove past on Crown Street, and the boy flinched and ducked out of sight. 'What are you wanted for? Busting out of preschool?'

'I damaged a court room, but I didn't mean to—' His irises flared red, and he looked away. A pile of trash on the ground started to smolder, and he scrambled to stomp it out. 'Normally, I can control this, but some moron judge wants to put me in a foster home! What happens if I burn down an entire house by accident or something? I don't want to hurt anybody—or end up in prison like my parents.'

'And who are they?'

He held up a crumpled remnant of newspaper, which had mugshot photos of Dominic and Dara Averelli. 'Everyone's calling my dad Chaosis now, but he never called himself that...not before...' He finally looked at me again, his eyes bloodshot and watery. 'So, scared now?'

'Eh, I've dealt with worse.' I held the shop door open so he could follow me inside, but he hesitated. 'When's the last time you ate? Don't worry, kid. I'm old and have very overpriced business insurance. If you end up burning this dump to the ground, we'll both be better off...'

CCA File 302940521__RMNRX20030706_MS_PA

Personal journal of Maggie Serrano
Loose pages found inside Perilous Island's cabin by Rachel McNabb/Rodoxian

CHAPTER TWENTY-SIX

EVERYTHING BASICALLY STARTED OFF the way we expected. Cyndero got the pizzas, placed one on top of the sedan in case I got hungry later, and then rang the doorbell with the other two.

Dominic answered—thinking he was the delivery driver at first. Cyndero mentioned the stuffed griffin—hoping that was the secret code word—and that he was a friend that his father sent over with food. For some reason, he never told Dominic the entire truth that day—maybe to avoid scaring him since he was in a hero uniform and not his normal clothes.

Once Terrashield arrived with a social worker, things got harder. Dominic didn't want to leave the apartment, and that took up a lot of time.

I waited inside the car—trying to resist the urge to run in and tell Dominic everything would be okay. Growing up, he'd been the bravest older brother I could have imagined. Seeing him taken away from his home at five years old—crying, screaming, begging...his eyes glowing bright red in panic but his laser vision completely harmless—gutted me.

They put him in another car, and the social worker drove away with Terrashield keeping watch over Dominic in the rear seat.

Once they were gone, I got out of the sedan and approached the apartment. From the furious expression on Cyndero's face, I wasn't sure if I wanted to see the condition of it.

"I'm not saying my mother and uncle were raised in a mansion, Caleb, but everything was at least clean at my grandfather's house. My mom gave me a hard time if I even left clothes on the floor instead of a hamper. This is disgusting, and it looks as if they've only been here for a few months. I know you don't know me that well yet, but I looked up to you growing up—and I promise this isn't what the rest of my family is like..."

The smell hit me before we reached the front door, and it took me a minute not to immediately want to throw up on the sidewalk. There was trash everywhere—old pizza boxes, empty soda cans and bottles, junk mail and newspapers scattered everywhere. The fridge had food, but most of it had expired...and all but a partial gallon of milk was in the same shape. Roaches and small mice darted as we entered rooms and turned on lights.

If there was anything here that could help us find Jhett, we'd have to wade through this dump to find it.

In an attempt to reach a bedroom window so he could open it, Cyndero kicked something.

"Tick tock, David." It was a recording from Chaosis. "Want to guess how I know you're here? I pre-recorded this message over a week ago with the help of our time traveling friend standing right behind you."

Cyndero turned around to face me.

I shook my head in confusion. "I was still in a coma then, right? You were all there?"

"It took you a few decades to finally come around, but better late than never, right?" The recording continued as if Chaosis was part of the conversation. "What was it you said to me the first time we met? Protect our family and stay out of your way? Well, I think Dara and I are fine with that now, too..."

Cyndero's cell phone rang—causing us both to jump. He answered it. "Rox, is that you? Caleb and I have a possible lead, but you and Terra need to get back here as soon as—oh, no...why the hell would he do that? I don't understand..."

"What happened?" I asked.

"My uncle just escaped Brunel Heights along with almost three dozen other prisoners and patients. He had help, Caleb."

"Dara?"
"No..." He shook his head in disbelief. "It was you."

CYCAD COVE ARCHIVES: ACCESS GRANTED_LEVEL 1

Over the course of exploring this island for decades, I've experienced things I otherwise wouldn't have believed.

Meeting another version of myself from within our timeline was technically dangerous. I remembered it happening the first time and then the other side of the same conversation a week later. Who I was as a person hadn't really changed in the span of a few days, but it was bizarre to be the one with a small extra grain of knowledge.

If I had warned myself about anything—even of some minor setback—could it have ended up affecting me later?

How addictive could an advantage like that become?

What you're planning, Caleb—what you feel like you have to do to correct everything for us—is terrifyingly desperate. You diverted me from probably becoming the worst possible version of myself, and I'm still grateful for it. You're my son-in-law—family—and Nadia and I care about you and your future.

I just want to understand all of this. Who were you before you helped me—in those scenarios you spoke about where my father survived Fortis's arrival instead of me? Nadia and I never would have met. Adira wouldn't have existed. I feel like events would have played out for you in a very different way, but I'm not sure how.

Do you even remember any of that anymore?

CCA File 49302849_MS19371018_RG_CS_NWPI

Message from Roman Greene
Recovered in Northwest Quadrant of Perilous Island by Maggie Serrano.

Note by M.S.—Showed this to Dad. He read it and seemed okay—just worried about a lot of things at once. Marked off location so we can send a reply later.

CHAPTER TWENTY-SEVEN

WHEN I WAS GROWING UP, Dominic had a saying I've never heard from anybody else:

Running equals guilt.

Because of him being Chaosis and Dara's son, nearly any mishap at school got blamed on him by default. Years before he rescued me, the fear of being locked away for life haunted him. At the first sign of trouble, he'd fly off and hide for hours—even if he'd been nowhere near whatever incident had happened. Eventually, he got tired of it and started holding his ground.

He taught me to do the same.

I'd just been accused of breaking out Chaosis and several other dangerous supervillains from Brunel Heights, and I really, really wanted to run.

Can time travelers feel guilt over things they technically haven't done yet?

I did—and more of everything the older me had done was somehow coming back to me.

In spite of becoming more cautious the longer he and Rodoxian spoke over the phone on speaker, Cyndero still tried to defend me. "You're sure that it was Fast Track? Could Dara have hijacked his suit somehow? Or that Samantha woman he keeps mentioning? He's been with me the entire time—still is..."

"That's the problem—his suit hasn't been moved," Rodoxian said. "It's still in storage at headquarters."

I started to say something, but Cyndero gestured for me to stay quiet before he replied. "Then how the hell could it be Caleb—at least this younger one? Is the older him still communicating with you and Terra—sending you messages?"

"No...he's stopped," Rodoxian explained. "I know he died in our past, but all those prerecorded messages he made to continue helping us out. I never thought they would just abruptly end like this. No goodbye. No explanation. No anything. It looks bad—like he was purposefully distracting us from the breakout, and now he doesn't need us anymore."

Cyndero stared at me. "I don't want to believe that..."

I slowly raised my hands and stepped back to give Cyndero some space. I didn't want a fight with him. Even without his visor, he had a lot more combat experience than me. In my imagination, he'd have the advantage.

Which made the fact he now seemed leery of me a little unnerving. Since I'd woken up from the coma, I'd caught quick flashes of fear in Terrashield and Rodoxian's expressions, too. I just didn't want to believe they were due to me.

I kept my voice quiet. "Look—I don't know any more about these villains escaping than you do. If I did, I wouldn't still be here."

Cyndero nodded, quickly ended the call with Rodoxian, and put his cell phone in his jacket pocket. "Rox is on her way with a copy of the security footage so you can see it for yourself. Maybe you'll notice something everyone else missed. I want to believe you."

I nodded but didn't relax. "I know I sound nervous, but it's because I don't know what to do right now. Rox could be right about this being the older me. I wouldn't know either way."

"Just don't bolt on us—please. We're about to have more than our share of trouble recovering all of these villains, and we may still need your help to locate them."

"You'll be way outnumbered—with or without me."

"As soon as word gets out, the mayor and governor will call in backup from other cities. I'm not saying it's why older you did this, but the chances of finding Jhett alive may get better now, too. It's the only motive I can think of that makes any sense to me."

I wanted to tell him more about the visions and what I thought had happened, but the timing seemed bad. "I really hope you're right..."

There was a frantic knock at the front door. Cyndero nodded that we were good, and I stepped out of his way and lowered my hands as he went to answer it.

It was Rodoxian, and she seemed surprised I was still there. "This mess isn't from you two fighting, is it?"

Cyndero gave an uneasy laugh. "I wish it was—place would be a lot cleaner. Let's talk outside. I left one of the pizzas on the roof of the car, but I don't really feel like eating until I get some fresh air..."

He led the way, and Rodoxian followed behind me. I didn't try to fly off once we reached the front yard. From what I'd witnessed at Perilous Island and the fairgrounds, she could fly faster than me and command certain elements to levitate. I wasn't in the mood to be brought down with the nearest combination of dirt and water. Most likely, her closest water source would be the sewer system—and I could tell she was seriously still considering it.

"You're really mad at me now, aren't you?" I asked. "I didn't do this—me personally at eighteen years old. If older me did it, I don't know why yet."

She didn't believe me, possibly thought I was taunting her. "I'm furious at whatever version of you thought this would be a great idea. Thirty-four dangerous and unstable villains, Caleb—one of them being Chaosis. When and where the hell did you take all of them? What are you planning?"

She handed me her phone. On the display was a paneled video from several security cameras synced to the same timecode.

It wasn't me.

Multiple robot demons appeared outside of the prisoner cells and patient rooms, manually punched in the correct key codes, and pulled their occupants into the hallway. Then they all disappeared in bursts of light almost simultaneously.

I felt a sense of relief. "I've been trying to tell you about these things! I think they work for Samantha—call themselves Messengers. I'm not sure if they're automated or if there's somebody inside them—would have to be a tight fit, or maybe they're some sort of advanced nanotech...?"

I stopped when I saw her and Cyndero's expressions.

At first, I thought it was because nanotechnology use by heroes and villains wasn't widespread during this time. Even Grandma rarely worked with it at the shop during my present, mostly for high-end clients like Roman.

This was something else, though.

"That's you—Fast Track," Cyndero said. "Either you have thirty-five identical suits lying around—including the one we have in storage—or you just coordinated a breakout with yourself and went back in time as many rounds as you needed. We had no clue you could do that—that anybody remotely human could even survive that. Who are you—really?"

"What are you?" Rodoxian added.

I shook my head. "What? No, my suit isn't even made like that."

Ever since the heroes had told me about the Fast Track alias, I'd imagined my suit to be the one Dominic would have built me—probably about half a foot shorter than the Griffin but with a similar design and weapons systems.

But Dominic had died on Perilous Island in my present. That suit would never be made...because my brother was gone.

And Robot Demon Guy—every instance of him—had been me...would be me.

I'd attacked myself multiple times, attacked Dominic at the shop, prevented myself from helping Fortis, broken my own arm...and now released a horde of dangerous villains for who knows what reasons...

"Caleb?" Rodoxian said in a much kinder tone. "Your nose again..."

I wiped the thin trail of blood off my lip with my hand. "I didn't know the Robot Demon Guy was older me! I swear I didn't know until now. I don't even know where that suit came from."

She nodded. "Cyndero, we need to get him back to headquarters—*willingly*—or this won't work out well for anyone." Then she addressed me directly. "Caleb—please, come back with us. Whatever is going on, we'll try to help you. You don't have to handle this alone. You can trust us."

"I know." I forced a smile and nodded in agreement, and they both relaxed a little. We'd almost reached the car. "The problem is I can't trust my older self anymore. I'm sorry, but I think the only person on the planet who can stop me is me."

Rodoxian's eyes widened. "Caleb, don't!"

Everything around me began to flow backwards.

CYCAD COVE ARCHIVES: ACCESS GRANTED_LEVEL 1

I get limited glimpses from before I was eight—nothing clear relative to the day Dominic found me.

Gregory Street in Cycad Cove never panned out as a clue when I was a kid, and the phone numbers seem to alternate between voicemails that are never returned and being disconnected altogether. My only guess with that is we've been checking everything at the wrong time.

I need to get better at controlling my abilities, and that will take both practice and experience. I don't literally see myself as different people, Roman, but from a practical standpoint for you and everyone else—you're asking the wrong Caleb at the moment.

As far as what I'm detecting as a concern, you're wondering if there's some worst-case version of me still out there, too? From an earlier loop? Someone who could be a threat to our timeline and family?

I'm afraid he exists, and we're all interconnected in a way I don't fully understand—shared memories and personality but very different goals. Son-in-law or not, it's not fair for me to ask you and Nadia for your absolute trust when I have my own doubts right now.

If I seem desperate, it's because I am. Every effort I've made to correct things on my own hasn't worked out, and every loop I make compounds the potential for unintended consequences.

If this is going to work, I need your help, too—all of you.

CCA File 49302852_RGNG19890418_CS_RG_NWPI

Message from Caleb Serrano
Recovered at Northwest Quadrant, Perilous Island, by Nadia and Roman Greene

CHAPTER TWENTY-EIGHT

I WAS BACK INSIDE THE CAR with Cyndero again about three hours earlier—after we'd left Brunel Heights but before we'd reached their headquarters downtown. I had the list of addresses from Doctor Brown in front of me.

"Everything okay?" Cyndero asked.

I scrambled to remember what I'd said the last time. "Um, yeah, I'm fine. I hate to say this, but it's none of these addresses. I'm not getting anything. Maybe something's wrong with me..."

"Do you sense that, or did you just go down that entire list and experience how things played out? Your nose is bleeding again. There should be some napkins in the glove compartment."

"Thanks," I mumbled. "Sorry about the upholstery."

"Don't worry about that." He looked worried about me. "Look, my mom is a medical doctor—kept track of everything right after we found you at the marina and while you were in a coma. I can call her. She works with people with secrets all the time, and older you trusted her."

I was about to tell him no but then thought about it. "Can she meet us at your headquarters? I've had enough of hospitals lately..."

He nodded. "Yeah, sure. It may be a while, but Terra and Rox can show you around in the meantime. You're not in any photos in the lobby—to protect you—but we've kept everything else the same. Your floor is the same as how you left it."

"My floor?"

"The building's so big that everyone has their own—

combination living quarters and personal offices. Mine's still pretty bare because I have another apartment, but you were old school—had a physical filing system and enough artifacts for your own museum. I loved visiting it and bugging the hell out of you with my history homework questions when I was a kid. You helped me a lot after my dad died, too...and I never really got to thank you for that."

I got the sense that I cared about the heroes, no matter how things kept playing out. I wasn't sure what to do about it. "It's okay...I'm sure older me knew, especially since you told me now. Crazy how all of that must work..."

"Is something wrong that you don't want to tell us? Is Jhett hurt or—?" He didn't want to say dead...just trailed off.

I shook my head. "I still don't know where Dara took her...just a few places where she didn't. I'm sorry."

He nodded but wouldn't let it go. "Something about my cousin then? Part of me hopes Dara has him and Jhett at the same place, and part of me doesn't—in the case that something goes wrong in front of him."

Even though the conversation had changed from before, I wanted to give him the opportunity to figure things out on his own again. "No...nothing about Dominic, either."

He sighed. "I don't know how much he saw or understood of what happened at the fairgrounds, but that could really mess up a kid that young. Anybody, really..." He stared straight ahead at the road. "It's weird to think about— that all the villains we've gone up against had to be kids once. I try not to think about it—probably because of everything I've seen in my own family. That could be me sitting inside a cell in Brunel Heights just as easily as my uncle. It could be any of us. We chose a different path with the same set of circumstances, and we have to keep choosing it day after day. Still feels more like a tightrope when things get this desperate...scares me sometimes..." He pulled into the reserved parking space in front of their headquarters and then got out of the car. "You coming? I'll have to let you in with my badge, but then you can get a temporary one from our receptionist. I need to check-in with Terra and Rox, anyway—wouldn't hurt to get my visor back, too, in case there's trouble."

I tried to give him a hint to what he figured out before. "Do you have any food here? Or could maybe order a pizza? I'll pay you back in future money."

He laughed. "You technically still have an account in this time, too—but I'll let Rox explain all of that. I'll order some for all of us before I leave. What do you like on pizzas?"

"Pepperoni, mushrooms, and green peppers. It's what Dominic used to order us all the time. The managers knew him well enough to always give us the same price as a 1-topping."

"Huh..." he said, and the question popped up. "Did he ever mention what pizza places he liked as a kid? It's a long-shot, but I have an idea."

I told him the same information, and he did the impersonation of Chaosis and got the address of the apartment again. The only thing different was that we were in the lobby instead of the car.

He also seemed concerned about me going with him. "With the whole nosebleed situation and the possibility of my cousin seeing you, you should sit this one out. I'll get Terra to go with me. He already has contacts with social services, and we'll make sure Dominic is safe. We may need Rox, too—just in case Dara and Jhett are nearby. I'll call my mom and have her come over as soon as she can to make sure you're all right. Are you good with waiting here for her?"

I planned to take the suit and leave before his mom arrived. "Yeah, that's fine."

"Let's still get you a keycard—in case you need to leave and come back."

The lobby appeared vacant at first—everyone else likely searching for Jhett—but at the reception desk was a dark-haired girl who looked around twelve or thirteen.

She seemed awkward, maybe a little annoyed. "Hey, Cyndero. Hey, Fast Track. Any news about Jhett?"

She looked familiar, but I couldn't place her. "Have we met before? I've been in a coma, so I'm a little scrambled up right now."

The girl crossed her arms as if I'd offended her, but then

she smiled. "Yeah—a few times here and there. You're really young this time, though. I'm Mags. It's short for Margaret. What can I do for you two?"

"Caleb needs a new entry and elevator keycard—and a quick tour couldn't hurt," Cyndero explained. "You up for the challenge, sidekick?" He faked as if he was going to punch her in the ribs.

She blocked him and moved around the desk. "I'll sidekick you in the shins if you keep that up, Laser Boy."

Cyndero laughed. "Mags is basically a deadly force of nature from the kneecaps-down—possibly a little higher on you. You're not quite as tall as you get once you're older, Caleb. I hadn't really noticed that earlier—like you must have had a surprise growth spurt in your 20s or something." He realized I wasn't listening. "Caleb? Earth to Caleb?"

Mags had to be over eighty years younger than when I'd first met her. Adira had mentioned the name Maggie when she talked about Roman and Nadia buying suits and other equipment from the shop before.

It was her...Grandma.

"How are you here?" I asked. "Are you okay?"

I didn't really give her time to answer before I hugged her.

She seemed startled for a moment but then hugged me back. "Long story. I can't tell you everything yet, but it's only because you made me promise not to foul up the timeline. That's apparently your job."

I nodded, but the math didn't make sense. "When you adopted Dominic and then me, you were—" I stopped myself from saying ancient. "—a lot older than you are now."

Her tone went careful. "Well, you're not exactly the only time traveler on the planet."

This did surprise me. "You're a time traveler, too? I hadn't even thought about other people being like me—being able to do this, I mean."

She nodded. "Well, I'm still an amateur compared to you, but almost any time traveler would be. You kept me safe, Caleb—seemed like the right thing to return the favor when you needed it the most. I've spoken to my older self once before. She's kind of crabbier than me, but most of it was to protect you and Dominic. Here's your keycard. I know you still need to find Jhett and stop Dara from whatever she's planning. We'll have plenty of time to catch up later. Everything will be okay. You told me that, too."

I hoped she was right—and that my older self hadn't lied to her.

I waved goodbye to her and then joined Cyndero at the elevators. He gave me instructions on how to get to my personal level of the building, which had been converted from one of the subbasements.

His tone was rushed, but I understood under the circumstances. "All of your biometric info shouldn't be affected by you being eighteen now. Swipe your card, press the button for your floor—this one—and then wait for the system to ask for everything else. Palm scanner is here. Retina scanner is there. Mags can page you overhead when either my mom or your pizza arrives. Once you're on your floor, getting back up to the lobby is just like any other elevator. Got it?"

"Yeah, I think so. Thanks—for everything. Be careful."

"We will," Cydero replied. "Hey, welcome back to the team. Even with everything else that's happened, I'm glad you're here with us again. I'll find you as soon as we get everything settled with Dominic. Have Mags contact me if you get any visions that might help us."

He took another elevator to go up. I got inside the one he showed me. Keycard worked. Palm scanner worked. I had to tiptoe to reach the retina scanner, which was apparently designed where the six-feet-and-over heroes didn't have to crouch very far.

There was a sudden jolt, but then the ride down was fairly smooth.

"Welcome, Caleb Averelli," a robotic voice said.

I laughed. "That's not my last name, but okay..."

"Four-digit numerical password will allow access to secondary level."

Cyndero hadn't mentioned this. Maybe Terrashield and Rodoxian had only given him a single floor because of his apartment—and the fact he wasn't sure he was staying. The problem was if my suit was stored there, I needed to get to it—not a bunch of artifacts and papers.

"Um…let's try my birthday without the year—0-2-1-7."

"Incorrect. Multiple failed attempts will temporarily shut out secondary level for 24-hours. Two attempts remain."

"I never got to ask Adira about her birthday…maybe Dominic's? 0-8-0-2?"

"Incorrect. Multiple failed attempts will temporarily shut out secondary level for 24-hours. One attempt remaining."

Technically, I still had unlimited attempts remaining—could just rewind and start the whole thing over again—but I had the edge of a migraine developing. It probably wasn't good for me to keep using the ability several times in a row without recovering, but I didn't see any other option.

I sighed, not expecting it to work. "Grandma's birthday? It was my key code to the cottage at Perilous, and she's here with the heroes now. 1-0-1-6."

"Processing…please stand by…"

There was another jolt and another smooth drop. Then the elevator doors opened.

CYCAD COVE ARCHIVES: ACCESS GRANTED_LEVEL 1

Maggie contacted me about Caleb's head injury the day my nephew found him, and I was able to meet them at the shop for a limited medical examination.

Since he was approximately eight years old, Caleb had no memories of when he was first part of my father's team or when he later reappeared in Cycad Cove around age eighteen. I considered explaining, but he already seemed scared and confused to be around who he considered total strangers.

Blood DNA tests matched his sixty-year-old, thirty-five-year-old, and eighteen-year-old samples I had available, though there was a dramatic difference in radiation exposure that may have impacted how his abilities presented at different ages. He still healed rapidly, and—at least physically—his injuries appeared temporary.

The long-term damage to Caleb's early memories, however—something Roman Greene was concerned about—may never correct itself. I personally don't have any way to determine how this impacted his time-travel and dimensional jumps from that point forward.

There's one other person on the planet who may be able to help us fill in those gaps, but my brother has refused to speak to me since the fairgrounds attack. Both he and Dara are insane murderers, so trusting them on anything is also a major issue.

We still need answers, especially if this somehow connects to the invasion. My father had to come from somewhere, and I'd be lying if I said he never kept anything from us.

I'm on your side. Please, let me help where I can.

CCA File 58197283_RMNRX20220902_CAS_FT_CCHQ_VM

Voice message from Dr. Catherine Averilli-Serrano to Rachel McNabb/Rodoxian and Ben Wallace/Terrashield

CHAPTER TWENTY-NINE

DIRECTLY IN FRONT OF ME in a massive transparent case was the Robot Demon—I mean, the Fast Track suit.

I still hated the damn thing, but I also needed it if I was going to prevent my older self from releasing Chaosis and the rest of those prisoners—if I even could.

I eased opened the case's door but hesitated on what to do next. There didn't appear to be any segments or seams to indicate how it came apart. How the hell was I supposed to get inside it?

I poked its shoulder to see if the metal plating had any give, and small bands of blue and white light began to spread throughout the metallic material—resembling something between a lightning strike and a circuit board pathway until the entire thing was lit up.

I jerked my hand away and took a few steps backwards—afraid the thing had been sabotaged and was about to explode. "This is crazy. I know I had to come here, but my older self can't kill me without it affecting everything after this, right? What am I doing?"

I looked down at my hands. A similar pattern of light was developing on my left side—originating from the two fingers that had touched the suit and spreading through my arm to the rest of me.

"Holy sh—!"

In front of me, the suit disintegrated into a pile inside the case—like someone had just dropped a jigsaw puzzle. Then tiny fragments started flying up and bonding to my hand—following the patterns of light on my skin like a blueprint. It stung—like getting pelted with sand. I tried to make it back to the elevator, but probably half the suit hit me at once—knocking me to the floor before I could reach it.

This all happened so fast I barely comprehended it. I managed to get to my feet. I could still breathe and hear, but I couldn't see anything. Some of the metallic fragments had sealed up an area in front of my eyes. The rest of me didn't feel uncomfortable—just odd as I moved around a small area and flexed my fingers.

"Hello?" My voice sounded modulated. "Anybody? Do I really have to sound like this all the time? It's creepy..." I started goofing around with it. "No, Dominic, I am your brother...he'd have loved this thing. Just wish I could see..."

In response to my voice, a small display activated in front of my eyes. It was a projection of what I would have seen normally—real enough for me to recheck to see if my eyes were still covered. I blinked a few times, too. It was a little off when I tried to walk—like looking through a high-def gaming monitor—but it wasn't so horrible that I felt motion sick.

"Okay...this thing likes voice commands. Evil Demon Guy voice off?"

"Warning," an automated voice replied. "Turning off voice enhancement may make it difficult for others to hear you in combat situations. Short-wave radio and limited frequencies will still be available. Confirm command?"

"Yes—for now, anyway," I said. "I'm not going to be talking to anybody but myself for a while."

"Processing..."

"I wonder how long this will—" It switched to my normal voice, just louder. "Oh, that's so much better..."

The next problem was how to leave the building without hurting anybody. Based on when Rodoxian had called Cyndero in my vision, I had maybe thirty minutes before the prison break—and flying to Brunel Heights would burn up at least ten of that.

Suddenly, Maggie paged me from inside the suit. "Hey, Fast Track? Doctor Serrano is here. Want to come up here or have her meet you? She already has access to your main office floor but not where you're at right now."

I cleared my throat. "Just a minute! I'll meet her up there!"

"Sorry, hold on a second...getting some interference for some reason..." She said something to Doctor Serrano and then lowered her voice to a whisper. "What are you doing inside your suit right now? Whatever's going on with your brain, that isn't going to help it! We don't want to lose you again. I don't..."

"I just touched it! Plus, there's something terrible that needs to be stopped. I—"

Her tone got flatter, reminding me more of her older self. "There's always something terrible that needs to be stopped. Using your abilities is hurting you—killing you little by little—and it hurts me to see you do it to yourself...I—I care about you very much, and I don't know if this is something you have to do right now. If you want to think about it, I can tell you how to shut off the suit. Doctor Serrano is a good person. She just wants to help you, too."

I sighed. "I'm sorry, but I can't. I wish I could explain everything to you right now, but I have to do this."

"I already know more than you do, and I know I can't stop you. I just still had to try. Be careful...I'll send Serrano down to meet you. Wait ten seconds for her to pick an elevator, and then use the other one to get to the roof. You'll just need your keycard. Nothing else."

"Thank you."

"Don't thank me until you make it back here. Just make it back this time, okay?"

"I will. I promise."

I watched and waited—taking the vacant elevator up once I knew Doctor Serrano was heading down. Instead of the rooftop, however, I stopped in the lobby.

Grandma—Mags—was at her desk and hurriedly wiped her eyes when she saw me. Then she forced a smile and pointed up. "The roof is that way the last time I checked. If you're still going to do this, you don't have much time."

"If I fail, I don't know how many times I can keep

rewinding and coming back here without making something else worse. The others won't understand. Is that why you don't want me to go? You already know what happens?"

"They're not dumb—you get that, right? You withheld things from the heroes and Roman before. They're all withholding things from you now. Everybody just wants to protect each other, protect the timeline, and protect the planet—but sometimes trying to do the right thing for one goal makes things worse for another. It's been a lot of spinning plates and going in circles for you—trying to fix everything by yourself. That's not even including Samantha and the other Messengers who want us all dead and out of their way. None of this will get any better until you and these heroes start trusting each other. That will mean you finally telling them the truth—all of it. Same goes for Roman and Nadia—when you see them again."

"Did you know you're really horrible at pep talks?"

She smiled. "Hey, I learned from you..."

I was about to reply when a page interrupted from above her desk.

"Hey, Mags, I don't see him down here. Try paging him again...just hope he hasn't passed out. With all the shelves and corridors, it will take me a while to walk the entire floor."

She tried to sound normal. "Okay. I'll try again." Then she looked at me. "If you're going to go, then go."

CYCAD COVE ARCHIVES: ACCESS GRANTED_LEVEL 1

'What happened to you, Mags? Your parents didn't just abandon you here, right?'

'My father used Perilous Island to send me back to when and where he believed I'd be safest—Metro Heights General Hospital about twenty years ago. He and Mom never wanted me involved in any of this. It just didn't work out that way...'

'Because you discovered how to time travel?'

'I had no choice. Between Samantha Fredricks popping up out-of-nowhere and targeting me and the Messengers attempting to abduct me, it was basically learn-or-die.'

'How long have you been running?'

'I don't even know anymore, Chuck, but I've pretty much seen everything. It's been like working a massive jigsaw puzzle across time and the entire planet. I eventually found my grandparents on Mom's side, so that helped, too. They caught me up and taught me a lot, but I couldn't stay with them forever without it causing a timeline collapse.'

'Why are you telling me all of this now?'

'You're a good listener—never pried too much—and I want you to know I've appreciated your friendship, even when it seemed like I didn't. Goodbye, Chuck. Thank you.'

'Mags, don't leave! Whatever's wrong, I know people. We can help you somehow. I can help.'

'Not with this part. I'm sorry.'

CCA File 112182738_FT19950802_DLBG_SF_CCHQ_MH

After-hours security footage from The Downlow Bar & Grill
Metro Heights, August 2nd, 1995
Sent to Fast Track by anonymous package.

CHAPTER THIRTY

WITHOUT COMPLETELY THINKING about it, I nodded and ran toward the exit doors.

The roof would have been a better idea—given there wouldn't be any civilians to stop and stare at me. At least I seemed scary enough that no one was approaching for an autograph.

An Al's Pizza delivery kid parked her bicycle a few feet from the lobby doors and wasn't completely paying attention. She bumped into me and went wide-eyed. "Are you Cyndero?"

I shook my head but opened the lobby door for her. She ran inside and nearly tripped on her shoelaces.

I walked around to the alley behind the building before I attracted any more attention. "Um, suit—can I engage autopilot? I need to get to Brunel Heights. The address is—"

"Denied. Engaging 'Catch Up My Idiot Self' Protocol."

I panicked. "No! Whatever that is, shut it down! I don't want—"

The small rocket boosters on the suit started operating by themselves, and I shot up to match the top of the headquarters building within seconds.

It was a higher elevation than I normally flew without equipment, and I felt off-balance and dizzy. "I want out! I want to land! Stop protocol. Override number 1-0-1-6."

Nothing worked. I just hovered there for a few seconds, but I'd lost all control of the suit. Then the view of the city flickered out. All I could see was black.

I was at least a hundred stories from the ground—now blind—and all the rockets stopped and went silent.

I went into a freefall.

My older self was going to kill me, and there was nothing I could do about it.

"Do I have your attention now?" This new voice didn't sound like the automated system, but it was too calm—like my older self may have prerecorded it.

"Go to hell!"

"I'm sort of rooting for us to end up in the other place—considering I'm dead by the time this happens."

"You're lying! I know about the prison break! I know—"

"Brunel Heights currently houses over six hundred supervillains. In my thirties, I *borrowed* thirty-four I could reason with—Chaosis being the most questionable. This wasn't about Jhett, but it was still necessary. I need you to understand that—and to stay clear this time. Stopping me today would have eventually erased me—and you—out of existence. I know it doesn't seem like it right now, but I have a great incentive for you to survive as long as possible. You're my last hope of setting all of this right."

The rockets reengaged and changed angles, but I still had no idea how far I was from the ground. I was being taken somewhere, but I doubted it was Brunel.

"Why? It's getting harder to separate who I know I am with everything else you did to the timeline. I can sense it—remember portions of it that other people don't. I feel it as if it was me personally. Are you taking over my life—my mind? Is that what all of this has been about? Tricking me into getting inside this suit? My head hurts so much right now..."

"Not that you want to take my word for it, but it does get easier—more manageable, anyway. I'm not trying to take you over, but we are connected. Think Voldermort and Harry Potter—only if they were the same guy, older and younger, and able to interact and affect each other's outcomes. I know what happens to you and what you're about to ask because I've already lived it. You're getting feedback and echoes from me because of our abilities and what we're both tapped into. Even when we change something in the timeline, all the alternate memories will remain with us. It's a gift and a curse wrapped up in one."

"Who...what are we?"

My older self laughed. "You're not quite ready for that yet. Just enjoy the ride. To modify the saying, this is going to hurt me as much as it's going to hurt you—but it's necessary to stabilize the timeline. Brace for impact."

There was a bright flash, and my entire body got a pins-and-needles sensation.

Then I ran into something—someone. The screens in front of my eyes started working again, and I saw myself with a confused expression. It was the day Dominic and I had first gone to Roman's house, and I'd been on my way back to the shop.

"What the hell? Who are you?"

I tried to shout and warn myself, but the suit still wasn't under my control. It used my own hand to grab my other self by the shirt collar and started forcing him to the ground. The warning about staying away from Perilous Island and Adira played, but that didn't come from me.

Then the other Caleb kicked me. The suit took most of the impact, but it still knocked the wind out of me and probably caused some bruising.

"Okay, next stop."

There was another bright flash, and I was in front of Grandma's shop. It was later that same night, when Dominic and I thought the thing was breaking in to attack or kill us.

"Please, don't do this," I begged. "You nearly killed Dominic—and that might have weakened him down before Samantha killed him at Perilous."

"You need to see what really happened for yourself, or you won't believe me."

Dominic confronted me without knowing I was inside the suit. "I don't know what Terminator cosplay party you just left from, but attacking a defenseless teenage kid and trying to steal from an old lady? Not cool, buddy. What's your problem?"

"Dominic, it's me!" I shouted, but he couldn't hear me without any amplification. "I—"

The suit's rockets engaged out of my control, and I flew away from the shop. Dominic followed but didn't fire on me with the Griffin suit.

Then the explosions started...but they weren't being caused by either of us. Someone else was suddenly targeting us both.

"What the hell?"

There was the sound of a laser blast, and he screamed. The suit turned me around just in time to see him fall to the sidewalk. Above him, another person in a similar suit to mine had a laser gun.

It was the same one Samantha had been using every time I saw her.

Before what happened at Perilous, she'd tried to kill Dominic earlier but failed. Before I could do anything, she disappeared again.

The suit brought me down to check on Dominic. He was still on his feet and hadn't fallen yet. He raised his wrist up to aim one of the Griffin's guns at my face.

My suit began to retract the material around my eyes, nose, and mouth—just enough for him to recognize me. His eyes widened.

"Caleb? You were just at the shop! How did you—?"

"I'm a time traveler. You can't tell the other me yet—long story, but I'm trying to fix this...I think."

He gave a reluctant nod. "Okay...just let me know when we can talk about it. I have more than a few questions. Are you okay? Who the hell was that? Why did you attack yourself earlier and try to break into the shop?"

He dropped to the sidewalk, but the suit let me catch him before his head hit the concrete. The metallic material began to form over my face again. I stood, and my slightly younger self and Adira were heading toward us. Just like I'd seen in the vision before, I pointed up to the street sign while inside the suit.

The bright light flashed again.

I was back at the fairgrounds, but the place was roped off and empty. A security guard was at the main gate but was watching something on his phone.

"That's enough for now," older me said. "We'll handle the rest at some point—just has to be done to keep everything stable. Are you getting that?"

"Dominic lied to Adira and me...made it sound like you...me...that Samantha and I were working together that night. He didn't know that it was her who shot him, but—"

"Dominic and I had time to catch up on a few things. It's the whole reason Roman had you two walk the length of the island. For now, you're free to go. The suit is back under your control."

"Why are you dropping me off here—not downtown?"

"One—the prison break still happened. With the suit being missing this time, that doesn't look so good on us. Two—this is where you need to be. You remember how you wanted Cyndero to figure things out with Dominic—not just give him everything?"

"Yeah..."

"Similar thing. You still need to stay sharp on your thinking, Caleb—not lean on these abilities like a crutch. They're not always a hundred percent reliable. Goodbye for now—and good luck."

"Good luck on what?"

No response. An indicator overlaying the display screens showed that the audio file had stopped playing. This must have been how older me had been communicating with the others, too—not exactly conversations, but close enough.

I was relieved to be able to move freely again, but my entire body ached—mostly from being kicked and the shockwaves of the explosions Samantha had attempted to use to take Dominic and me out. I was thankful I hadn't had to relive Fortis's death and breaking my own arm...but apparently that had to happen at some point.

I still didn't want to be at the fairgrounds—at all. Even if it was just a tire shop, the idea of returning home again occurred to me.

Only that wasn't my home in this time. Even Grandma—however many versions of her that existed—wasn't there yet.

No matter what my original motivations for joining them, the heroes were my friends now...and they needed me. Jhett needed me...

I looked around, and there was a single exterior light turning on and off again at the funhouse. Other than the guard shack, nothing else seemed to still have power going to it. It would have been easy to dismiss it as damage from the attack, but the light seemed to be blinking with a pattern.

"Chaosis said something to Doctor Brown about not being affected by funhouse mirrors. I don't think it's Morse Code, but is the blinking a pattern?"

The automated suit voice responded. "It's binary but with some errors...analyzing...Do not help. Trap. Dara and Chaosis know everything. Made deal with Samantha to regain Dominic and flee city soon. Do not help...and it repeats again from there. Would you like me to send a message to headquarters?"

"No—not yet. I need a minute to think."

"Message sent to headquarters with GPS coordinates and all known data. Advised to wait until backup arrives."

This frustrated me. "Then why the hell did you just ask if I—"

"I have limited programming to protect you and maintain the stability of the timeline. Jenny Weiland a.k.a. Jhett's survival is a key event. You will still need to proceed before others arrive, or the overall damage to the timeline will be unrepairable."

"Why? I mean, I want to save her. I wanted to save Fortis, too, but somehow some events are more important than others? How is that even determined?"

"Full parameters are not known. Jhett's survival determined as key event in relation to your existence. She and David Serrano a.k.a. Cyndero later become one set of your biological grandparents. Would you like more information on this?"

"Not right now. Did they already know this—Cyndero and Jhett?"

"Unknown."

I sighed. "Can I save her? Get past whatever this trap is?"

"Your continued existence tends to indicate this has already occurred, but the alternative would be a paradox."

"Okay. Then how did I do it?"

"Information currently restricted under 'Cheating Damages the Timeline' safeguard protocol. Will be available for review in twelve hours."

All the funhouse lights and music activated.

Whether Dara had seen me or not, someone now knew I was there. The lights reflected off my suit, creating a disco ball-like pattern around me. The suit reacted to this, and the metal turned darker and less reflective.

I was terrified, but I didn't see any other options. "Okay, let's do this..."

EXTINGUISHED WORLDS: WHAT GOES AROUND

CYCAD COVE ARCHIVES: ACCESS GRANTED_LEVEL 1

'A visitor? I'm surprised the warden approved this. Or are you here to kill me, Buttercup? Be a shame to ruin that frilly yellow suit and cape.'

'I could just shoot you right now, Dara. This thing seemed to work well enough on your son.'

'Oh, you break Nicky's heart in the future and then shoot him? That's brutal, even by my standards. It doesn't matter, though. Fast Track will reset everything again soon.'

'You know about the multiple time loops? How?'

'Don't remember them personally, but my husband always finds me and gives me the recap. He believed killing Fortis at the fairgrounds would repair everything this round, but apparently this timeline's problems originated long before that. Maybe it's you and your little revenge spree. Ever think you may have caused your war with Fortis and Fast Track—gotten your own family killed for it?'

'I didn't start this. I'm just finishing it.'

'I'm sure they're telling themselves the same exact thing. You murdered Virginia Averelli and then threatened Adira and Maggie across multiple timelines. How else were they supposed to react?'

'My parents and brother are dead, and they're somehow behind it! I know they are, but I can't prove—"

'Who are you trying to prove it to? Your hero friends? You think they'd help kill Fast Track even if you did?'

'Probably not. That's why I'm here. I have an offer for you.'

CCA File 49283944494_CW20130418_DA_SFP_BHAA_SF

Brunel Heights West, Women's Facility
Security Footage Recovered by Dr. Colleen Watkins
April 18th, 2013

CHAPTER THIRTY-ONE

"TICK-TOCK, FAST TRACK." Dara said over the loudspeaker. "Even Messengers have limits. You'll learn that tonight..."

Jhett was barely alive—still in her purple and gray hero uniform from the fairgrounds attack. Dara had blindfolded and tied her to a chair anchored in the middle of the funhouse.

Five feet above her head hung a converted wooden platform braced in position with metal corner railings. Its bottom had been embedded with dozens of knives—smaller than the machete Roman had given me but just as sharp.

The only things preventing it from falling on Jhett were four stainless steel cables—one at each corner. Their releases connected to receivers similar to those used to sabotage the rides.

The entire contraption looked like a cross between a medieval torture device and a guillotine. All Dara had to do was press a button, and Jhett would be dead before anyone could reach her.

Even me.

The suit amplified my normal voice. "What do you want, Dara? I'm not like Samantha. Are you working with her now? Is that something she told you?"

Dara didn't answer—at least, not verbally.

The cables released, and the platform dropped. Jhett let out a partial scream from the shock of the sound, but it was over in less than a second.

Time went backwards.

It was the fourth time I'd witnessed this. Each round I'd reversed time had made me gradually weaker.

I'd realized this far too late, and going back further in time—even half a day—would have probably killed me before I could warn anybody. I was trapped now, too—able to recover just enough to repeat this same thirty-minute loop.

If Jhett died, I'd disappear from existence. Perilous Island would destabilize and launch the probes, and I could only guess at the other timeline consequences that would follow.

"Tick-tock, Fast Track. Even Messengers have—"

"I'll take Jhett's place!" I shouted in desperation. "Just let her go! You'll still have leverage against my older self—maybe even more than you have with her."

This seemed to be what Dara actually wanted. "Get out of your suit, and leave behind your shock batons and knife. I'll know it if you don't."

"Okay...okay..." I replied and then addressed the automated system. "Please, don't make this difficult...suit off."

The entire thing fell off me, the pile of metallic segments becoming reflective again.

A single baton had remained solid—hadn't even realized they were attached near my calves before. I'd lost the other one in the future—the one Dominic had found and brought with him to the shop.

I stepped forward out of the pile and then removed the machete's holster from my belt. Its handle must have been inlaid with the same mineral as the batons because it lit up blue for a split-second and then faded. I placed it in the pile and then approached the funhouse's entrance for the fifth time.

The doors opened on their own.

CYCAD COVE ARCHIVES: ACCESS GRANTED_LEVEL 1

'What did Samantha Fredricks offer you?'

'A way out of here and a 'get-out-of-invasion-free' card from her new Messenger friends. Poor thing didn't realize I already had the same deal with you. How are you here now? You're looking much younger to be a dead man.'

'I'm still dead—technically—but that doesn't mean I have to give away all my secrets. Did you accept her offer?'

'She claims she's gained access to portions of the island that you apparently haven't. I told her I was intrigued and would think about it. She'll be back soon for my answer.'

'If you betray me, Dara—'

'The way it sounds, it's your so-called allies you should be worried about. They allowed you to turn this timeline into your personal playground for centuries, and now they're here to collect. What the hell do you owe them for all of that?'

'Not what—who. Goodbye, Dara. Do whatever you want—while you still can.'

'Oh, I will...'

CCA File 49283944495_CW20130418_DA_SFP_BHAA_SF

Brunel Heights West, Women's Facility
Security Footage Recovered by Dr. Colleen Watkins
April 18th, 2013

Note by C.W. to Roman and Nadia Greene—I don't recognize the man Dara is talking with. Do you? Any family relation to Caleb? I think you should warn him.

CHAPTER THIRTY-TWO

I DISCOVERED IT DID NOTHING to help me recover, but pausing everything each time I entered the funhouse had given me a few minutes to think between each loop.

Other than seeing Dara at the fairgrounds when Terrashield asked me to point her out, we'd only interacted once before this—in the future when Dominic got permission to speak with her via video chat.

He was eighteen, and I was ten.

"You can't tell Grandma about any of this—got it?" Dominic said. "I know she'll act as if it's not a big deal in front of you, but she's never liked the idea of me communicating with either of my parents...closest I've ever seen her genuinely upset with me. I'm not going to make a habit of it, and I just don't want her to worry."

I nodded. "I won't say anything. Do you want me to leave? I can go upstairs with my laptop if you don't want your mom to see me or—"

"Hey, you're my family, too. If she starts acting weird, though—hearing voices or anything like that—you don't have to stay. This is kind of scary for me compared to a normal phone call. I may need you to bail me out with an excuse—shout that dinner's ready or something."

I was worried that Dara would escape and somehow find us. "Does she know about Grandma and me? Where we live?"

"I don't believe she'd ever hurt us, but I'll never tell her anything she might be able to use later—just in case she's ever released. She knows I'm still in Cycad Cove—probably thinks I'm in a foster home or something. You and Grandma mean a lot more to me now than she does. It's just complicated...she's still my mother, even with everything she and Dad did when I was too young to understand. I still have some memories and questions that I want to work through, but I never want to be anything like them, Caleb. I hope you know that."

"You're not."

There was a process to Dominic logging-in and then speaking to several other people—Dara's lawyer, the women facility's director, and then a psychiatrist...who I now recognized was Doctor Brown. She explained that the call would be monitored—that Dominic could end it whenever he wanted—and she would be inside the cell to keep Dara's abilities suppressed for the duration of the conversation.

Then we had to wait for about another fifteen minutes for other precautions they wouldn't tell us.

"Mom has this extrasensory connection with technology. Dad had the showmanship, but she was behind all the designs of his magic act—before they both turned evil overnight..."

"Do you know what happened to them? What caused it?"

Dominic shook his head. "Portions of their court cases are sealed, and I still don't know everything. They murdered a hundred and seventy-four innocent civilians—that I know about—seemingly just because they wanted bait for Fortis and his hero teams to show up for a trap at the fairgrounds. Dad and Fortis were enemies before I was even born—but I've hit nothing but dead ends there, too. I've asked a few heroes about it, but they just change the subject—but I get that it's painful they lost their leader and a lot of their friends. I'm probably the last person they want to talk about it with...I wouldn't expect anybody else to care about the why thirteen years later, but it matters to me. If they're both just psychotic monsters...I guess I should know that, too. As much as it would terrify me, I'd check myself into Brunel before I'd allow myself to get to that point. That's why most people react to me the way they do. I look a lot like Dad now, and they're scared of who I could become down the road."

"You're a good brother to me," I replied, but this didn't

seem to make him feel any better. "You're a good person."

"So were they—once. Either that, or I just remember a lot of early things wrong." His tone turned frustrated. "Other than my parents, I have nobody else to verify anything with one way or the other. It was just the three of us before that attack happened."

When the camera switched to Dara's prison cell, she seemed calm. She looked about forty years old, red hair pulled back in a ponytail, and had a white patient's uniform instead of an orange one usually designating prisoners.

Between her and Chaosis, the police and court system had considered Dara the less dangerous threat—possibly even a victim drawn in by his personality—along with the other villains he'd convinced to help them that night.

When she saw Dominic, Dara's hands went to her face—and she started to cry. "Oh, Nicky. You're so grown up now! I'm so sorry—for not being there for you this entire time. If it wasn't for you, I wish I'd never met your father. Do you understand that he brought all of this upon us? I wanted to leave—for the three of us to get as far away from Cycad Cove as possible. He just couldn't let it go with Fortis—wanted to do it personally. He brought us back here when we could have just trusted his contacts to follow the plan..." She trailed off, and her tone changed when she remembered Dr. Brown was nearby. "I now understand that was wrong on many levels, morally and practically."

This got to Dominic—the fact Dara had genuine remorse for abandoning him but not for killing all those people.

He glanced over at me watching his computer's display and took a deep breath. "I'm okay. As far as everything with me, I forgave you both long before I got in touch with your lawyers. I had to...or I think it would have made things worse for me. Life isn't easy, but it's not terrible, either. I'm with good people, and I'm safe. I don't agree at all with what you and Dad did—including what happened with Fortis—but I hope you both somehow find a way to work through it, too. If you were both sick—are still sick and need help—"

"Do you know how many people Fortis murdered without ever getting caught? Your father saw it happen—

more than once—but he could never prove it. No one in Cycad Cove would believe him, so eventually he ran—and he found me. I believed him, and I helped him put an end to it. If you had the choice between an uncontrolled train killing less than two hundred people or killing billions, wouldn't the responsible thing be to redirect it—or to stop it once and for all? We did what was necessary, and we're paying the price for it. So are you."

Dominic frowned. "You're saying Fortis was the train? But he was a hero. I remember—"

Dara's tone hardened. "You remember what *they* want you to remember."

"They?" Dominic asked in confusion. "As in Fortis's remaining team? I've barely even spoken to them. They all kind of avoid me now—leave me alone and don't hassle me, at least."

"Not them—the Messengers. Alien scouts. They manipulate people's lives for their own goals—invading other worlds and then altering them. I was an aerospace engineer once. Your father was a hero—Fortis's..." She suddenly trailed off.

I'd gotten curious about all of this and had made my way behind Dominic's chair to see better. "Sorry. Hi, I'm—"

Dara began screaming and cursing hysterically. "You took my son! I'll kill you, Fast Track! I'll kill all of you if it's the last thing I do, you son-of-a—"

Dominic's eyes widened as he muted the sound. Dara continued to scream at the camera until a couple of guards brought her under control.

I backed away—terrified.

Dominic put a hand on my shoulder. "It's okay, Caleb. She can't hurt you. I'd never let her hurt you—I promise."

The camera panned to the left, and Dominic unmuted the audio when Doctor Brown's face appeared.

"Who was she talking to?"

Dominic lied, probably to keep me from being taken away. "Our neighbor's kid. He comes over to use my computer for homework sometimes. Caleb, this is Doctor Brown."

I was more reluctant this time. "Hi."

She waved at me but still seemed upset. "I'm very sorry, Dominic. She'd been doing so well with her treatments, and I thought this might be beneficial—give her motivation to move in a positive direction. Are you all right?"

Dominic shrugged. "I'm fine, but I don't think this is a good thing to keep trying—for either of us. Maybe when I'm older and can handle it better. I need to get Caleb home, but I'll stay in touch."

"If you ever want to come to my office to talk—the one downtown, not at Brunel Heights—I won't charge you anything. This entire situation has been one of the most difficult cases I've ever dealt with. For you to be in the middle of it at eighteen—"

"I'm okay," Dominic interrupted quickly. "Sorry—I mean, I have people. Thank you, though. I appreciate the offer...honestly hope I never have to take you up on it—no offense." He shut down the video window before Doctor Brown could respond. "So, yeah...that's my mom. I think this calls for pizza *and* ice cream—my treat. Let's just get the hell away from these computers for a while. You okay?"

I tried to calm down so he wouldn't feel bad. "I'm fine." Something confused me at the time, though. "Who's Fast Track?"

"I've heard the name before—some hero on Fortis's team who died a long time ago...not at the fairgrounds but before that." Dominic sighed. "She was out of her mind, Caleb. Don't worry about it."

CYCAD COVE ARCHIVES: ACCESS GRANTED_LEVEL 1

'You don't look so good, Buttercup. What happened?'

'The Messengers told me who came to see you right after I did. What are they planning? Tell me, or I'll kill you right now!'

'I don't think you have the time for all of it. Bit of advice. Killing Fortis or Fast Track directly never works out. Fast Track always finds some way to reset everything again. You want a more permanent revenge? Go after who they care about the most—who they can't protect no matter how many times they try.'

'I don't have time, Dara!'

'Then do what they do—go back and find some version of yourself who does. I'll see you again soon, right?'

'I don't understand.'

'Then you better find one of your alien friends who does.'

CCA File 49283944496_CW20130418_DA_SFP_BHAA_SF

Brunel Heights West, Women's Facility
Security Footage Recovered by Dr. Colleen Watkins
April 18th, 2013

Note by C.W. to Roman Greene—Got your reply and the sample of cape fabric you found. I'm so sorry about Nadia. Yes, it looks like Samantha Fredricks had a stab wound, but she didn't have any machete with her. Maybe she lost it during the struggle, or maybe Nadia got it away from her in time to hide it? If that's the case, Caleb is probably the only person capable of locating it. Again, I'm so sorry for your loss. If you or Adira need anything, let me know.

CHAPTER THIRTY-THREE

THAT CHILDHOOD FEELING OF TERROR resurfaced with the memory, and I had to fight to reign it in.

The first section of the funhouse was a hall of mirrors. I could navigate it rapidly now after the first four attempts—only because I'd initially believed the release for the platform was on some sort of automated timer.

It wasn't. Wherever Dara was hiding, she could see me on cameras—and manually released the platform once Jhett was in my line of sight. It didn't matter what path or angle I took to get to her. Even flying in from above wouldn't have worked.

"Take your time. I'd rather you not be in here while I get her free and outside. You honor your word. I'll honor mine. Plus, finding her will keep your ex-friends occupied for a while—if the heroes even choose to believe your message begging for their help right after betraying them. They may even think this is all your doing—not mine. She's in no condition right now to tell them otherwise...hope the baby still makes it, and I'm sure you do, too. She grows up to be your mother, correct? Do you remember her?"

I resisted the urge to quicken my pace, but I kicked through a couple of the mirrors. They shattered, and the pieces fell to the floor. I walked through the gap as a shortcut to the next section.

"Temper. Temper. You're so self-righteous that it's sickening. Just because you no longer remember who and what you are doesn't give you an automatic pass for everything you've ever done."

"Then tell me."

"I'll do better than that—but not until you're restrained. Be right back. Feel free to have a seat if you make it there before I return—for her sake. You try anything out-of-place, and I still have ways to kill her long before her rescue arrives—maybe take a few others out with her. Understand?"

"Yeah...I understand."

The next section was a black-lit psychedelic tunnel with a series of spinning rollers—very disorienting, and I already felt light-headed. I shut my eyes and managed to stumble through it.

After that was a room filled with dozens of punching bags—which had been lit the first four rounds—but was now in total darkness. I started to feel my way toward a wall when someone pushed one into me, knocking me off balance.

"You should have listened to me, Caleb! You could have had everything—your wife, your daughter...a peaceful life together in exchange for your cooperation."

"Cooperation?" I asked. "You mean selling out everyone else on the planet? Are you really from Earth—or from somewhere else? Is that what you did where you're from?"

The edges of her suit lit up in the darkness, and she grabbed me by my throat and lifted me off the floor. "I had no choice! You did—and you're going to have to live with it...or more accurately die with it in the next hour or so. I don't need you anymore. I've found another way, so I guess this is goodbye. The way I see it, the Caleb I knew is already dead."

She disappeared in a burst of light, and I collapsed to the floor.

Then Dara's voice came over the speaker system. She sounded irritated. "When I said, 'take your time,' I didn't mean 'take all night.' Here..."

Based on her tone, Dara didn't know Samantha had just been in the room with me. The lights came on, and I finally made my way to the door. It led to the auditorium-like room where Jhett had been held.

Dara was there—holding a laser gun like Samantha's. It might have possibly been the same one. "You don't look so good."

"I've been better."

"Your Messenger friend told me one blast from this thing could kill you right now? That true?"

I sighed. "Probably..."

"Have a seat."

"Samantha is using you. You know that, right?"

"She told me you'd say that. She didn't kill me when she could have, and the thing is I'm smart enough to take the deal you wouldn't. Once you're out of the way, she's going to help me get my family back and give us a great life. Could you promise me that?"

"Not without lying," I replied. "You could just shoot me—would save me from sitting beneath that thing."

"You're not the main target—just better bait. Sit—or I'll shoot you in the leg and go back outside to Jhett next. Understand? There's no winning for you from this point forward. It's just how much and how badly you want to lose."

CYCAD COVE ARCHIVES: ACCESS GRANTED_LEVEL 1

We finally found the machete today.

Samantha Fredricks doesn't murder me five years from now. It was someone else.

We were wrong, Caleb. Someone fooled all of us and tricked you into making all those time loops to try to save me. Roman and I now believe they hoped that would have weakened and eventually killed you, too.

You have to stop this—please. At least until we know more.

The yellow fragment of cape with my blood on it must have been planted.

Will let you know blood test results as soon as we have them. In the meantime, watch your back.

CCA File 893027483932_MS20130819_NG_SFP_NWOI

Message from Nadia Greene
Recovered on Orchid Island, Northwest Quadrant by Maggie Serrano

Reply from M.S.—Will relay this message to the other known drop-off points. The Caleb in my timeline currently isn't old enough to do anything about this yet. Will keep him safe. Thank you.

CHAPTER THIRTY-FOUR

I RELUCTANTLY TOOK A SEAT in the chair. Its wrist and leg restraints were automated—something I hadn't been able to see before—and Dara rechecked them and adjusted the last one around my neck. I could glance and see the glint off the knives but couldn't fully tilt my head up.

"Your older self will come for you like you came for her. It's a matter of self-preservation."

She hit the release, and the platform started to fall. I cringed and had to strain to focus.

Time went backwards, and the moment repeated.

"It's just how much and how badly you want to lose. Oh, you poor thing...this will be over soon enough. It's so easy to be angry. You're him—and yet you're not. Not yet, anyway."

She wiped a trail of blood off my nose and mouth with a handkerchief.

I suddenly felt a puncture of a needle at my neck and something cold shot into it. My heart started beating faster. "What the hell was that?"

"Something Samantha said would help you remember—and make it easier for me to kill you. She didn't tell me how long it would take, but it's not as if you have anywhere else to go."

I was disoriented and tried to stay conscious. "Dominic rescued me when I was eight. He was like my older brother for ten years. I loved him—and the woman you're trusting shot him in the back twice, killed him, and then tried to kill me. I escaped and ended up here. I just wanted to save him and everyone else Samantha manipulated into being there. That's the truth. That's who I am."

Dara smiled. "I know—but it's not all of it. Everything that caused you to come back here won't matter soon. Samantha will fix everything for us."

"How?"

"By destroying the island instead of trying to gain control over it. Apparently, you're not needed for that."

I shook my head. "Pretty sure Cycad Cove is still within the blast radius..."

"That's the beauty of it." She laughed. "We—as in my husband, son, and me—won't be here when it happens. She's going to take us into the past first. We'll be safe—will even be able to live out our lives in peace before the invasion. Not a bad deal. You should have taken it."

She released the platform again.

I rewound time again, but something else happened.

I saw a flash of Dominic with the mercenaries—Patterson, Kaylor, and Hackney. He was working with them on Perilous Island.

"Boss, we've got incoming," Hackney said.

"Good. Let them come." Dominic was leading them—and had no issues killing Rodoxian and Terrashield with his laser vision the moment they touched down on the beach just to talk.

Once I was dead, Samantha would go back and turn Dominic evil, too...and she wanted me to know it.

Everything with Dara repeated again. "It's just how much and how badly you want to lose. Oh, you poor thing..."

"Whatever that stuff was, don't put more of it in me!" I shouted. "You've already done it once. I think it stays in my system, even when I go back in time."

Dara was either indifferent or just didn't believe me. "No puncture wound, though. Maybe it's all in your head. What did you see?"

"You never get Dominic back, and I think he ends up worse than Chaosis. You need to let me go. I don't want him to turn out like that. Do you? Do even care about him at all—really?"

This offended her. "Nice try. He's not your brother. He's not your family. He's my son—and you're never getting near him again."

She injected me a second time. It glowed blue and then white as she brought it closer to my neck—like it must have contained the mineral suspended in some sort of liquid solution.

The floor started to tremble.

It was an earthquake. Perilous Island was becoming unstable again.

"Samantha isn't coming back for any of you!" I strained. "Don't you get that?"

She released the platform again. I didn't have enough strength left to rewind it—just paused the moment it released.

***

"Do you want to hold her, Caleb?" Adira asked.

Whatever revenge Samantha had wanted out of this, my mind refused to do a final replay of all the terrible things I'd done.

It just brought me back to Adira and our daughter.

That moment drove out everything else—all the fear...all the hate and anger at the Messengers for abducting me...

In everything else I'd tried, I'd never thought death was the answer to getting back to them.

Now there were no other options. I looked into my tiny daughter's eyes as she held onto my finger. "I love you, Maggie. I'm so sorry..."

I released the pause, and the platform fell for one last time.

CYCAD COVE ARCHIVES: ACCESS GRANTED_LEVEL 1

No matter where I was on the planet and without fail, my father would send me a birthday card every October 16th. I always found it nearby but never saw who delivered them.

Once I discovered I could time travel, I began searching every October 16th across known history—testing if he could still locate me and hoping this was a turning point where he'd actually stop and explain everything. I finally caught a man in a futuristic metallic suit just outside of Paris in 1921.

'I'm just a messenger, Maggie.' His tone seemed sad even through the modulated voice. 'I'm a version of your father—like an alternate universe twin with a weird mental connection across dimensions. He loves you. He misses you. If he could be here right now, he would be.'

'Why can't he be?' I asked. 'What happened to my mother?'

'There's already an invasion on the Earth where you came from, and they lost. Adira—his Adira—died in an attack not long after you were born. I can see your father's memories as if it was my wife and...' He trailed off but retracted a portion of his helmet where I could see his face. 'She loved you, too. More than anything. They just wanted you to have a good life here—not to be alone.'

'But what's going to happen here? Same thing—eventually?'

He looked away from me. 'I don't know yet. I want to protect everyone and keep this Earth safe, but your father made a promise to you that I don't know if I can keep. I'm sorry. I have to go.'

Then he disappeared in a burst of light.

CCA File 4702934859_RMNRX200307106_MS_EC_FT

Personal journal of Maggie Serrano
Loose pages found inside Perilous Island's cabin by Rachel McNabb/Rodoxian

CHAPTER THIRTY-FIVE

THE BLAST CAME FROM OUTSIDE the building and was hot enough to singe my hair.

The flaming platform tumbled and landed a few yards in front of me, the knives liquefied and beginning to cool into one massive metal blob.

A second blast followed—nearly missing Dara—and Roman Greene walked through the opening it left. "Leave, lady—or you're next."

Startled and apparently not expecting this, Dara dropped the laser gun and ran out a side exit door.

Roman picked up the laser gun and approached me with a cautious expression. "Hi."

I sighed in relief. "Hi, Roman. Thank you. How did you even know I was here? Did my suit send you a message, too?"

"Not exactly. The machete contains a tracker for when one of us gets into trouble. You gave it to Nadia and me first...long time ago. We heard about the prison break at Brunel Heights, and we didn't think you'd return to the fairgrounds a few hours later just for the fun of it. I knew you were telling us the truth before, but it's an entirely different thing to see it. You're still you, right? I made it in time?"

This confused me. "What are you talking about? It's me—Caleb."

He walked over and only released the neck restraint. My wrists and legs were still bound, but I could look down again.

Intricate patterns of blue and white light pulsed beneath my skin. They weren't fading like when I'd left my suit—and I realized they reminded me of the egg-like probes in my vision...some sort of symbols or language. More than that. An interface—to the island and everything contained within it.

I was connected to the probes—could have released them at that moment, if I could recall the right set of commands. The exact details were still blocked from me. I'd taken extreme steps to hide information from my younger self, but Samantha wanted to reverse it all—wanted me back to who the Messengers had altered me into.

She'd almost succeeded.

I shuddered. "Dara injected me with something Samantha gave her—had the mineral from Perilous Island in it, I think...the one Nadia named Adiralite."

"Does it hurt?" Roman asked.

"No. Just feels strange—cold. Maybe you should keep me restrained and go get some help. Terrashield and Rodoxian might know something."

"Nadia has our car—drove Jhett to the hospital when we found her. All your hero friends are on their way there. Nadia will explain, but we don't know if they'll believe her. You—older you—seemed pretty clear that I needed to get you back to Perilous Island as soon as possible. He's waiting there and can probably help you."

"Why didn't he come himself?"

"He knew this was a distraction—that Samantha was planning something larger there. It was a risk, but he trusted me to help you. I hope you can trust me, too." He forced a smile. "Otherwise, I'd feel like a terrible father-in-law..."

"I told you everything?" I asked.

"I figured it out when I saw the wedding ring. He—you have always been protective of us. Nadia and I aren't even married yet, but you slip on details sometimes. You're a good man, Caleb, and I know you'll love my daughter and grandchildren. I suppose I can learn to overlook the minor things like you being from the future and looking like a walking alien glow stick."

I laughed nervously. "I'm really hoping this isn't permanent...not exactly going to be able to blend-in at the marina."

"Everything up there okay, though?" He relaxed a little and tapped the side of his head. If I'd asked him, he probably would have released me.

I felt conflicted. "I know we need to get back to the island to help, but I don't know if we should leave right this second. Maybe this was what Samantha really wanted. I keep feeling as if she's a dozen steps ahead of us."

"You want me to shoot you first then?" He was joking. "Sweep up your suit in the parking lot and load you and everything else onto the *Kairos*? I think this thing may have a stun setting, but it would probably be better to confirm the translation first. It may say 'disintegrate' for all I know..."

I strained and gritted my teeth. "If you have to, do it..."

His eyes widened. "What?"

I started feeling warmer—really warm—and the remaining restraints on the chair started to weaken. I snapped them and then stood up. "Roman, get clear! This isn't me. I don't know what's happening..."

He wasn't Adira's father anymore.

He wasn't even recognizably human to me.

He was a target.

"I don't want to hurt you, Caleb..." Roman backed away and wavered on whether to use the laser gun or not, finally building up a small reddish ball of energy in his hands instead. It was enough to knock a normal person with powers off their feet.

It did nothing to me.

Roman flew toward the room with the punching bags to get some distance. I followed—all the sand in the bags turning to glass when I got close to them.

Part of me was still aware of everything—screaming for my body to stop—but it wouldn't respond. I was going to kill Roman, and Adira would never be born. That had been my original mission, but I'd stopped myself. I just couldn't remember how...

I had him cornered, and he didn't have time to blast another way out.

"If you can hear me, Caleb—forgive me. I know it's not

you."

He aimed and fired the laser gun at my chest as I rushed toward him, and I dropped to the floor in pain.

CYCAD COVE ARCHIVES: ACCESS GRANTED_LEVEL 1

Received the test results back from our Doctor Catherine Serrano. She ran them three times—I think in part because she didn't want to believe it.

The DNA matched her father—Fortis. He's dead in our timeline, too—murdered by Chaosis—so how does some version of him still end up attacking Nadia in five years? And why her? To manipulate me into tracking down and murdering our Pacer out of revenge? Did you ever see that scenario in any visions?

I don't know what to do with this information, Caleb.

Is there any way to still save Nadia in any timeline without Adira dying?

If it's me instead of them, I'm willing.

I know I'll never get the answer out of you, but isn't that exactly what my father did for me when I was sixteen? I was the one who was supposed to die when Fortis first arrived—not him. My father was your friend, and you agreed to change what happened?

How is this any different?

CCA File 60024453009_CA19870403_SEOI_RG_NG_SFP

Message from Roman Greene
Recovered on Orchid Island, Southeast Quadrant by Caleb Averelli

Note by C.A.—I had a vision once of Adira having two younger brothers, and there's at least one timeline where all of them survived. I just don't know how—or if it's something I changed or something I managed to correct compared to an original timeline. I can't tell the difference anymore.

CHAPTER THIRTY-SIX

IN ALL THE TIME LOOPS I'd done in Cycad Cove, I never lived at 319D Gregory Street. My mind had burned that address into my earliest memory, but it hadn't been familiar when Grandma took Dominic and me there when I was eight.

Seeing the apartment and surrounding neighborhood as an adult didn't prompt anything new. Fortis was still alive and with me this time.

He rang the doorbell and waited. "You didn't have to tag along on this one, Fast Track. If you want, Terrashield or Rodoxian could probably use the help closer to downtown. I'll be fine."

No one seemed in any hurry to answer.

"It all sounds crazy—I know," I replied. "You've given me every answer I could possibly imagine about our family and where you came from—and I'm grateful I found you here. I just wish I could remember why this place was so important to me before. Who lives here now?"

"The wife and children of one of my informants," Fortis explained. "He's currently undercover, and his wife is worried he hasn't checked-in with them for their son's birthday. The kid's a fan—thought making a quick appearance might cheer him up. Both of us showing up at their door this late might be a little excessive, though. I don't want to scare them into thinking something's wrong."

Fortis was acting odd, but I couldn't place why.

"*Is* something wrong?" I asked.

Fortis shook his head. "No. Pacer is fine—just doesn't want to put his family at risk. I'll explain as best I can, say hello to the kids right quick, and then I'm done for tonight.

Seriously—if I can't handle that on my own then Cycad Cove is going to fall apart soon."

"It's not that. It's just this address has always been personal to me, and I've never fully figured out why. Maybe we should get the kids something—say it's from the team? It won't be the same as having their dad here, but they'd know whatever he's doing matters to us."

"People already think I've gone soft. That would just prove it." Then he sighed. "Go on. I already see I can't talk you out of this."

Just before Pacer's wife reached the door, I went back in time a few hours and bought out a fourth of Cycad Cove's only toy store—filling the apartment building's hallway with bicycles, action figures, dolls, and outdoor toys they could share with the other kids living in the complex.

Even though Fortis knew what was coming, he still pinched the bridge of his nose. "They're not exactly in witness protection, but they're trying to keep a low profile here. After everything you've experienced with Adira and Maggie, I get why you're like this sometimes. You just need to work at not going overboard..."

"Oh—oh, sorry! This visit isn't on-record—to protect them in case your database gets compromised?" I asked. "Damn...should I take most of this stuff back then? Maybe donate it to somewhere else? I'll feel terrible if these kids see all of this and then don't get to keep most of it..."

The door opened before he could answer.

Pacer's wife seemed startled to see us. "Wow...I didn't even hear you two bring all of this up. Thank you so much...I'm not even sure if it will all fit in here..." She gestured for us to come inside. "The kids are asleep—finally crashed from all the sugar. I kept things small today—had a cake and invited a few neighbors who seem nice. Did George ask you to do all of this, Fortis? Have you heard from him?"

"Not in a few days, but he talked to me about you and the kids often. I put a reminder in my calendar today for Ryan's birthday—and my friend here accidentally thought it was case-related. Fast Track, this is Becky Fredricks. Becky—Fast Track."

"My real name's Caleb if that's more comfortable to you," I explained. "I'm retired—for the most part. I still help out Fortis and his team when they ask me—and sometimes just to keep myself busy between other projects."

She looked back and forth between Fortis and me. "You're brothers, right? Not twins, but there's definitely a family resemblance."

I had no idea how to explain. "We're distantly related. I'm—uh—"

"That's a long story that would keep us here all week," Fortis interrupted. "I'm sorry if we upset you by showing up unannounced—and you don't have to wake up your children because of us. We'll carry all of this inside before it causes you any problems, and it will be a nice surprise for them in the morning. Just say it's from George—not us. He'll probably never let me hear the end of it once he's in the clear again, but I don't mind."

"That's very generous of you—both of you. Hopefully another time—when things are safer—we can plan and invite your core team over for dinner. Would either of you like some coffee or bottled water? We're kind of cleaned out of everything else—and so sorry for all the mess. I was cleaning up the kitchen when you rang the doorbell. I thought it was something on TV at first. We almost never get visitors here."

Fortis smiled. "My wife Virginia and I are dealing with two superpowered teenagers. I hate to say it, but it doesn't get any less messy once they're older. Catherine is divided between art and veterinary school, so we've got a house scattered with rescued animals and paint supplies. Dominic believes his laser ability is for incinerating his dirty clothes so he can just go buy new ones. We own a washer and dryer just like everybody else. I just can't get him to understand he doesn't have to shortcut everything in his life, you know?"

She gave a reluctant nod. "Neither of ours are showing any signs of George's abilities—yet. No offense, but I'm sort of thankful for that. What all of you do carries a lot of responsibility—and a lot of stress. I love George, and I know he loves us. Being Pacer—helping people—that drive will always be there. It's a part of him, and I admire and love that about him, too. It upsets him when I worry, and I try not to show it. It's hard, though—and of course everything else that comes with protecting ourselves and protecting him when he's on an assignment. It can make you paranoid about everyone and everything." She paused, more focused on Fortis than me. "May I ask you how you found us? If I've made some accidental mistake, I don't want to repeat it. We were lucky it was you two and not some villain out for revenge. You caught me off-guard, and I honestly wouldn't have been prepared if this was something terrible."

"You didn't make any major mistakes or slip up," Fortis replied. "George did—but we'll have that conversation the next time I see him and set it right. You're safe. He's safe. That's all that really matters. Caleb and I still probably shouldn't stay long—just in case any villain gets the idea of tracking us."

I'd mostly been moving toys and books from the hallway to the living room while Fortis and Becky talked on the sofa. There was one family photo on the coffee table, but I didn't feel right about picking it up to look at it—given how nervous Becky seemed.

Fortis was right. Even with my suit's helmet retracted where she could see my face, she kept staring at the two energy batons mounted on my calves. Shock weapons—deadly, if I needed them to be.

I had just finished bringing in a small soccer net—the last thing left in the hallway—when George and Becky's daughter entered the living room. She yawned and rubbed her eyes. I'd tried to work quietly, but the noise had woken her up.

Based on the girl's hesitation, she must have thought she was dreaming. "Hi."

She looked somewhat familiar, but I couldn't place how I knew her. It was weird.

"Hi. I'm Caleb—Fortis there with your mom is a friend of your dad's. We brought you some presents from him. He's sorry he couldn't be here in person for your brother's party."

She was still half-asleep. "It's okay—he missed mine, too, but he came back the next week and spent a whole day with just me to make up for it. Is he coming back soon to surprise Ryan? Even if he spends the day with just him, I'll get to see him again when they come home..."

I looked over at Fortis and Becky. Fortis gave me a warning look to not make any promises. It bothered me that he seemed to be withholding something—even though I sometimes had to do that to him and the others with what I knew about their futures.

My attention went back to the girl and her question. "I haven't met your dad in person—yet—so I'm not sure. I'm sorry. Um, do you like Rodoxian? She's not here right now, but there's one of her dolls around here—just need to find it again. Want to help me?"

She smiled at me but then ran back toward what I assumed was her bedroom. She returned holding a photo of her and her dad. They were in front of a carnival booth...with wooden puzzles and stuffed dogs, dragons, and griffins as prizes.

Her father was the booth operator—the same one Chaosis had murdered. Running the shooting game was some sort of cover for Pacer—not his actual job—and his rude personality might have been an act, too. Fortis already knew him—knew the guy's entire family—and he hadn't told any of us about it.

The fairgrounds attack would happen on the Fourth of July—almost six years later from that point. We had the time and opportunity again to change it—to prepare for it. I'd already told everyone on the team what I thought could be helpful to save as many people as possible.

I hadn't known to tell them about this.

"What's your name?" I asked.

The girl found another doll in the pile I'd created—another hero I didn't recognize instead of Rodoxian—and hugged it. "I'm Samantha. It's nice to meet you, sir—and thank you for protecting us...the whole city, I mean. If I ever get powers, I hope I can be on your team someday, too...like my dad. He told us Fortis is a great trainer—especially with teleporting..."

Fortis was apparently great at lying, too.

I restrained my anger before it slipped into my tone. "Yeah—yeah, he is...Excuse me, but I have to go. I just remembered something important I need to do back at headquarters. Nice meeting you both. Have a good night."

"Caleb—wait!" Fortis shouted from the couch.

Time flowed backwards.

We were in front of the apartment's door again. Becky hadn't answered it yet, and all the toys were back in the hallway.

I freaked out, wondering how it had happened. "Fortis, I didn't do this—not consciously, anyway."

His tone turned sad. "I know. I did. I was just hoping you wouldn't remember any of it..."

He'd stolen both my shock batons.

Before I could react, he jabbed them into the chest of my suit.

They both faded within seconds—the energy dissipating evenly throughout thousands of tiny metal scales. It stung physically and wasn't pleasant, but it wasn't going to kill me like he'd intended.

Not even close.

I glared at him, and his eyes went wide. He tried to rewind the moment again to attempt something else, but I had enough experience and developed power to block him from it—now that I knew he could do it in the first place.

I placed my hands on his shoulders—resisting the urge to move them closer to his neck. I needed to calm down and focus if I was going to take him with me. "We need to talk—just not here and now."

By the time Becky Fredricks reached the apartment's door and opened it, we were gone.

EXTINGUISHED WORLDS: WHAT GOES AROUND

CYCAD COVE ARCHIVES: ACCESS GRANTED_LEVEL 1

This message is for Fast Track—Caleb Serrano in my timeline, but I think there's somehow more than one of him. I don't know if this will make it to you at the right time or if you'll understand, but I have to try.

My name is George Fredricks. In my timeline, I'm a hero working in Cycad Cove under the name Pacer. I also work with an organization Senator Horace McNabb founded to maintain hero accountability—like the law enforcement equivalent of Internal Affairs.

It's not what I believed it was when I first agreed to join. If anything, this organization has been covering up 'inconvenient' events for decades—all under the guise of maintaining the stability of the planet.

Two weeks ago, I followed Fortis to Perilous Island—ended up getting lost and missing my daughter's birthday. What I couldn't tell my family was that I almost didn't return at all.

I've discovered where Fortis came from, and it's not an alien planet like he claimed. It's a version of Earth, but it's been invaded by some outside force—possibly his species? Most of the humans there are dead, and who's left...there's nothing human about them. I was attacked by these altered creatures and nearly died.

Another version of you saved me. He told me how to get back home—and a few other things about the future that will take time to process.

He was dying...asked for me to relay to you and Adira to please take care of his Maggie...that he won't be able to send her anymore cards. I'm sorry. I've attached a storage drive with copies of photos and videos so you can see for yourself.

CCA File 7110293849_MS20210801_FT_CS_GFP_NWPI

Handwritten note recovered on Northwest Quadrant of Perilous Island by Maggie Serrano.

CHAPTER THIRTY-SEVEN

I HEARD FUNHOUSE MUSIC AGAIN, followed by a blast.
The music groaned to a stop.
Roman sighed in relief. "That's better. Not as creepy as snakes, but still..." He walked closer to me. "Well, you're looking less florescent—will hopefully feel a lot less murderous once you wake up. That was close..."
I was eighteen again...back at the funhouse. I could hear Roman, but I could barely move and couldn't speak yet. My ribcage felt as if it was burning from the laser gun blast, but my body was distracted with healing the chest wound instead of attacking him.
Roman didn't want to kill me. He was trying to help me regain control over what the Messengers had programmed into me.
The funhouse trembled again, sending most of the superheated sandbags crashing to the floor around us. This seemed milder but more directed than the previous earthquake.
Terrashield and Rodoxian had gotten my message but had no idea Roman was my friend and Adira's father in the future.
Roman anticipated what was coming and primed his ability. It made the hair on my arms stand on end—like the charge from a lightning storm.
"Step away from Fast Track and stand down—now!" Rodoxian shouted.
"That's not happening, Sparkles," Roman replied. "As

soon as Caleb cools down where he won't give me fourth-degree burns, I'm taking him back to Perilous Island. His older self can help him sort this out. Not me. Not you and your hero buddies. We literally don't have time for this."

There was a whooshing sound—like multiple knives hitting a wooden board.

Rodoxian pinned Roman to the wall—the hardened glass shards from the sandbags penetrating his clothes like knives.

He glared at her but then realized I'd regained consciousness. "Caleb, please tell me you're back to being you again..."

I was still in too much pain to speak or stand, but I nodded and gave a longer blink than normal. He relaxed as Rodoxian and Terrashield cautiously approached me.

"What the hell did you do to him?" Terrashield asked.

"I didn't do this," Roman explained and pointed outside. "The psycho magician's assistant made a deal with the Messenger called Samantha—thinks she and her husband will be spared from the invasion and get their son back if she cooperates. She ran west if you two want to do something useful and capture her."

"You let Dara go?" Rodoxian asked in disbelief. "After everything she's done? She's just as responsible as Chaosis for what happened at the fairgrounds—and then torturing Jhett and Caleb—"

Roman's tone turned irritated. "She wasn't my priority. Do you not get what's happening? If this Caleb dies or turns brainwashed alien permanently, this planet and our timeline will collapse. I'm not saying everything he's ever done has worked out perfect, but this future is a hell of a lot better than what those monsters have planned for us. I need to get him to the island—and you two are doing nothing but slowing us down. My fiancé took your other friend to the hospital the moment we found her. We're not the enemy here..."

Rodoxian hesitated. "They just arrived a few minutes ago, but Cyndero said he didn't see who dropped Jhett off. Did your fiancé just leave Jhett there at the ER and then drive away?"

Roman's tone turned sarcastic. "Maybe, but I can't imagine why. You're all such a warm and welcoming bunch." His expression relaxed when he looked at me. "Nadia is probably heading to the marina, Caleb—thinking she's catching up to us. I don't want her to be there alone on the *Kairos* without backup, and we should have already left by now..."

"Rox, drop the shards." Terrashield said and then approached Roman. "Whoever you are, go—but Caleb isn't going with you. There's nothing left on the coast of Perilous anymore, and he needs an actual hospital."

The building shook—not from Terrashield's ability but another major quake originating from the island.

Whether from that or Rodoxian willingly releasing him, Roman broke free—and launched a primed ball of energy from each of his hands.

Terrashield and Rodoxian were knocked backwards—almost out of the building.

I shook my head at Roman and tried to get up before collapsing again.

"Take it easy," Roman said. "I didn't hurt them. If I max out at ten, that was a three—just enough to stun them for an hour or two while we—" Before he could finish his sentence, Rodoxian had pinned him with the shards again. "Oh, come on! I just bought these clothes last week!"

This time she had a larger shard hovering near his throat. I still couldn't tell her to stop—was barely able to shake my head again—but she wasn't focused on me.

She was out of breath and strained. "You're not taking Caleb anywhere. Do *you* understand? Until we sort this out, for all we know you're working with Samantha, too. You have a gun just like hers."

"This thing?" Roman asked. "Her minion dropped it! I wasn't going to leave it on the floor—not in the state Caleb was in when I got here! I don't know how much of this you understand, but bed rest and fluids won't fix him this time. He's a potential threat to us right now—not that he means to be—and I know *when* and where to take him for help. Let me, or I won't hold back next time."

In response, Rodoxian brought up every remaining glass shard from the floor—hovering dozens of them inches from Roman's face and chest. "You want to repeat that again? We have a doctor who can help him, too—someone who'd never harm him. If Caleb's younger self is compromised right now, his older self could be, too. The prison break at Brunel Heights and him cutting off all contact with us makes no sense. If you do care about him, think this out. You may not work for Samantha, but you may be delivering Caleb right to her without realizing it."

"And maybe you're the ones helping her but are too damn stubborn and arrogant to believe you can't make a mistake! Fortis had you all fooled from the start, and you blindly worked under his command for years. He used your good intentions and this city's vulnerabilities to protect himself from ever being questioned, and this isn't much different. Do you want everyone in Cycad Cove to die while we waste time here? If I don't take Caleb with me, we're all dead in a few hours, anyway..."

While all of this was happening and I was struggling to do anything to prevent them from killing each other, tiny metal scales of my suit came to me from the parking lot and began bonding to my skin.

Similar to what happened the first time, a majority of the suit covered me at once. Then its flight-assist rockets engaged and had me upright a few feet from the ceiling. I was still injured, but the external support from the suit helped me breathe.

"Stop—both of you!" The suit's voice had reset to a default, and I'd startled them...and myself, a little.

Rodoxian changed her aim of all the glass shards from Roman to me. Roman dropped to the floor and had his ability primed again—also targeting me. Even with the suit, I probably couldn't have handled a fight with either of them— much less both of them at the same time.

My heart started racing so fast my chest hurt. I raised my hands and flew backwards away from them.

"You okay inside there?" Roman asked. "Back in control?"

I nodded. "Robot demon voice off. Retract helmet." My voice sounded normal but panicked. "Hey, I'm back! I think I'm back. Don't kill each other—or me, unless you have to, I guess. We're all on the same side. Roman—we may need Terrashield and Rodoxian to help, too. We'll bring them with us and explain on the way. You okay with that, Rox?"

Roman nodded in reluctant agreement.

Rodoxian just stared up at me as if she still didn't trust us. "Was Fortis like this, too, Caleb? Your being from Perilous Island makes some sense, but what Fortis told us about how he first arrived on Earth doesn't add up with that...not anymore..."

Roman gave a disgusted laugh. "Fortis didn't flee some distant planet in cryostasis and gently land his escape pod in the Pacific. He faked that whole event and story just to gain an entry point into this dimension without having to hide. Caleb is a lot more merciful than I am, or I'd have killed that coward a long time ago for his part in all of this. It's probably the only thing Chaosis has done right—other than making it quicker than he deserved."

This confused me. "I thought Fortis and I were friends—allies, at least—but he was doing something behind all of our backs. I think he got Samantha's father killed on purpose. That's why she hates us so much—thinks we're tied to him and were in on it, too."

Roman nodded. "Fortis sold out his own family to save himself—got his wife killed, and his son is insane. You're all wrapped up in guilt because of what you've seen in your visions, but I don't believe you caused as much of this as you think you did. You actually care about this planet and all of us. Fortis never did—just acted the part to leverage what he wanted out of people."

"Where do you fit into all of this?" Rodoxian asked Roman. "We knew the older Caleb for over a decade, and he never mentioned you or your fiancé until we found this younger version of him."

Roman didn't immediately answer—just walked up to a still-unconscious Terrashield and picked him up in a fireman's carry. He didn't seem strained at all, even though

Terrashield probably weighed over two hundred and fifty pounds—likely closer to three hundred with his suit and gear. "I met Caleb roughly nine years ago from my perspective—and I'm pretty sure he was around eighty and hasn't experienced that part of his lifetime yet. Time travel is weird—still makes my head hurt the more I think about it."

"Caleb pulled you out of your original timeline?" Rodoxian asked. "Like he pulled all those prisoners and disappeared from Brunel Heights? Why?"

The answer came to me—not as a memory or vision but almost a resolve of what I needed to do...what I'd have to eventually do to end this.

It would kill me...just not today.

It was everyone and everything else it would cost that weighed on me. This wasn't about winning against the Messengers and gaining some kind of revenge. It was about how badly I didn't want to lose it all...my wife and daughter...my friends...our home...the desperate possibility of somehow protecting the planet and our timeline from further attacks...

"My older self is building a team...an army not bound by time or place because this enemy will never fight fair," I explained. "No matter what happens today with Samantha—no matter what happens to me—Earth is still going to need protection. And it's going to need all of you to lead it after I'm gone..."

EXTINGUISHED WORLDS: WHAT GOES AROUND

CYCAD COVE ARCHIVES: ACCESS GRANTED_LEVEL 1

'Tell me about this plan of yours with the fairgrounds booth. I'm recording.'

'In every vision you have of the attack, thousands of people die—correct? All murdered by Chaosis and Dara trying to draw Fortis out into the open? My daughter Samantha is one of them?'

'Unfortunately, yes. Chaosis takes her hostage, and he somehow remembers every move we make trying to save her—even after I go back again. He knows me—Rodoxian and Terrashield, too.'

'But he doesn't know me—not out-of-costume.'

'He'll kill you, George—and there's no guarantee he still won't take Samantha again. I won't be able to stop him.'

'He's already murdered my wife and son, Caleb. I can't prove any of it, but I hope you can believe me. He has to be captured, and this may be the only chance my daughter has for survival. Please, I'm begging you. Help me save her.'

'Let me think it out. One more thing—if we manage to pull this off, how much do you want Samantha to know?'

'When she's old enough, tell her the truth—that I loved her and wanted her and all those other innocent people to be okay. She's just like me, Caleb. She'll want to be a hero, and I trust all of you to watch out for her. Thank you.'

'I haven't agreed to this yet.'

'You're a father, too. Of course, you have...'

CCA File 29304000293_BWTSRMNRX20020114_FT_GFP

Video recording from Fast Track suit camera, archived January 14th, 2002.
Recovered by Ben Wallace/Terrashield and Rachel McNabb/Rodoxian in Caleb/Fast Track's office files.

CHAPTERT THIRTY-EIGHT

ONCE RODOXIAN AND ROMAN DECIDED on an uneasy truce, it didn't take us long to fly to the marina. Nadia was already preparing the boat, and Roman dropped Terrashield off in one of the beds down below.

The increase in seismic activity made the water rougher than normal. As the *Kairos* moved, I hovered just above the deck instead of trying to stand on it.

I tried to recap Rodoxian on what I'd been able to recall about the apartment and Fortis's attempt to kill me, but she acted as if she didn't want to hear it.

"I remember around that time, and I do believe you," she said. "It wasn't long after that when you split up the team and took over leading and training our division of it—from a practical standpoint. Fortis was still around publicly—was too good at playing the part, I guess. You allowed him to save face...maybe because of his family being yours, too. Cyndero was just a kid. Griffin wasn't Chaosis yet. You probably tried to help him, too. It just didn't work out..." She frowned and shook her head. "You could have trusted Terra and me, though. We could have helped you with the burden of it—tried, at least."

"You both would have quit the team if I exposed Fortis as a fraud to the general public, and I wouldn't have blamed you at the time," I said. "I think you would have regretted it later, though. Across all these loops, you and Terrashield have always been genuine...wanted to help people and protect the city—the entire world, if you could. I didn't want to destroy that part of you, either. Who Fortis really was and what he tried to do had nothing to do with either of you. I handled the problem...tried to repair as much damage to the timeline as I could. I just don't know if it will ever be enough..."

"What are you going to do about Samantha?" she asked.

"Locate her—try to reason with her—but I don't think it will go well." I looked down. "I don't want to kill her, Rox. I don't want to kill anybody...but if she's found some way to override the island's systems without me...Perilous Island is a lot more than a big chunk of space dirt with veins of the mineral. In the wrong hands, it could be an entry portal for us to be invaded without a single alien ship appearing in the sky. Even with some of us having powers, humanity as a whole is nowhere near prepared for that. It could also be turned into a gigantic bomb—and nothing could survive the fallout. Everything we know would either die immediately or just go extinct within days. It's a sort of last resort option for planets initially deemed viable candidates but turn out to be too much hassle. The aliens don't want potential enemies to develop down the road, either."

This scared her. "How do you know all of this?"

"It's probably been inside my head the entire time. I just couldn't recall it. Don't worry—it's still me. To be honest, I'm pretty terrified right now, too. I hope older me can show me how to block all the insane alien assassin stuff out—hopefully keep what could be useful to us. I still want to help you—if you can trust me."

"I want to...I really do." Her tone turned awkward, almost sad. "I need to go check on Terra...don't want him tearing the boat apart if he wakes up alone. We'll find you again once I'm able to explain. Okay?"

"Yeah...okay. Thanks, Rox."

Nadia Greene waited until Rodoxian left before she came to talk to me. "Roman's pushing the engines—trying to stay just under burning them out, but he knows we need to hurry. You might have to fly the rest of the way, but it looks like you're already prepared for that."

"I didn't want to add getting seasick to my list of problems," I explained. "Are you okay? Seem like a pro on keeping your balance."

"I'm fine—just worried," she replied. "About you. About your hero friend who's apparently your grandmother? Life must be so dizzying to you sometimes. I don't see how you keep track of it all."

I laughed. "I don't—not completely. I think that's part of the problem."

"I think you do just fine. I know it's difficult—trying to scramble and save everyone across multiple decades—but you've never been alone. We're all here, and we'll help you."

She took out a folded paper from her sketch book. It was a highly-detailed map of Perilous Island—a tangled maze of trails and underground passages that became pathways to other times and places if you knew where to go. She and Roman had been working on it for years.

Before I put it away in one of my suit's compartments to keep it from getting wet, I noticed the date in the bottom corner. It was the same day she'd died. This Nadia was younger—near the same age as Roman, which meant she'd somehow gotten it from her older self.

She knew she'd die in ten years—that I couldn't prevent it for some reason—and she and Roman were still helping me, anyway.

"I'm so sorry," I said. "If there was any way I could change it..."

"You tried, Caleb—so many times." Her tone was gentle without any trace of being upset with me. "The instability to the timeline would have caused Adira's death instead...or Roman's...or yours...and Maggie would have never existed. Even to survive, I'd never want that to happen. You do find a way to let me see Adira with Maggie, though—for a few minutes. That's more than I ever could have asked. Thank you—and never feel guilty about it. We both still have a lot of life left to go right now. Time traveler or not, it's all precious, Caleb. It's all worth fighting for. You can do this. Roman and I know you can."

She grabbed my hand, placed something inside it, and walked back to the front of the boat. It was Maggie's other baby sock—the one I thought I'd lost. Inside it was the engraved ring I'd given Adira at our wedding. I put them with the other sock holding my ring.

Terrashield cleared his throat to get my attention. "So, if Rodoxian and I take the next two decades to decide *not* to fight Roman on the island—not even show up for a fight—will that mean you'll never come back in the first place to warn us? What about the day Dominic finds you? Similar situation? That still seems like a paradox problem—just like you multiplying yourself and your suit a few dozen times and having those same wedding rings over and over again. Somebody had to make those in the first place, right? I didn't take college physics for nothing, did I?"

I was glad to see he was okay. "You weren't a geology major?" I asked, knowing those kinds of jokes annoyed him. "Did you wake up to logic me out of existence or to give me a pep talk? I think I'm in good shape on motivation—other than I feel sorry for the person trying to murder us all. Samantha Fredricks and her father were a part of your and Rox's team, too—at least in most loops. It's all a big mess in my head right now. I must have trusted her enough to show her how the island worked—at least enough of it for her to see what happened to her father. There's no scenario where she would have come to us for help or an explanation...it just tore her apart inside. She trusted us. She trusted *me*. I just wanted to help her after what Chaosis did at the fairgrounds, and I didn't remember about the rest until now."

"You do realize there are a few options in between letting Samantha destroy the entire planet and killing her, right?" He asked. "You just have to stop her, Caleb. Teleporters aren't the easiest people to go up against, but you're a time traveler. Aren't you technically faster—or will at least know where she pops up before she does it?"

I shook my head. "The Messengers altered her, too. I don't know when—technically could have happened at any point after we brought her into this mess. They're using her, and I don't know a way around that—not right now. Maybe my older self will."

CYCAD COVE ARCHIVES: ACCESS GRANTED_LEVEL 1

'Name?'

'Oh, come on! You know who I am! It's why you brought me in, isn't it?'

'Name, please. It's for the record.'

'Who's record? I want a lawyer. I have a card for someone. Here—just call her.'

'She represents your father, too. Not sure if that will be a conflict, Mr. Averelli...'

'Why are you trying to set me off? I don't want to hurt anybody! I'm not like him! I'm not like either of them!'

'Then why the hell did your girlfriend publish this to warn everyone? She got it through just before someone killed her.'

'Girlfriend? You mean Samantha? Sam's dead? How? What happened to her?'

'That's what we'd like to know...'

CCA File 30029388192_CA20230406_DAJR_CCPD

Interrogation of Dominic Averelli, Jr.
Archive file from Cycad Cove Police Department

Note by Caleb Averelli: I averted this scenario but still wanted you to see it for yourself. Someone intends to murder Samantha Fredricks in the future and frame Dominic for it.

We have to protect them both somehow.

CHAPTER THIRTY-NINE

AFTER WE MADE LANDFALL and made sure the *Kairos* was anchored, Roman left us to go into the woods. It wasn't long before he returned—with a version of me who looked around thirty.

"This is still weird, I know," he said. "I can remember being where you are right now. We need to get you somewhere level—maybe get a cot or reclining chair from the boat? You need to get out of your suit, too. It's okay. We're about as safe as we can be right now—under the circumstances."

I listened, but a lot of my earlier pain returned the moment the suit became a pile again.

Roman found a cot and quickly assembled it where I could lie down on the beach.

"Okay, what now?" I asked.

The older version of me seemed uneasy. "You know that glowing stuff Dara injected us with at the funhouse?"

"Yeah—it nearly caused me to kill Roman."

"Well, I have to give you more of it—a lot more. This would have been easier if other people hadn't come with you, but we can't help that now. Roman and I won't let you hurt anybody—I promise. It's still going to get worse for a little bit before it gets better, though. You're going to have to trust us, or you won't make it long enough to even reach Samantha."

I looked over at Terrashield and Rodoxian. Neither of them liked the idea but were going to let it be my call. "I didn't know this was the plan. You two and Nadia need to get clear of me. It's not abandoning me. It's keeping yourselves safe so I don't do anything horrible by accident."

"There is somewhere I can take them on the island—

temporarily," Nadia offered. "I left it off the map in case we ever needed a place to hide. Roman knows where—can find us once you're better."

"If I'm better..." I replied.

"It's not a toxin to us or something designed to turn people evil," my older self explained. "The Messengers use it to heal physical injuries, mostly during combat. We're part-human, and using our abilities puts a lot of pressure on our brain and body. That's why you've been getting nose bleeds and have always had memory issues. This will help you—there's just some unwelcome side effects because of what happened to us before."

"Like trying to kill the same people I care about?" I asked. "Maybe getting all my memories back isn't worth it anymore."

"Hang on," Roman said. "I have an idea—won't take but a minute. Nadia, go ahead and take the heroes where you need to go. I'll be there as soon as we confirm Caleb's good."

Roman returned with a blanket—it was about ninety degrees on the beach—and what looked like a lifetime supply of duct tape.

"You're serious?" I couldn't help but laugh.

"That's not a normal blanket and duct tape." Older me nodded to Roman that he approved of the idea. "There's Adiralite integrated into the fabric fibers. You won't catch them on fire or melt them, and it will help dissipate the extra energy. It worked for me before—in the last loop I remember."

Another earthquake hit in the middle of them basically wrapping me into a duct tape cocoon.

I felt ridiculous—given everything else that was happening—but I was worried, too. "I turned sandbags into glass spikes a few hours ago, and now we're on a freakin beach..."

"More incentive to get control sooner," Roman replied. "I promise we'll let you out once you're better.

"You ready?" older me asked.

In the daylight, the mineral solution looked pale blue in the syringes—almost clear as my older self brought them closer to me. I shut my eyes—and lost track after about the fifth injection.

I really hoped I didn't kill them both...

My mind started to drift.

"This little guy is so tiny." It was Roman's voice, but this was a memory or vision. He was referring to a small brown-haired boy inside a clear containment pod. "You're sure that's you—and that you're eight at this point? Caleb?"

I nodded. I wasn't sure if we had time traveled or were in some sort of nearby dimension.

We were inside some sort of cavern network, but there was alien tech inlaid everywhere in the stones. It was a medical facility...filled with abducted victims...and I'd recently found a way to locate myself.

"There's so many more than I expected—all children. They took us all when we were children, Roman. What kind of sick—"

"I know you want to save all of them, but it has to start with saving yourself before they turn you completely," he interrupted, trying to keep me focused. "We can't get out of here with anyone else—not this time. You knew that from the start. This was your plan."

I nodded, but I was disoriented from being in two places at once within close proximity.

As an eight-year-old overhearing the conversation, I felt Roman pick me up. I'd been in some sort of stasis pod or chamber, and I wanted them to put me back. It was peaceful there. No voices. No dreams. No monsters. I started crying, and Roman put his hand around my entire head.

"Shhh...it's okay, kid. You're going to be okay. Caleb? You coming?"

I hesitated. "I'm forgetting something else, Roman—something important."

He was getting worried and frustrated. "That happens when you get older. You can remember while we get away. Come on!"

I followed Roman but started to fall behind. "I came through remembering my name and a few other things—319D Gregory Street and two phone numbers. I still don't know what those mean yet. No one ever answered them."

"What were the numbers?"

I told him, and he was able to repeat them right back on the first try.

"That's impressive."

"Not really," he replied. "They're not phone numbers. Take away the extra zeroes on the ends, and they're the latitude and longitude of my house. You were trying to lead yourself to us before I had Adira contact you. We can try that again, I guess. Couldn't hurt anything. What do I do? Just have the kid repeat them over and over again? It won't hurt you?"

"No worse than what these things have done...Roman?"

"Yeah?"

"I need to stay—not exactly planning on dying yet, but I need to get as many of these kids out of here while we still can. Thank you—for everything."

He seemed to expect this. "We'll all take good care of mini-you—I promise."

"I know you will. You did..."

Roman hugged me and patted my older self's back.

For a brief moment, I could see both sides of my life simultaneously. Older me blasted a pathway for Roman to escape. Then he blocked it behind us as alarms began to sound.

For my eight-year-old self, it felt as if we were in pure darkness for hours, Roman saying nothing to me but the address and the numbers until I began repeating them back to him.

Roman had flown and exited Perilous Island at a fast speed on purpose, letting me go at a safe moment and covering for my body's response to being ripped out of the timeline I'd just been saved from.

The implosion I'd later created had brought a skyscraper down on me, and we knew the rest from there.

Remembering this wasn't so bad, but then other things began to creep in...the aliens' original plans for me. Even though I'd been rescued, a lot of remnants remained as if I hadn't been.

They'd made me powerful. Messenger was the wrong term. We were world-killers—solitary beings altered to create extinction-level events if a planet refused to comply.

Weapons turned against our own planets and people.

Earth and humanity were particularly stubborn...about 5% successful planetary assimilation versus 95% total destruction. These weren't hypothetical odds. A war was raging that just hadn't reached us yet—across multiple Earths...multiple timelines...multiple versions of me and my family.

I could sense a connection to them—even the ones I'd never be able to reach.

They were fighting.

We would be, too—soon enough.

CYCAD COVE ARCHIVES: ACCESS GRANTED_LEVEL 1

When Cyndero found the booth operator's daughter and passed her to safety, I was the undercover police officer. When I first met Caleb—from my perspective—he warned me this girl needed to be protected and to contact you.

Earlier that day, a little boy had done some slight-of-hand magic near the booth. I gave him fifty dollars and told him to go home. I just wanted him safe from the attack—didn't realize at the time he was Chaosis and Dara's son.

It's not that I didn't believe Caleb before—about this whole time travel multiple dimensions thing, I mean—but then a woman in a yellow suit and cape teleported into the passenger seat of my car and aimed a laser gun at my head.

'Pull over—now!' she ordered.

I kept calm, in part because Caleb had warned me this would happen. 'She's you, right? The kid sleeping in the back is you?'

'H-how did you?' the woman stammered. 'Who sent you?'

'Fast Track asked me to get her away from Cycad Cove before someone kills her,' I explained. 'I have connections who can get her a new identity and protect her.'

She might have actually shot me for a few loops—that part is kind of hazy for me—but I found myself outside the car with the little girl holding my hand tight.

'What happened?' I asked.

'The metal man took her away,' she replied in a stunned tone. 'They're gone.'

CCA File 930200049550_RG20030417_AB_SFP_FT

Message from Andy Brant to Roman and Nadia Greene
July 17th, 2003

CHAPTER FORTY

I WOKE UP ON A COT, still wrapped in the blanket and duct tape. The sky was dark and cloudy, and the light pollution from the city was missing.

At first, I thought I'd been carried somewhere else on the island—I assumed by Roman and the other me. "Hello? Anybody?"

Ziggy—or another ancient dog-like creature like him—showed up. It sniffed and licked my face before sneezing on me. I didn't try to move or talk to it—just in case it was hungry.

It left me for the woods again. No one else responded.

I concentrated—carefully—and was able to heat my body and the blanket up without setting it on fire. The adhesive portion of the tape weakened, and I was able to break and slip out of it.

I felt good—physically, anyway—but I wasn't sure what had happened while I was out.

"It's straining, but I can take people with me when I teleport, too." Samantha said from behind me. "You were basically gift-wrapped, so that made it a little easier. How's your memory?"

As I turned around, she kept her distance and raised her hands. She didn't appear to be armed.

"It's coming back—slowly," I replied in a cautious tone. "Listen, what happened with Fortis and your father—"

"Did you know heroes have their own version of Internal Affairs?" she interrupted. "I didn't—not until I started digging into my father's murder case...and the fairgrounds attack as a whole. My father worked for them—joined

Fortis's informant network to investigate him."

"And Fortis found out?" I asked.

She nodded. "Dad found evidence that Fortis was working with an alien syndicate calling themselves 'Messengers'—a handful of them scoping out Earth's defensive capabilities. Dad assumed your entire family and the main team over Cycad Cove were a part of it, too. It frightened him—but he had no one to go to for advice or help. As far as he was concerned, all of you were compromised—corrupted. I lied to Dominic—told him I dated him for a college paper. It was more than that. I thought he had answers that he didn't...and eventually he would have figured out that his father murdered mine...and you and the others stood by and allowed it to happen. You didn't even try to go back and fix it. The Messengers returned and abducted me in a later time loop—altered me—just like they did you when you were a child. I've watched my father die hundreds of times now—unable to stop it. You always get to forget with each loop. I don't."

I had wanted to save her father—had spent multiple loops trying—but nothing had worked out. "Samantha, I—"

"I don't care about your excuses or apologies or whatever damn rationalizations you've told yourself. Fortis set him up to be there—set me up to be there, too. I was twelve, Caleb! And that was three years after losing Mom and Ryan in a so-called 'mysterious' car accident. Clear day. No traffic. Mom swerved and plowed into a light post—as if she'd suddenly been blinded. Do you know what Chaosis did to my father right before he killed him?"

My tone went quiet. "He blinded him..."

"With my mother, it could have been Chaosis...or Fortis himself...Cyndero...you—for all I know about your actual abilities. I hate you. I hate all of you—and the worst part is your team was all I had left after I lost my family. I wanted to be just like all of you. It gave me some purpose—some hope for the future. You took that, too. Once you learn the truth, you can't unlearn it—even when you get so desperate you drop a building on yourself trying to forget. I'm not going to let you forget anymore—not until you set this entire mess right again."

"I don't know how!" I shouted. "I—"

Samantha's expression turned pained, and she suddenly dropped to the ground. Confused, I approached her and checked her pulse.

Nothing—and she wasn't breathing, either.

I started chest compressions and breaths, but she was cold—as if she'd been dead longer than when we'd been talking.

As if time had been moved by someone else...

"What the hell? Samantha? Samantha, come on! I don't understand this..."

"She served her purpose, Caleb—bringing you here." Fortis wasn't dead—or at least this version of him wasn't. "Everything she said was true. The only thing that kept her going was the possibility you could go back and save her father. At least now, they're reunited. She got what she wanted—just not how she wanted it. Life is like that sometimes."

I didn't understand how he was still alive. Fortis's remains had been found at the fairgrounds scene—and there had been a funeral of some sort.

I'd been on the island during all of that, so I wasn't sure if or how he'd somehow faked his death.

"You killed her?" I asked. "Convinced Chaosis to kill her whole family?"

Fortis nodded. "As if he ever needed convincing. I just nudge him in a general direction, and he takes care of the rest. The more he thought he was disappointing me, the easier it was. Hell, even Dara tracking him down after he left Cycad Cove was my idea. She worked for me—still does. Their son Dominic shows a lot of promise—as do you."

I shook my head. "Why? Why do all of this?"

He stepped closer, his skin glowing blue and white with the alien language similar to mine. I backed away, and he seemed amused.

"We all have a common goal here, Caleb—to keep this particular Earth protected from invasion and to keep our family safe."

I shook my head. "No—not like this…"

"If I had allowed things to play out how you think you want them, you wouldn't even exist to have this conversation. I would have been killed, and my children would have been turned into science experiments—at best. I settled on this Earth because I was tired of running and tired of fighting. There's a balance to this that you can't comprehend—and even if you could I don't think your humanity would endure it for very long. It doesn't bother me. It never has. If a few humans here have to die to ensure the rest of the planet survives, there isn't a choice. If they understood the overall picture, most of them would make that sacrifice. I respect that about them, and I respect that about you. We're enough to protect them—if we work together. You don't have to ask or know my side of things—at all. Enjoy your life. Get married to Adira. Watch Maggie grow up and grow old. Buy random children gifts if it eases your conscience. But if you ever try to move against me, Caleb, you won't win. Not in any time. Not in any place. You have no idea what you're dealing with. Am I clear?"

"You turned me over to the same aliens you're running from?" I asked. "As what—appeasement? There were other children there, too—human children."

"Mostly human," he replied and looked down at his suit. "That's been an advantage of being a hero. If a colleague or enemy has a useful ability, it's usually passed on in some capacity to their offspring. It won't last forever, but scouting potential candidates for their experiments is buying us time. I want to end this, Caleb—destroy the Messengers and their alien commanders. All I'm asking from you is a little patience and understanding. Think about Adira. Think about Maggie."

He already knew what my answer would be—was just stalling to figure out my next move. I thought I would have been going up against Samantha, but I'd still made an effort not to look at the map Nadia had given me too closely.

I needed to get clear of Fortis first—then learn what my options were. "No."

"No?" He laughed. "No, what? If it came down to either

saving some dying stranger or Adira—or Maggie—you wouldn't hesitate."

"That's not the same as throwing innocent people into a situation so it gets them killed or tortured instead."

"Morally, I see no distinction in the long-term—and I think this world may be better and safer if we just end this now." He sighed and shook his head at me. "I'm sorry, Caleb. I did try."

I had a slight lead on him—and I took off in the direction I'd last seen Ziggy enter the woods. It at least indicated a pathway that wouldn't launch me clear of the island. I needed to keep Fortis contained there long enough to think of a better plan.

It didn't help that his laser vision could take out tree trucks.

CYCAD COVE ARCHIVES: ACCESS GRANTED_LEVEL 1

'What is this place? Let me out!'

'It's a time prison—technically a pocket dimension where you can't hurt anybody or teleport. I just want to talk. Are you the same Samantha who murdered Virginia Averelli?'

'Fortis and Chaosis killed my parents and brother first! They deserved—'

'Using Perilous Island as a means of revenge is exactly what the Messengers wanted. These aliens keep manipulating and altering us—you, me, Fortis, maybe some others—over and over again. I'm trying to figure out why. This cycle has to stop, or billions of innocent people across multiple Earths will continue to die. Do you understand that? The combination of our actions is giving them entry points to destroy everything.'

'It doesn't matter anymore. It's already happened to my Earth, and I'm dying, too. Our world's Fortis caught up to me about a half-hour ago—stabbed me with your knife. Did you give it to him after I tried to reason with you?'

'No. I left it with Nadia Greene on the island later—thought it could protect her. Fortis murders her, too—a few years from now—and frames you for it to set off Roman and me. We know the truth now, but I still can't avert it.'

'So, what are you going to do? Just allow him to kill your younger self, too? It doesn't matter if you're related or not. You're a threat to him now. All of you are.'

'I know.'

CCA File 1099330493849_CA20030704_SFP_FTSCA

Fast Track Suit Camera Archive
Copies sent to all known allies.
Message from Caleb Averelli—I have a new plan. Details on the way.

CHAPTER FORTY-ONE

I BARELY HAD TIME TO PROCESS any of it, but as I flew and dodged his attacks we traveled through different time periods. Massive dinosaurs with feathers followed us several steps before giving up on us being prey. Snow and ice pelted me seconds later, and I nearly crashed landed into a herd of mammoths before I recovered.

Another circle around the island's center put us in a modern city where Perilous Island had never been shut out from development. People screamed and stared up at us as if they'd never seen anyone with powers before.

By that point, Fortis and I didn't exactly look human, either.

He sounded deranged. "Even with being altered, you're not enough to stop me, Caleb! No one is!"

There had been at least a few time loops where Fortis had been good—and he'd wanted Chaosis to stop him before the Messengers changed him.

That hadn't worked this time, and now Fortis wouldn't stop until one of us was dead. If I could find my suit, it had limited firepower—but not enough to stop him. I even had doubts about thirty different versions of me attacking him at once. Our bodies absorbed and released massive amounts of energy.

We were living batteries.

I spent several frantic minutes getting myself oriented on when and where we were relative to the overall timeline and the other versions of Earth. I had to find the night when Roman, Adira, Dominic, and I were all on the *Kairos* but before Scott and Andy had made it back to Roman's house with the Griffin suit.

The defenses around Roman's house were still in place, but I flew in through a small checkpoint near the guard shack. That still released Ziggy from his cage, and he started to chase me even before Fortis caught up to me.

"Run, Ziggy! Go far away! You don't want to be around for this!"

The surface-to-air missiles and laser weapons didn't do much to slow Fortis down, and he'd seen me enter the hangar behind the house—Ziggy refusing to leave my side.

"There's nowhere on Earth you can run, Caleb. Go on. Look ahead. You know that."

Ziggy tried to place himself between Fortis and me, and I had to fly around him. I wish he didn't stay, but I couldn't get him to leave me.

"I did look ahead—and I'm not running."

I placed my hand on the first unstable piece of tech I could find. It rapidly went bright—and I grabbed onto Ziggy's fur and focused—pausing time but not rewinding it.

Ziggy and I could still move. Fortis was frozen in place—angry and horrified by what I'd just placed into motion. Chasing me all over Perilous Island had worn him down—much like Dara had worn me down trying to save Jhett.

It was the only major advantage I had over him with me being eighteen.

Time flowed backwards.

He tried pulling us back again—trying to hold Ziggy and me there with him once the hangar exploded.

I paused everything again, walked us clear to the front gate, and let him do it again—and again—and again—until he finally let go. The hangar exploded in a deafening boom, knocking me unconscious.

I woke up to Ziggy licking my face and nudging me to get up. Andy and Scott arrived seconds later and helped me to my feet.

"Roman knows about this—downplayed it as a small fire while you were on the boat," Scott explained. I had to read his lips at first because of my ears still ringing. "This was your plan—your older self's plan. Do you understand?"

"I'm starting to..." I replied, barely able to talk. Andy walked away and returned with several bottles of water—handing one to me and pouring the others into a bucket for Ziggy. "Thanks." As I cooled down, I started to look closer to human again.

Fortis was gone—likely for good this time. I knew that from the earthquake that followed. Roman's house was miles from Cycad Cove and Perilous Island, but the shaking affected the house and the guard shack—causing portions of it to almost buckle.

"Ziggy, please stay here with them. I'll be back as soon as I can."

I could see ahead that Fortis's death had triggered the launch of the probes.

EXTINGUISHED WORLDS: WHAT GOES AROUND

CYCAD COVE ARCHIVES: ACCESS GRANTED_LEVEL 1

'You can't hold me here forever, Caleb!'

Fortis—the version of him who'd first tried to kill me at the Gregory Street apartment—was right. In this dimension, I had maybe a few minutes before he'd break free.

His future was my past, so I also knew how things would play out after he attacked my younger self.

I wasn't sure if he knew—or if he believed killing me when I was eighteen would change the entire timeline again.

'Samantha Fredricks is dead,' I replied. 'She told me it was you who stabbed her—that you originally wanted to frame Dominic for it. I couldn't save her, but she didn't want his life destroyed over his father's actions—or yours.'

'Dominic was who the Messengers originally wanted—until you popped up.' Fortis shook his head at me. 'I don't even fully understand how or why you exist, but I'm going to correct it—for good.'

He disappeared, and I allowed it to happen—along with what followed at the hangar at your house.

All the other loops where I tried to reason with him—before Samantha murdered his wife—are still stuck in my head, too. As much as I tried, he kept getting worse.

I don't know what the Messengers promised Fortis or if he was always using them just as much as he was being used.

The enemy of our enemy is definitely not our friend. You can't trust anything they tell you.

It doesn't matter that my father may have been one of them.

CCA File 1099330493850_CA20030704_FTS_FT_RG

Message to Roman Greene from Caleb Averelli.
Archive Access Restricted to Level 1 Only

CHAPTER FORTY-TWO

BY THE TIME I FINALLY reached the island again, the original fight during my present appeared to be over.

I'd already vanished right as Samantha shot me, and she'd disappeared, too. That left just Dominic, the heroes and their team, Roman, and the mercenaries. Part of me wondered if I'd find any of them left alive.

Roman was still throwing balls of energy at Terrashield and Rodoxian, but he stopped when he saw me approaching. "Everybody, stand down! He's back!"

Heroes and villains who I'd thought were dead were getting to their feet, which made me go to Dominic.

Samantha had shot him, but he wasn't dead.

"Roman and some guy who looked a lot like you told me to play dead if Samantha shot me—didn't exactly get a lot of time to explain why." He winced in pain. "For future reference, Roman—this shirt probably saved my life, but it gives you a minor burn across its entire surface. Still—thanks."

He had a shirt made with the mineral underneath his other clothes. Probably everyone did—except for me.

They had to leave me out of that plan—or I never would have gone back in the first place. Between Roman, Terrashield, and Rodoxian, they'd worked something out together—all to protect me.

Part of me had hoped that the earthquakes would stop with my return to the island—similar to before—but the next one hit with such brutal force I thought the ground was about to split in half.

Everyone looked at me for an answer on what to do next,

and I wasn't sure. I took out the map Nadia had given me and started to scan it for a possible answer. Roman didn't appear upset anymore, so I'd assumed Adira had survived, too. Even with the pressure of what was happening, I finally relaxed the moment I heard her voice.

"Wow, that was crazy..." Adira said, and she smiled at me. "Not so sure what I think of the bald look and all the light tattoos, but as long as it's still you..." There was so much I wanted to tell her—so much I wanted to explain—but she just grabbed one of my hands and squeezed it. "It's going to be okay, Caleb. You've got this. Just think it out. I'm fine. We're going to be fine. Just tell us how we can help."

"In other visions, we were all older when this happened. There are probes beneath the island—hundreds of them. If any of them break through, they'll send a signal for the aliens to find this dimension and timeline—indicate that we're a major threat and a priority to destroy. We won't be able to stop them then—not yet."

"So, we either take them all out or find some way to delay them launching in the first place," Dominic replied. "We have a lot of people here at least. Samantha probably wasn't expecting everyone to be working together. What happened to her? She disappeared right after you did. Is she coming back, too?"

I shook my head. "I don't think so..."

He and Adira looked over my shoulder at the map. Adira recognized it was sketched by her mother, gave me an odd look, but said nothing. Dominic pointed to an area near the island's center. "Command center, maybe? Might be easier to shut the probes down than chase them. I'll go, too—try to help you."

The mineral in his shirt wasn't glowing—which made me think he didn't have the same alien genes from Fortis that I did...plus the Messengers had never taken him...thankfully.

"I think I have to be the one to do it," I explained. "The core of the island has some sort of biological control or security system. If all of you could stay out here—just in case I can't shut it down. I'm not trying to keep you out, but—I don't want to risk anybody else for no reason."

Rodoxian and Terrashield approached us as Roman went to update the mercenaries.

"We have more friends on standby—just had to wait until you left. You remember us now, right?"

Based on his and Rodoxian's expressions, they still didn't know about Samantha's origins—or that Fortis had survived the fairgrounds attack.

For some reason, I'd never told them the entire truth. Maybe to keep the timeline stable?

All of that would have to wait.

I forced a smile. "Of course. Rox hasn't changed a bit—but you look older than dirt, man."

Terrashield groaned. "It's definitely him and not some brainwashed version. Just be careful, okay, Caleb? We don't want to lose you again."

I nodded and took off on the path I needed before anything else came up. It was somewhat disorienting compared to even when I'd been running from Fortis. This island—the tech it contained—was never meant to be accessed by anyone willing to sabotage it. I wasn't sure what to expect—and that was a good thing.

If I'd known, terror would have held me back from ever exploring any passage beneath the island.

CYCAD COVE ARCHIVES: ACCESS GRANTED_LEVEL 1

Dr. Greene,

I hope this message finds you and your family well. We haven't met yet, but my son commissioned your help in exploring this island.

I have been searching for Caleb since he was taken from my wife and I in 2053—believed he was dead or worse for decades. Now that I know what happened, I feel he's much safer in the past with you.

I don't want anything from you or him. This isn't some deception, and I don't have much to offer—other than maybe a small fraction of hope for your Earth and timeline.

The war is close, but I'm doing everything I can to hold things at bay for as long as possible.

I also have a lead on some potential allies. It's complicated, considering they have no good reason to trust me. Caleb will likely experience a similar problem, though he won't have the background to realize why.

Once we have a safe opportunity to meet, I'll try to explain as best as I can.

For now, please burn this letter. I don't want Caleb to search this current future for me. It will likely get him killed.

CCA File 417283940003_RG20200930_FT_CA_CG

Scanned copy of hand-written document. Recovered from Northwest Quadrant of Orchid Island by Roman Greene.

Note by R.G.: The handwriting on this is difficult to read, and the letter wasn't signed. I did show the original to Caleb once I believed he was old enough to see it.

He immediately burned it and hasn't mentioned it since.

CHAPTER FORTY-THREE

THE COMMAND CENTER RESEMBLED a natural cave, but a path lit up as soon as I touched the walls. That was useful. What greeted me at the end of that path—not so much.

The things had been human—once—but the closest references I had were some zombie and alien invasion movies combined. They were behind a series of force-field barriers—not clawing and scrambling to get through, though. They were calm—standing in formation like rows of robots, but I could see them breathing.

As I passed each set, they followed me with their eyes—turning their heads and then facing straight forward again as soon as I was out of their periphery.

It was the creepiest thing I'd ever experienced—because under another set of circumstances, I could have been one of them.

And if I didn't keep going, I would be.

Everyone on Earth would be.

Once I reached the island's main control room, there was another problem.

Similar to how missile silos required two people to initiate and confirm a launch, the interface required two people...two aliens.

Fortis was dead. Samantha was dead. One of my other selves might have worked—as long as the system didn't care about both of us having the same DNA. If that was a viable option, I would have thought I'd have met myself before that point.

I was stuck—and those probes would continue launching in wave after wave if I didn't figure something out. I started to go back the way I'd come when I saw the alien drones turning to face another person.

Grandma.

"Just hold your horses, Caleb. I had a few other errands to do, and it takes longer when you and Dominic aren't around."

I ran to meet her, and she grinned at me.

"Did Adira and I name our Maggie after you?" I asked. "Or are you our—?"

"What do you think?" She smiled and crossed her arms. "Oh, don't worry—either way, I'll brandish this over you and Mom for my entire childhood. You want me to go to bed at nine, Dad? Remember that time I helped you save the planet after raising you and Dominic with no bedtime restrictions at all? You're going to get so annoyed, but you'll love it, too. Let's get to work. Everybody up there is getting nervous while we're down here catching up. Put your palm there. I'll take this side."

"You know what to do?" I asked in confusion.

She nodded. "Good news is if we screw this up, we're not going to be around to know it. Comforting, right? Now the moment this goes active, you need to access the probe launchers. That's on your side. I've got a few things to do over here, but I'll walk you through everything."

A jolt rattled through the underground structure. We were already too late. The initial wave of the probes had already launched, and the next set was priming.

"Don't panic," she said and continued working. "We have everyone up top, too—and they knew this was coming. Plus, you're bringing in some extra help from about twenty years ago."

I thought a moment. "The patients and prisoners from Brunel?"

"You know all those kids you were able to save just before you died? Well, they grew up here. Some are heroes now. Some ended up in Brunel—but you're going to help them...and they're going to help us in return. That's the first lesson you taught me. Our actions aren't just linear. They circle and grow—compound into something much greater with each additional loop. A lot of what we do comes back to either help us or haunt us. It's the same with normal people, but they can't sense what we can."

I gave a reluctant nod. I had so many questions, but I didn't want either of us to lose focus. After about fifteen nerve-wracking minutes, we had stopped the probe system.

Maggie stepped away from her console, taking her palm off of it. I did the same with mine.

As we passed the alien creatures for the second time, they were now in a frenzy—ramming themselves into the force fields keeping them contained.

"We have to shut them out from the rest of the island," Grandma explained. "I can show you how to do that, too."

She told me another set of instructions and showed me another panel to place my palm. She went to a second panel—much closer to the creatures.

I didn't like that. "Grand—Maggie, we should trade. Just tell me what to do over there. I'll—"

It turned out she had some of Adira's abilities, too. My entire life, I'd never seen Grandma blast anything from her hands. It would have been an immediate give-away, and I would have asked questions right after meeting Adira.

She sent me flying backwards. By the time I recovered—more from shock than physical pain—she'd brought up another force field to seal the tunnel entirely.

I pounded on it.

I tried to rewind time again, but it didn't work.

She was trapped in there—with those things—and she gave me a minute before she approached the field. She was muffled, but I could see and hear her through it. There was an alarm, too—similar to the one I'd heard in the medical facility before I'd rescued the kids.

I realized how I'd gotten them out of there.

"I still have a lot of work to do—and they could probably use your help up top—" Grandma started.

"No—I'm not leaving you! Maggie, I can't. You're—"

"If you don't leave soon, I'll never exist. You know that. I know what I'm doing, and we're going to meet again. You and Mom and me will have a life together. It won't be what

Fortis planned—or these things—or even what you saw in some of your visions...but it will be a life! Caleb...Dad...I don't want you to see this. Please, just go. They're about to get out, and I know what I have to do. It was either one or both of us—and it couldn't have been you. Do you understand?"

I understood perfectly—but I wasn't going to leave her there. Not alone. With the way she'd acted sometimes, it was almost as if she'd been alone for a very long time. I was never sure why—hadn't wanted to hurt her by asking.

"How long can I stay?" I asked. "How long will it take you to create an explosion? That's what you're planning, isn't it?"

"Thirty seconds—a minute at most." She dropped the act of seeming annoyed, and her expression turned frantic. "Dad, you have to go! I love you! I love you, and I don't want you to die!"

"I know...and I love you, too. Maggie, listen—"

"What?"

"Just listen..."

The alarm had stopped. The creatures were contorted but frozen in their efforts to break free. Maggie looked at me wide-eyed.

I must have never told her about this.

"We will find a way to get you out of there, too. Tell me everything you can. We'll figure this out together—I promise. Just start with the first thing you can remember..."

There's a lot of tragedy and pain with being a time traveler, and sometimes there are events you can't change no matter how badly you wish you could.

But it's not the entirety of it—and I carry with me just as much joy and amazement in the events that work out right.

In a single immeasurable moment to the outside universe, I learned my daughter's entire lifetime—and a lot of how my own connected to it.

It's all precious...

It's all worth fighting for...

And I kept my promise.

EPILOGUE

ONCE MAGGIE AND I REACHED the surface and headed for the coast, what had felt like days for us had been minutes to everyone else. The final cycle of probes had just launched, but they were being destroyed almost instantly by nearly a hundred heroes, villains, and civilian allies I'd gathered together from multiple loops.

"Hey, took you two long enough! You've been missing out!" Dominic shouted. "It's kind of fun—in an 'if-we-miss-we're-all-gonna-die' sort of way. Thanks for repairing the visor and dropping it off, Grandma. I thought you'd be pissed at me for holding out on you."

After everything she and I had talked about, it took a moment for Maggie to recover and remember when and where we were.

She smiled at me and then Dominic. "Oh, we'll discuss the basement-level drop in your pay rates as soon as we get home. You both better hope Roman has more jobs for you after this is over."

Dominic laughed. "Aww, you know you love me."

"Have you seen Cyndero?" I asked. "I need to talk to him about something..."

"Yeah—he's over there with a hero I'm afraid might sue me for trademark infringement. I swear the name Griffin was inactive when I started creating my suits, but apparently one of your duplicates brought some guy with a big vintage logo of one plastered on his chest. He's kind of snobby, too—just flew away from me when I tried to talk to him. At least Cyndero seems decent in person—said he's good with me keeping the visor, anyway."

I nodded. "I'll be right back. Even if those things seemed to stop launching, don't let your guard down until I give an all-clear."

"Wasn't planning on it. Be careful, kid."

Before I even reached Cyndero and Griffin, Terrashield and Rodoxian blocked me.

"What the hell, Caleb?" Rodoxian said. "Even if he's somehow fooled you into believing he's stable again, all those people he killed at the fairgrounds are still dead! You can't just—"

"He's literally not Chaosis—not the one you knew," I explained. "In the past, did he help you capture Dara? To keep her away from Dominic?"

"Yes—right after you put him and a few of the others back in Brunel. The ones you couldn't help, right? We weren't entirely sure what you did to Chaosis, but with anything regarding Dominic, he seemed pretty lucid—wanted to protect him, at least. Occasionally, he'd do something crazy to get himself put into solitary—and then he murdered that guard just before the other guards had to kill him."

"That's what's bothering me. With what I did, that never should have happened. Let me talk to him."

By the time they let me pass—having to focus on more of the probes again—Cyndero had already figured it out.

"Caleb, who is this? That's definitely my uncle's old suit—and it looks and sounds like him—but this guy has no idea what happened at the fairgrounds and has never even heard of Dara."

Griffin wasn't exactly happy to see me again. "You were the one in Brunel Heights, Fast Track—not me! Now my own nephew is looking at me as if I'm some mass-murderer, and I'm assuming that's my future son over there? Does he think that, too? I don't give a damn if you're a teenager now. You're going to fix this you little—"

I shook my head and tried to keep my tone level. "I'm so

sorry, but your Earth and timeline are gone—wiped out by the aliens. Another version of me pulled you from there before its invasion and hid you here—a few others, too. You've been helping me gain intel—were undercover and pretending to be a psychotic version of yourself after I returned him to Brunel."

"What?" he asked in disbelief. "Why?"

Before I could reply, a brief vision hit—a single orb escaping orbit and broadcasting a signal before Cyndero and Griffin would destroy it.

Even with extra help this round, it would still be close.

As I snapped back to reality, everyone's attention was drawn to the city across the water from us. All the lights in Cycad Cove went out in a wave, similar to what had happened at the fairgrounds twenty years earlier.

Dara had escaped, and something had made her ability more powerful than it had ever been in previous loops.

"Because this isn't over yet," I answered Griffin and commanded my suit's helmet to cover my face again. "I'll explain as soon as I can. Both of you—I need you to follow me."

ABOUT THE AUTHOR

Patricia Gilliam is the author of *The Hannaria Series* (sci-fi) and *Heroes of Corvus* (urban fantasy/superhero). She is also a contributor to several anthologies and the creator of *Seriescraft 101* character and world-building resources.

Along with many global writers, artists, musicians, and other creatives, a collection of her works will be included in three lunar time capsules (Intuitive Machine's Nova-C, Astrobiotic's Peregrine, and Astrobiotic's Griffin landers) through *Writers on the Moon* and *The Lunar Codex* archives in 2022 and 2023.

She and her husband Cory live in Knoxville, TN with their cat, Butterscotch.

Made in the USA
Columbia, SC
18 April 2023

53d822ea-affd-4cbb-ac8d-946655fa6941R01